"Are you going to use the shotgun on me?" he taunted.

"Then take your best shot, sweetheart, because I'll be back."

Dee lashed out in retaliation. "You overestimate your charm. I'd always wonder what you really wanted, me or Angel Creek."

"Both, sweetheart," he said, and crashed his mouth down onto hers. It was a rough kiss and she tried to bite him, but he jerked his head back, then returned to kiss her even harder . . .

He unbuttoned the shirt she wore and opened it, baring her breasts. Her breath caught in her throat as his hard, warm hand closed over one of the soft mounds.

"This is what it would be like between us," he muttered. "Hot and wild. Think about it. Remember that when you think about using the shotgun on me."

Praise for Linda Howard's *A Lady of the West*

"A powerful, emotionally intense, very sensual tale . . . as . . . untamed as the wild New Mexico landscape."
—*Romantic Times*

"*A Lady of the West* is marvelous. Textured with gritty reality, riveting action and sizzling sensuality, it still manages to capture moments of heartwarming pathos and tenderness. I read it through at one sitting because I couldn't put it down. . . . Wonderful."
—Iris Johansen

Books by Linda Howard

A Lady of the West
Angel Creek

Published by POCKET BOOKS

ANGEL CREEK

LINDA HOWARD

POCKET BOOKS

New York   London   Toronto   Sydney   Tokyo   Singapore

An *Original* Publication of POCKET BOOKS

POCKET BOOKS, a division of Simon & Schuster Inc.
1230 Avenue of the Americas, New York, NY 10020

ISBN: 0-671-66081-0

First Pocket Books printing November 1991

10 9 8 7 6 5 4 3 2 1

POCKET and colophon are registered trademarks of
Simon & Schuster Inc.

Cover art by Greg Gulbronson

Printed in the U.S.A.

1

Lucas Cochran had been back in town for almost a month, but it still amazed him how much the little town of Prosper had lived up to its name. It would never be anything more than a small town, but it was neat and bustling. A man could tell a lot about a place just by looking at the people on the streets, and by that standard Prosper was quiet, steady, and—well—prosperous. A boomtown might be more exciting than a town like Prosper, and people could make a lot of money in such places, but mining towns tended to die as soon as the ore played out.

Prosper, on the other hand, had started out as a single building serving triple duty as general store, bar, and livery for the few settlers around. Lucas could remember when the site Prosper now occupied had been nothing but bare ground and the only white men for miles had been on the Double C. The gold rush in 1858 had changed all that, bringing thousands of men into the Colorado mountains in search of instant wealth; no gold had been found around Prosper, but a few people had seen the land and stayed, starting small ranches. More people had meant a larger demand for goods. The lone general store/bar/livery soon had another building standing beside it, and the tiny settlement that would one day become Prosper, Colorado, was born.

Lucas had seen a lot of boomtowns, not just in Colorado, and they were all very similar in their frenzied pace, as muddy streets swarmed with miners and those looking to separate the miners from their gold: gamblers, saloon owners, whores, and claim-jumpers. He was glad that Prosper hadn't been blessed—or cursed, depending on your point of view —by either gold or silver. Being what it was, it would still be there when most of the boomtowns were nothing but weathered skeletons.

It was a sturdy little town, a good place to raise a family, as evidenced by the three hundred and twenty-eight souls who lived there. All of the businesses were located on the long center street, around which nine streets of residences had arranged themselves. Most of the houses were small and simple, but some of the people, like banker Wilson Millican, had already possessed money before settling in Prosper. Their houses wouldn't have looked out of place in Denver or even in the larger cities back East.

Prosper had only one saloon and no whorehouses, though it was well known among the men in town (and the women, although the men didn't know it) that the two saloon girls would take care of any extra itches they happened to have, for a price. There was a church on the north end of town, and a school for the youngsters. Prosper had a bank, two hotels, three restaurants (counting the two in the hotels), a general store, two livery stables, a dry goods store, a barber shop, a cobbler, a blacksmith, and even a hat shop for the ladies. The stage came through once a week.

The entire town was there only because the Cochran family had carved the big Double C spread out of nothing, fighting the Comanche and Arapaho, paying for the land with Cochran blood. Lucas had been the first Cochran born there, and now he was the only one left; he had buried his two brothers and his mother back during the Indian wars, and his father had died the month before. Other ranchers had moved in, but the Cochrans had been the first, and had bought the security the town now enjoyed with Cochran lives. Everyone who had been in town for long knew that Prosper's backbone wasn't the long center street, but the line of graves in the family burial plot on the Double C.

Lucas's bootheels thudded on the sidewalk as he walked toward the general store. A cold wind had sprung up that had the smell of snow on it, and he looked at the sky. Low gray clouds were building over the mountains, signaling yet another delay to spring. Warmer weather should arrive any day, but those low clouds said not quite yet. He passed a woman with her shawl pulled tight around her shoulders and tipped his hat to her. "Looks like more snow, Mrs. Padgett."

Beatrice Padgett gave him a friendly smile. "It does that, Mr. Cochran."

He entered the general store and nodded to Mr. Winches, the proprietor. Winches had done right well in the ten years Lucas had been gone, enough to hire himself a clerk who took care of most of the stocking.

"Hosea," Lucas said by way of greeting.

"How do, Lucas? It's turning a mite cold out there, ain't it?"

"It'll snow by morning. The snowpacks can use it, but I'm ready for spring myself."

"Ain't we all? You need anything in particular?"

"Just some gun oil."

"Down the left, toward the back."

"Thanks."

Lucas went down the aisle Hosea had indicated, almost bumping into a farm woman who was fingering the harnesses. He muttered an absentminded apology and continued without more than a glance. Farming was hard on a woman, making her look old before her time. Besides, he had just spotted a familiar blond head over by the sacks of flour, and a sense of satisfaction filled him. Olivia Millican was just the type he would want when he got around to getting married: well-bred, with a pleasant disposition, and pretty enough for him to look forward to bedding her for the rest of his life. He had plans for the Double C, and the ruthless ambition to put those plans into effect.

There were two other young women standing with Olivia, so he didn't approach, just contented himself with a tip of his hat when her eyes strayed his way. To her credit she didn't giggle, though the two with her did. Instead she gave him a grave nod of acknowledgment, and if the color in her cheeks heightened a bit, it just made her prettier.

He paid for the gun oil and left, not getting the door

shut good behind him before a muffled flurry of squeals and giggles broke out, though again Olivia didn't contribute.

"He danced with you twice!"

"What did he say?"

"I was so excited when he asked *me*, I almost fainted dead away!"

"Does he dance well? I swear I had butterflies in my stomach just at the thought of having his arm around my waist! It's just as well he didn't ask me, because I'd have made a fool of myself, but at the same time I admit I was powerfully jealous of you, Olivia."

Dee Swann glanced at the knot of three young women, two of whom were taking turns gabbing without allowing Olivia a chance to answer. Olivia was blushing a little but nevertheless maintaining her composure. They stood off to the side in the general store and were making an effort to keep their voices down, but their excitement had caught Dee's attention. It took only a moment of eavesdropping to discern that the gossip was, as usual, about some man, in this case Lucas Cochran. She continued to listen as she selected a new bridle. The stiff leather straps slipped through her fingers as she searched for the one that was most pliable.

"He was very gentlemanly," Olivia said in an even tone. The banker's daughter was seldom ruffled. Dee looked up again with amusement sparkling in her eyes at Olivia's unwavering good manners, and their gazes met across the aisles in silent communication. Olivia understood Dee's mirth as plainly as if she had laughed aloud, just as she understood why Dee not only didn't join them but preferred that Olivia not even acknowledge her presence beyond a polite nod. Dee jealously guarded her privacy, and Olivia respected her old friend enough not to try to include her in a discussion that wouldn't interest her and might actually irritate her.

Even as small as Prosper was, there was a definite social structure. Dee wouldn't normally have been welcome in the circles in which Olivia moved, and she had long ago made certain her friend understood she didn't want to be made an exception to the rule. Dee was totally disinterested in such socializing. Her penchant for privacy was so strong that though everyone knew they were acquainted, since they had attended the local school together, only the two of them knew how close their friendship really was. Dee never visited Olivia; it was always Olivia who rode out, alone, to Dee's small cabin, but it was an arrangement that suited both of them. Not only was Dee's privacy protected, but Olivia in turn felt a certain freedom, a sense of relief in knowing herself unobserved and unjudged at least for a few hours by anyone other than Dee, who was the least judgmental person Olivia had ever met. Only with Dee could she truly be herself. This wasn't to say that she was in reality anything less than a lady, but merely that she enjoyed being able to say whatever she thought. In their shared glance was Olivia's promise to ride out soon and tell Dee all that had happened since they had last seen each other, which had been over a month ago due to the late winter weather.

Having made her selection, Dee took the bridle and her other purchases up to the counter where Hosea Winches waited. He painstakingly tallied her selections on the ledger page that bore her name at the top, then subtracted the total from the amount of credit remaining from the year before. There was only a small amount left, she saw, reading the figures upside down, but it would last her until her crops came in this summer.

Mr. Winches turned the ledger around for her to double-check his arithemetic. While she ran a finger down his columns he eyed the group of young women still standing at the back of the store. Bursts of stifled laughter, high-pitched with excitement, made him snort. "Sounds like a fox got in the chicken house, what with all that squawking," he mumbled.

Dee nodded her satisfaction with his totals and turned the ledger back to its original position, then gathered up her purchases. "Thank you, Mr. Winches."

He shook his head absently. "Be thankful you're more levelheaded than some," he said. "You'd think they ain't never seen a man before."

Dee looked back at the others, then at Mr. Winches again, and they both shrugged their shoulders. So what if Lucas Cochran was back in town after a ten-year absence? It didn't mean anything to either of them.

She had recognized Cochran when he had bumped her in the store aisle, of course, but she hadn't spoken because recognizing someone wasn't the same as knowing him, and she doubted that he had recognized her. After all, he had left Prosper shortly after her folks had settled in the area. She had been a fourteen-year-old schoolgirl, while he had been eight years older, a grown man. They had never even met. She knew his face, but she didn't know the man or much about him.

Dee made it a practice to mind her own business and expected others to do the same, but even so she had been aware of what was going on at the Double C. It was the biggest ranch in the area, so everyone paid some attention. Ellery Cochran, Lucas's father, had died a few weeks before. Dee hadn't known the man personally, only enough to put a name to his face whenever their paths crossed in town. She hadn't thought anything unusual of his passing; death was common, and he'd died peacefully, which was about as much as a body could ask for.

The matter was of only mild interest to her, on the level of hearing that a neighbor had a new baby. She had never had any dealings with Ellery, so she didn't expect to have any with his son. She had already forgotten about the Cochrans by the time she stepped out into the icy wind. She tugged her father's old coat more snugly around her and jammed his too-big hat down around her ears, ducking her head to keep the wind off her face as she walked hurriedly to the wagon and climbed up onto the plank seat.

It began snowing late that afternoon, but the swirling of the silent white flakes was one of her favorite sights and filled her with contentment, rather than restlessness at yet another delay of spring. Dee loved the changing seasons, each with its own magic and beauty, and she lived close enough to the land to become immersed in the inexorable rhythm of nature. Her animals were snug in the barn, her chores finished for the day, and she was safe in the cabin with a brisk fire snapping cheerfully, warming her on the outside, while a cup of coffee warmed her on the inside. She had nothing more pressing to do than sit with her feet stretched toward the fire and read one of the precious few books she had obtained over the winter. Winter was her time of rest; she was too busy during the other three seasons to have either the time or the energy for much reading.

But the book soon dropped to her lap, and she leaned her head against the high back of the rocking chair, her eyes focused inward as she planned her garden. The corn had done so well last year that it might be a good thing to plant more of it. Corn was never a waste; what the townspeople didn't buy, she could always use as feed for the horse. But extra corn would mean that she would have to cut back on some other vegetable, and she couldn't decide if that would be wise. By careful planning and experimentation she knew to the square yard how much she could tend, and tend well, by herself. She didn't intend to expand at the expense of the quality of her vegetables. Nor did she want to hire a young boy to help her. It was selfish of her, perhaps, but the greatest pleasure she got from her garden, other than the primitive satisfaction of making things grow, was her complete independence. She stood alone and reveled in it.

At first it had frightened her when she had found herself, at the age of eighteen, totally alone in life. When Dee was sixteen, only a couple of years after they had settled in the narrow, fertile valley just outside Prosper, Colorado, her mother, a schoolteacher, had died, leaving her daughter a legacy of books, an appreciation of the benefits of hard work, and a level head. Barely two more years had passed before her father, George Swann, had managed to get himself kicked in the head by a mule, and he died in his bed the next day without regaining consciousness.

The silence, the emptiness had haunted her. Her solitude, her vulnerability had frightened her. A woman alone was a woman without protection. Dee had dug her father's grave herself and buried him, not wanting anyone to know she was all alone on the homestead. When she had to go into Prosper for supplies she turned aside friendly queries about her father, saying only that he couldn't leave the ranch just then, and she comforted her conscience with the knowledge that she hadn't lied, even if she hadn't told the exact truth.

George had died early in the winter, and during the long, cold months Dee had grieved and pondered her situation. She owned this fertile little valley now; it was too small to support a large-scale ranching operation, but too large for her to work herself. On the other hand, the soil was lush, fed by crystal-clear Angel Creek as it poured out of Prosper Canyon and ran right down the middle of the valley. She could never remember deciding on any exact day what she was going to do with the rest of her life; she had just done what she had to as each day presented itself.

First and foremost had been the necessity of learning how to protect herself. With dogged determination each day she set out her father's weapons: a Colt .36 handgun, an old Sharps rifle, and a shiny, year-old double-barreled shotgun. The handgun was rusty with disuse, as George hadn't gotten it out of the holster where it had been hanging on a peg since they'd settled on Angel Creek. He hadn't been any good with a handgun, he'd often joked; just give him a shotgun, so all he had to do was aim in the general direction of something.

Dee had felt much the same way, but she cleaned and oiled all three of the weapons, something she had often seen her father do, and practiced loading and unloading each weapon in turn, hour after hour, until she could do it automatically, without thinking. Only then did she begin practicing with targets. She began with the handgun, because she thought it would be the easiest, and immediately she saw why George hadn't much liked it. Over any distance at all it just wasn't accurate enough to count on. She experimented until she knew the distance from which she could reasonably expect to hit within the circle of the target she'd painted on a big tree trunk. With the rifle it was much easier to hit what she aimed at, and from a much greater distance. But, like her father, she liked the shotgun best. A man up to no good might reason she wouldn't be able to hit him with a pistol, or even a rifle, and take his chances, but no man with a brain between his ears was going to figure she was likely to miss with a shotgun.

She didn't waste her time trying to build up any speed with the pistol; that was for fast draws, gunslicks looking to make a reputation, and wasn't what she needed. Accuracy was her goal, and she worked on it day after day until she felt satisfied that she was competent enough to defend herself with whichever weapon was at hand. She would never be more than competent, but as competency was what she wanted, that was enough.

The garden was something that had seemed necessary, too. She and her mother had always planted a garden and worked long hours every summer canning the vegetables for use during the winter. Dee liked working in the garden, liked the rhythm of it and the way she could actually see the fruits of her labor. Losing both of her parents so close together had stunned her with the realization that human life was temporary, and she had needed something permanent to get her through the desolation of grief. She had found it in the land, for it continued, and the seasons marched on. A garden was a productive thing, returning a bounty for the most elemental care. It eased her grief to see life coming out of the ground, and the physical labor provided its own kind of relief. The land had given her a reason to live and thus had given her life.

By early spring it was known in town that George Swann had died during the winter, and she had had to weather the storm of questions. People with no more than a nodding acquaintance would ask her outright what her plans were, if she had any folks to take her in, when she'd be going back East. She had cousins in Virginia, where she'd been born, but no one close, even if she had been inclined to go back, which she wasn't. Nor did she consider it anyone's business except her own. The townfolk's nosiness had been almost intolerable for her, for she had always been a private person, and that part of her personality had grown stronger during the past months. Those same people were scandalized when she'd made it plain she had no intention of leaving the homestead. She was only a girl, not yet even nineteen years old, and in the opinion of the townsfolk she had no business living out there all by herself. A respectable woman wouldn't do such a thing.

Some of the young cowhands from the area ranches, as well as others who hadn't the excuse of youth, thought she might be pining for what a man could give her and took it upon themselves to relieve her loneliness. They found their way, singly and sometimes in pairs, to her cabin during the summer nights. With the shotgun in hand Dee had seen to it that they had even more quickly found their way off her property, and gradually the word had gotten around that the Swann girl wasn't interested. A few of them had had to have their britches dusted with shot before they saw the light, but once they realized that she wasn't shy about pulling the trigger they hadn't come back. At least not in the guise of generous swains.

That first spring she had, by habit, planted a garden meant to provide enough for two, as that was what she had planted before, and the crops had been on the verge of bearing before she realized she would have a large surplus. She began taking what she couldn't use into town to sell it off her wagon. But that meant that she had to stay in town all day long herself, so finally she arranged with Mr. Winches that he would buy her vegetables, sometimes for cash and sometimes for credit on his books, and resell them in his general store. It was an arrangement that worked out for both of them, as Dee was able to spend more time in the garden and Mr. Winches could sell the vegetables to the townspeople—the ones who didn't have their own small garden plots—for a neat little profit.

The next year, this time deliberately, Dee planted a huge garden and soon found that she couldn't properly take care of it. The weeds outstripped her efforts to destroy them, and the vegetables suffered. Still, she made a nice profit through Mr. Winches and put up more than enough to feed herself over the winter.

The next spring, as Dee planted her third garden, a new rancher moved into the area south of Prosper. Kyle Bellamy was young, only in his late twenties, and too handsome for his own good. Dee had disliked him on sight; he was overly aggressive, riding roughshod over other people's conversations and opinions. He intended to build a great ranch and made no secret of it as he began acquiring land, though he was careful to avoid stepping on Ellery Cochran's toes.

Bellamy decided that he needed another good water source for his growing empire, and he offered to buy the Angel Creek valley from Dee. She had almost laughed aloud at the ridiculously low offer but managed to decline politely.

His next offer was much higher. Her refusal remained polite.

The third offer was even higher, and he was clearly angry when he made it. He warned her that he wasn't going to go any higher, and Dee decided that he didn't quite understand her position.

"Mr. Bellamy, it isn't the money. I don't want to sell to anyone, for any price. I don't want to leave here; this is my home."

In Bellamy's experience, he could buy anything he wanted; it was just a question of how much he was willing to spend to get it. It came as a shock to him to read the truth in Dee's steady green eyes. No matter how much he offered, she wasn't going to sell.

But he wanted that land.

His next offer was for marriage. Dee would have been amused if it hadn't been for the abrupt shock of realization that she was as disinclined to marry *any-one* as she was to sell her land. Whenever she had thought of the future she had always vaguely assumed that she would someday get married and have children, so she herself was surprised to learn that that wasn't what she wanted at all. Her two and a half years of complete independence had taught her how entirely suited she was to solitude and being her own mistress, answerable to no one but herself. In a split second her view of life was shattered and rearranged, as if she had been looking at herself through a distorted mirror that had abruptly righted itself, leaving her staring frankly at the real woman rather than the false image.

So instead of laughing, she looked up at Kyle Bellamy with an oddly remote expression and said, "Thank you, Mr. Bellamy, but I don't intend ever to marry."

It was after her refusal that some of the cowhands began to think it would be fun to ride through her vegetable garden, firing their pistols into the air to frighten the animals, laughing and shouting to themselves. If they expected her to be hiding under her bed, they soon found out, as had her erstwhile swains, how dangerous it was to underestimate her. That vegetable garden was her livelihood, and she protected it with her booming double-barreled shotgun. She never doubted that most of the cowhands were from Bellamy's ranch, but more and more small ranches were springing up, bringing in strangers who had to be taught to leave the Swann woman alone. During the growing season she learned to sleep with one eye open and the shotgun at hand, to ward off the occasional band of hoorahing cowboys who saw nothing wrong with harassing a nester. She got along just fine except for that, and she felt she could handle the hoorahing. If they ever became more than a nuisance, if she felt threatened herself, she'd start doing more than dusting them with buckshot.

It was six years since her father had died. Dee looked around the small cabin and was satisfied with what she saw, with her life. She had everything she needed and a few small luxuries besides; she had a slowly growing nest egg in the bank, credit at Mr. Winches's store, and a fertile little valley in which to grow her vegetables every year. There were two cows in the barn for milk, and a bull to make certain that she always had a yearling to provide beef. Eventually the bull and cows would be replaced by those yearlings, and life would go on. She had one horse, a sturdy animal who pulled the plow and the wagon and occasionally bore her on his back. A small flock of chickens kept her in eggs and provided a change from beef. It was all hers, and she had done it all herself.

When a woman married, whatever she owned automatically became her husband's property, subject to his will rather than hers, just as the woman herself did. Dee saw no reason ever to give up control of herself and her land. If that meant she would be an old maid, well, there were worse things in life. She was truly independent, as few women were, working her own land and supporting herself. The people in Prosper might think she was a little odd, but she was respected as a hard worker and an honest business-woman. She was satisfied with that.

2

THE TREES ON THE DOUBLE C WERE FINALLY SHOWING new growth, a sure sign of spring. Despite the lingering chill in the air, borne on the winds sweeping down from the mountains that still wore their white winter caps, Lucas Cochran could smell the indefinable fragrance of new life, fresh and green. He had spent ten long years away from the land he loved, and now that he was back he felt as if he couldn't get enough of it, as if a part of himself that had been lost was now restored.

He had been born on this land in a mud dugout only a scant five months after his father had brought his small family west from Tennessee and settled on the broad valley that became the center of the Double C. He sometimes wondered at the courage it had taken for his mother to come out there with one baby just barely a year old and another one on the way, to leave her comfortable house and live in a hole in the ground, and all of that a time when they were the only whites for hundreds of square miles. Those early days had been the safest, however, because the Indians hadn't yet been alarmed by the strange people moving into their territory.

Looking back, he thought that probably the '49 gold rush in California had been the beginning of the real hostilities between Indian and white. Thousands of people had poured west, and after the gold rush had ended few of them had gone home. The number of white men wandering west of the Mississippi so increased, and the tension between the two peoples had naturally increased as well. Then the Colorado Territory had had its own gold rush in '58, and the second big increase in the population of whites had pushed the situation into open warfare.

By then the Double C had grown to its present size and employed almost a hundred men, and the mud dugout had long since given way to a rough-hewn cabin. Ellery Cochran was in the process of building a big, ambitious house for his wife and family. Lucas had been fourteen that year, already pushing six feet in height and with a man's strength from a lifetime of hard work. His older brother Matthew had been almost sixteen, with all the wild impetuosity of any young male on the verge of adulthood. The two boys had been inseparable all their lives, with Matt's cheerfulness balancing Lucas's darker nature, and Lucas's levelheadedness reining in the worst of Matt's adventurousness.

The youngest Cochran, Jonah, was six years younger than Lucas and had always been excluded from the close relationship between the two older boys, not from any maliciousness on their part, but because of the simple, unbridgeable distance of age. The closeness in their ages meant that Matt and Lucas had been together from babyhood, had always had each other as a playmate, had slept together under the same blanket. Those were things that Jonah could never share, and he was largely left to his own devices. He was a quiet, withdrawn boy, always standing on the fringes and watching his two older brothers but seldom included in their rough activities. It was odd, Lucas often thought, that as close as he had been to Matt, it was Jonah's thin, solemn face that had remained clearest in his memory.

The Indians had attacked the ranch house one day while most of the men were out on the range, something they had evidently known. Matt and Lucas had been there only by chance, having ridden in early only because Matt's horse had thrown a shoe, and where one went, so did the other. Alice, their mother, had insisted that they eat lunch before riding back out. They had been sitting at the table with her and Jonah when they had heard the first shouts.

The Indians hadn't had any firearms, but they had outnumbered the few defenders by five to one, and it took time to reload the muzzle-loaders the Cochrans possessed. The speed of the attack, an Indian specialty, was dizzying. All Lucas could remember was a blur of noise and motion, the explosions of gunpowder in his ear, the panic as he tried to reload while keeping an eye on the Indians. He and Matt and Alice had each taken up a position at a window, and he remembered Alice's sudden scream when she had seen eight-year-old Jonah standing at an unguarded win-

dow, bravely sighting down the barrel of a pistol so
heavy it took both hands for him to hold it. Lucas, the
closest, had tackled his baby brother and stuffed him
behind an overturned table with orders to stay there.
Then he had turned back just as the front door was
kicked in and Matt met an Indian warrior in a
chest-to-chest clash, muscles straining, hands locked
together. The Indian had held a club in one hand, a
glittering knife in the other. Lucas grabbed up the
pistol Jonah had dropped and whirled on one knee,
trying for a clear shot, when Matt went down under
the warrior's greater weight and the long knife buried
itself in his chest. Lucas had shot then, his aim true,
but too late for Matt.

The attack was over as fast as it had started,
perhaps because the Indians had known the men out
on the range, alerted by the gunfire, would be riding
hell for leather for the ranch house. The entire fight
had lasted less than five minutes.

Losing Matt had left Lucas like a wounded animal,
unable to find comfort. His parents had comforted
each other over the loss of their firstborn; Jonah,
accustomed to being alone, had pulled even deeper
inside himself. Lucas was the one who had been cast
adrift, for he had always had Matt, and now his entire
world had changed. He had truly grown up that year,
for he had seen death, and he had killed, and without
Matt to buffer those experiences the hard edges of his
character had grown even harder.

The Civil War had started in 1861, and the army
had pulled out of Colorado Territory to fight it, in
effect leaving the citizens of the Territory on their own
to face the increasing Indian attacks. Only the few

settled towns were safe; Prosper by then had been big enough to protect itself, but the wagon trains and outlying ranches had to defend themselves as best they could. The Double C was an armed camp, but then it had to be to survive. Alice Cochran hadn't survived, but not because of the Indians; a cold had turned into pneumonia during the winter of '63, and within a week of first taking sick she was put in her grave. The second mainstay of Lucas's life was gone.

The Indian wars were even worse in 1864. In November of that year Colonel John Chivington led his Third Colorado troops against a group of Indians at Sand Creek and massacred hundreds of women and children, causing an explosion of violence that spread from Canada to Mexico, uniting the Plains tribes in the fury of revenge. Troops began returning after the end of the Civil War in '65, but the Territory was already locked in its own war.

Even with all the danger, settlers had poured west. Prosper had quickly become a busy little town, even hiring a schoolteacher, which was a sure sign of civilization. A community had to have a school as a means of attracting new settlers. Boulder had built the first schoolhouse in '60, but the people of Prosper were proud of the fact that it only took them five more years to get one, too. Lucas and Matt had been taught at home by their mother, but Jonah's schooling had been cut short by her death. For the first time in his life Jonah began attending a school at the age of fifteen, riding into Prosper every day.

Jonah never said much; he just watched. As Lucas had grown older he had regretted the lack of closeness between himself and his remaining brother, but Jonah didn't seem to want that kind of relationship. The boy lived within himself, keeping his dreams and thoughts private. Sometimes Lucas wondered what went on behind the boy's somber blue eyes, so like his own in color. He never found out.

Jonah's horse brought him home from school one afternoon. The boy clung to the saddle, an arrow all the way through his chest. Lucas had been the first to reach him, and a look of acute embarrassment had crossed Jonah's white face as he had fallen off the saddle into his brother's arms. He had looked up at Lucas, and for the first time his blue eyes weren't somber, but lit with a kind of fierce love, a joy. "I wish . . ." he had said, but what he wished had gone unsaid because he died on the next breath.

Lucas had knelt on the ground, rocking his brother in his arms. What had he wished, this young boy who hadn't had time to live much? Had his wish been something simple, a wish that it would stop hurting? Or had he wished for a girl's kiss, for his own future, for the pleasures that he hadn't yet been able to taste? Lucas didn't know; he only knew that in the last instant before death Jonah's eyes had held more life than ever before.

The Double C had soaked up Cochran blood as well as Indian blood. Cochrans lay buried in its soil. And now Lucas was the only Cochran left.

His dreams centered around the Double C, just as they always had. That was what had led to the rift with his father. Maybe if Jonah hadn't died Lucas wouldn't have felt so raw, so violent, but that was a big maybe, and he'd never let himself fret about it. The simple fact was that a ranch could have only one boss, and the two remaining Cochrans had butted heads time and again. Ellery had been content with what he had, while Lucas had wanted to enlarge.

The Double C had, after all, belonged to Ellery, so Lucas had been the one to go. Father and son had made their peace, but both knew two stallions just couldn't live in the same pasture. They regretted the break but accepted that, for both of them, it was better that Lucas lead his own life away from the Double C. They had written and even visited a couple of times in Denver, but Lucas hadn't returned to the ranch until Ellery's death.

He hadn't spent those ten years living in the lap of luxury. He had supported himself in various ways: as a cowhand, gambling, even as a lawman for a while. He knew ranch work inside out, and he was handy with a gun, but that alone hadn't kept him alive. A cool head, sharp eyes, and iron determination had served him well. Luke Cochran wasn't a man to mess with; he didn't let anything stand in his way when he wanted something. If the cost was high—well, he was willing to pay it if he wanted something bad enough. There wasn't much that could stop a man who was willing to pay the price, in blood or money, to get what he wanted, and he knew it.

But with Ellery's death the Double C had become his. It was already profitable, but he meant to make it even more so. Colorado was on the brink of statehood, which would open up a gold mine of opportunities to a man smart enough and tough enough to take them. He hadn't spent all of those ten years working at rough jobs; for the past two he had been in Denver, working with the territorial governor to secure statehood, learning how power worked, instantly seeing the vast applications of it. He had been part of the convention that had met in Denver the previous December to draft a constitution, and it was due to be voted on in July.

The value of statehood to the Double C was almost incalculable. With statehood would come settlers; with settlers would come the railroads. The railroads would make it infinitely easier for him to get his beef to market, and his profits would soar. He wanted the Double C to be the biggest and the best. It was all he had left now; the soil embraced his family in death even as it had sustained them in life. And as the Double C became richer he would work within the lines of contact he had already established in Denver. The two would feed each other: The Double C would make more money, and he would have more influence in Denver; the more influence he had in Denver, the more he could sway decisions that would affect the Double C, thus making it even richer.

He wasn't ambitious for the political aspect of it, but he needed to make certain the ranch would continue to prosper. He was willing to pay the price. The ten years out on his own had taught him some hard lessons, finishing the process of hardening that had begun in boyhood. Those lessons would come in handy now that he had an empire to build.

An empire needed heirs.

He wasn't in any real hurry to tie himself down, but he hadn't been back long before Olivia Millican, banker Wilson Millican's daughter, had caught his eye. She was pretty and cool and refined, socially adept and always well-mannered. She would be a perfect wife. A woman like her had to be courted, and Lucas was willing to do it. He liked her; he figured they would get along better than most. In another year or so she'd make him a fine wife.

But this year he'd be busy putting his plans into action.

There were so many things that he wanted to do. One of them was improving the herd, bringing in new bulls, trying new crossbreeds to produce a hardier steer without losing any quality in the meat. He also wanted to try different grasses for grazing, rather than letting the herd graze on whatever happened to be growing.

And he wanted to expand. Not too much right away; he didn't want to start off by overextending himself. But after producing a better herd he wanted to produce one that was bigger as well, and that meant more land for grazing, more water. He well knew the value of a good source of water; it could mean the difference between life and death for a herd. Many a rancher had gone under when the water dried up.

Building the ranch up would give him the solid base he needed to fulfill the rest of his ambitions. It was the first step, the most necessary step.

He had a good water source now, a small, lazily moving river that wound around the ranch. It had never gone dry that he could remember, but there had been a couple of summers when it had slowed to little more than a trickle. It had always rained before the situation became dire, but someday the rain might not come in time. Rainfall wasn't heavy in Colorado anyway; most of the water came from the snowcaps. A good year depended more on the winter snows than the summer rains, and it hadn't snowed much this past winter. A smart rancher always had more than one water source, just in case. Some streams would continue to run while others dried up.

One of the things he'd argued about with Ellery was the need for another good water source, Angel Creek specifically. Angel Creek and the river on the Double C came from the same source, a larger stream that divided in two and flowed down opposite sides of the mountain. But at the point of division the bed of Angel Creek lay lower than the other riverbed. Thus what runoff there was from the mountain during the dry weather would flow into Angel Creek, leaving the other dry until the water level in the stream rose enough to overflow into the higher riverbed.

Lucas had wanted to claim the narrow Angel Creek valley just for its water, but Ellery had refused, saying that the Double C had enough water to take care of its own, and anyway, Angel Creek was on the other side of the mountain with no good way to herd the cattle across it. They'd have to be moved *around* the mountain, and that was too much trouble. Besides, the valley was too small to support a large herd. Lucas had disagreed with his father's reasoning.

Angel Creek. Lucas narrowed his eyes, remembering how lush the valley was. Maybe it would be Cochran land after all.

He sought out his foreman. "Toby, didn't someone settle on Angel Creek some years back?"

William Tobias, who had been ranch foreman as far back as Lucas could remember, grunted an affirmative. "Yep. Nester by the name of Swann." A slight curl to his lip indicated how much he disliked even saying the word "nester."

Lucas grunted back, a scowl settling on his face. Like all cattlemen, he didn't care for nesters or the fences they put up on what had been open range. But maybe the nester on Angel Creek would consider selling. From what he'd seen of nesters, though, they were as hardheaded as mules.

Maybe this one would have more sense. It was worth a ride over to Angel Creek, at least, because he'd never know unless he asked.

A man on horseback could pick his way through any of the narrow passes, though trying to move a herd over them would have been stupid. Lucas eyed the sun and calculated that he had plenty of time before nightfall to ride over there and back, so there wasn't any point in waiting.

He wasn't optimistic about talking the nester into selling, and it put him in an irritable mood. If Ellery had listened to him, Angel Creek would already be his. Or he could have claimed it for his own before the settlers had started moving in if he hadn't been too young and hotheaded to plan ahead. Looking back and realizing what he should have done was just a waste of time.

The little homestead surprised him as he rode down the broad slope toward the farm buildings. There were only two cows and a bull, but they were fat and healthy. A lone horse in the corral looked sleek and well cared for, even if it wasn't a prime specimen of horseflesh. Chickens pecked contentedly at the ground, scarcely paying him any attention when he rode up and dismounted, tying the reins to a post while he looked around with interest. The small cabin, though roughly built, was neat and sturdy, as were the barn and fences. In the back was a plot for a large vegetable garden, the ground recently broken in preparation for spring planting, though it was still a bit early. He couldn't see anything out of place or untended, and his slim hope that the nester would sell disappeared. If the place had been rundown he would have had a chance, but this homestead was prospering. There was no need for the man to go anywhere else.

The cabin door opened, and a slim young woman stepped out onto the porch, a shotgun in her hands. Her face was calm but alert, and Lucas saw that her finger was on the trigger.

"State your business, mister."

A shotgun made him wary at any time, but he was doubly edgy facing one in the hands of a woman. If she got excited, she might accidently kill either him or his horse, or both. He tamped down a quick rise of anger and made his voice low and soothing. "I don't mean you any harm, ma'am. You can put that shotgun down."

The shotgun didn't waver. The twin barrels looked enormous. "I'll make my own judgment about that," she replied calmly. "Too many cowboys think it's funny to trample my garden."

"You don't have a garden yet," he pointed out.

"But I do have livestock to run off, so I'll keep this gun right where it is until you answer my question."

He could see the green of her eyes even in the shadow of the porch where she stood. There was no fear or uncertainty in her gaze, nor any hostility, come to that, only a certain purposefulness. A little bit of admiration tinged his anger. The nester was one lucky man to have a wife with this sort of gumption, he thought. Lucas was abruptly certain that she would hit whatever she aimed at. He was careful not to make any sudden moves as he reached up and took off his hat. "I'm Lucas Cochran from the Double C. I came over to make your husband's acquaintance, Mrs. Swann, and talk a little business with him."

She gave him a cool, level look. "George Swann was my father, not my husband. He died six years ago."

He was beginning to get irritated at being held at bay. "Then maybe I could talk to your husband. Or your brother. Whoever owns the place."

"I don't have a husband or a brother. I'm Dee Swann. This is my land."

His interest sharpened. He looked around the tidy little place again, wondering who helped her do the work. Maybe there were other women on the place, but even that would be unheard of; women simply didn't work a homestead on their own. If their men died, they went to live with relatives somewhere. He listened but didn't hear any voices or movement inside the cabin. "Are you alone here?"

She smiled, her expression as cool as her eyes, challenging him. "No. I have this shotgun."

"You can put it down," he said sharply, his irritation now plain. "I just came by to get acquainted, not to do you any harm."

She looked him over carefully, and he had the feeling it wasn't what he'd said that reassured her, but rather her own private assessment of him as a man that prompted her to lower the muzzle of the shotgun toward the floor and nod at him. "It's dinnertime," she said. "I eat early. You're welcome to join me, if you'd like."

He wasn't hungry, but he seized the opportunity and followed her into the cabin. It was only two rooms and a loft, but it was as neat inside as out. The kitchen was on the left; what he assumed to be her bedroom was on the right. There was a comfortable chair pulled over next to the fireplace with an oil lamp on a small table beside it, and to his surprise a book lay open on the table. He looked around, noting some rough, handmade shelves lined with books. She wasn't illiterate, then.

She had gone straight to the wood stove and was ladling steaming soup into two big bowls. Lucas took his hat off and sat down at the sturdy table just as she placed the bowl in front of him. A plate of biscuits was already on the table, as well as a pot of coffee. The soup was thick with vegetables and tender pieces of beef. Lucas found himself going at it as if he hadn't had anything all day.

Dee Swann sat across from him, eating as composedly as if she were alone. Lucas watched her, studying her face. She intrigued him. She didn't flirt with him the way he was used to women doing, or even seem to be aware that he was a man beyond the simple fact of identification. She was straightforward in her speech and actions, but he thought that calmness just might be a cover for the heat underneath. It was in her eyes, long and green, with banked fires in them.

At first glance she was plain, but closer examination made him realize it was an impression created by her utilitarian clothing and severe hairstyle; her black hair was pulled back and twisted into a tight knot at her nape. She had an exotic sort of attractiveness, with high cheekbones and a wide, soft mouth, but they weren't the kind of looks that were blatantly fetching. The heat of sexual arousal began to build in his loins and belly as he watched her eat, dipping daintily into the soup without any indication that she even remembered he was there.

"Don't you have any other family?" he asked abruptly, determined to make her pay attention to him.

She shrugged and put down her spoon. "I have cousins, but no one close."

"Wouldn't they take you in?"

Those green eyes studied him for a long time before she deigned to answer. "I suppose they would have, if I'd asked. I preferred to stay here."

"Why? It has to be lonesome for you, as well as dangerous."

"I have the shotgun," she reminded him. "And no, I'm not lonesome. I like it out here."

"I suppose you have plenty of men friends." How could she not have? A young, attractive woman, alone at that, would attract all sorts of attention.

She laughed. It wasn't a maidenly giggle, but the full-throated sound of a woman who knew how to enjoy herself. "Not since they learned I know how to hit what I aim at. After I peppered a few, the others decided to leave me alone."

"Why did you do that? You might have been married by now." Her laughter made the heat intensify. Whatever her reason, he was glad she hadn't married, because he'd always made it a point to stay away from other men's wives even when the wives in question were willing.

"Oh, I've had some marriage proposals, Mr. Cochran. Three, I think. I'm not married because I don't want to be. I don't plan on ever getting married."

In his experience, all women wanted to get married. He sipped his coffee and eyed her over the rim of the cup. "If you got married, you'd have a man to do the work around here."

"I can handle the work just fine. And if I got married, it wouldn't be my land any longer, it would be his. I'd rather be my own woman."

They were sitting alone in her cozy cabin eating food she had prepared. The conversation had without effort become far more personal than it ever should have been on first meeting. An aura of intimacy wrapped them, making him think of reaching out for her and drawing her onto his knee, the way he would if she were his woman. It was a fantasy, though, because her composed green gaze invited nothing more than conversation. It irritated him, because he was used to women paying him more attention than that. Even Olivia, with her perfect manners and composure, responded to him in the way he expected.

It was probably the last thing Dee Swann intended, but her disinterest provoked the opposite reaction in him. Lucas had always enjoyed a challenge, and she was certainly that; any woman who used a shotgun to discourage suitors was bound to keep him on his toes. Maybe she didn't need a man to work her land, but a woman sure needed a man to take care of her other needs. It was fine with him that she didn't want to get married, because she wasn't the type of woman he would ever select to be his wife. Dee would, however, he thought, make a fine bed partner.

Lucas had gotten out of a lot of tight situations by using his head, and he was too smart to let any of his thoughts show. He knew that if he even hinted at anything sexual between them right now she'd have that shotgun pointed at him faster than he could blink. Let her get used to him first, accept him as a friend, then they'd become really *close* friends. So he kept his face blank as he turned the conversation to his original reason for being there.

"You've gotten by okay because so far all you've had to deal with are a few liquored-up cowhands with nothing more than hoorahing on their minds. But let a man come up on you without all the yelling and shooting to warn you, and he'd be on you before you could get to your shotgun. Or a bunch of them could decide to get even with you; there's no way you could guard both doors and every window. It's dangerous for you out here," he said persuasively. "With the money you could get for this land you could set yourself up in town in any kind of business you wanted, and you'd be safe. Think about it. I'm willing to give you more than a fair price."

"I don't have to think about it," she said. "I don't want to sell. This is my home; I like it here. I tend my garden and sell vegetables in town and get along just fine. If I'd wanted to sell, I could have sold to Mr. Bellamy a long time ago."

He frowned. "Bellamy's offered to buy you out?"

"Several times."

"You should have taken his offer. You're a woman alone." He didn't like the idea of Bellamy owning Angel Creek, but he was serious about the potential danger she was in. A good-looking woman living by herself like this was just asking for trouble from any no-good passing through.

But Dee only shrugged, dismissing his warnings. "So? I'd be alone no matter where I went, so I might as well stay here."

"You'd have other people close by if you lived in town, in case you needed help. You'd be safe instead of working yourself half to death out here."

"And just what would I do in town?" she demanded, getting to her feet and placing her empty bowl in the big wash bowl. "How would I earn a living? The town doesn't need another dress shop, or another hat shop, or another general store, and the money from selling the land wouldn't last forever. There's nothing I could do except maybe take one of the rooms over the saloon, and somehow I don't think I'd be a success at that."

Luke was jolted at the thought of her working as a whore. No, he couldn't see it either. She was too proud and independent. A man didn't want a challenge when he went to a whorehouse; he wanted simple, unthinking relief. He pictured her taking her clothes off, her eyes flashing green heat in a dim room, and his blood started pounding through his body. Mounting this filly would take a strong man, but it would be worth it when he was locked deep inside her, feeling her heat, riding her hard and fast. Only a strong man would be able to handle her, keep her satisfied.

He was a strong man, and he liked a challenge. His earlier thoughts hardened into determination. He was going to teach Dee Swann that she needed a man for one thing, at least.

But because he was smart, he didn't say anything on the subject or push her anymore to sell her land. He thanked her politely for the meal, offered his aid if she ever needed it, tipped his hat, and left like a gentleman. He didn't feel the least bit gentlemanly, though, as he rode back toward the cut over the mountain. He felt tense and alive, his senses alert, his loins stirring with anticipation. No, there was nothing gentlemanly about his thoughts or his intentions; in both he was purely male, scenting female and wanting her. The only thing was, the female didn't know yet that she was being pursued, so she wasn't even running.

Dee went to the door and watched him ride away. She felt strangely disturbed and too warm; she loosened the top buttons of her blouse to let the cooling air waft over her throat. So that was Lucas Cochran. That brief glimpse of him in the general store hadn't prepared her for a face-to-face meeting. She hadn't realized that he was quite so tall, or so strongly built, or that his iron will gleamed so plainly in his blue eyes. Lucas Cochran was used to getting what he wanted, and he hadn't liked it at all that she had turned down his offer for the land.

She would bet all the money she had that he would be back.

3

OLIVIA MILLICAN HAD SPENT HER ENTIRE LIFE BEING
the perfect daughter and the perfect lady. It wasn't
difficult; she was by nature both kind and composed.
Sometimes she felt guilty that she had had such an
easy, privileged life when she could see how so many
other people had to struggle to have even a fraction of
the luxuries to which she was accustomed, but she was
also intelligent enough to see that neither was it her
fault. Her father had worked hard to make his bank
successful; any child of his would have had the same
comfortable life. She tried to do what she could to
help with the few small charities around town, and she
tried never to be mean or rude. Her rules of conduct
were simple, and she truly tried to adhere to them.

All she had ever wanted was to fall in love with a
good man and have him love her in return, marry her,
and give her his children. When she was younger she
had never thought that it was such an unreasonable

thing to expect from life; heaven knew it seemed an easy enough thing for most of her friends. She still didn't see that it was anything but an ordinary wish, yet somehow it had never happened.

She was twenty-five now, virtually an old maid, though there again her father's money was shielding her. A poor woman of twenty-five would have been an old maid; a wealthy woman of twenty-five was still "a good catch." Yet somehow, though there were good men in town, she had never loved any of them, and none of them had ever seemed to be wildly in love with her, and now just about all of those her age were married to someone else.

Except Lucas Cochran.

His name ran through her mind as she worked with her mother on the fine embroidery of a linen tablecloth, and she shivered a little. It wasn't that she disliked him; he was handsome in a hard sort of way, wealthy, intelligent, well-mannered, and certainly eligible. It wasn't her imagination that he had singled her out in some small way every time they had met since his return to town, for other people had remarked on it. He danced well and treated her with respect. Her feminine instincts also told her that after they had known each other a respectable length of time he would ask her to marry him. She was very much afraid that, because she was twenty-five and this would likely be her last chance at marriage and a family, she would say yes. But Lucas Cochran didn't love her. Despite all of the little attentions he paid her, despite the faintly possessive expression in his blue eyes whenever he looked at her, as if she already belonged to him, she knew that she aroused none of the passionate emotion in him that she had always longed for from the man she would marry.

And he was a hard man, hard in a way that her father, who had a forceful personality himself, couldn't even begin to match. Lucas Cochran would never allow anyone to stand between him and anything he wanted. Olivia knew herself to be no more a match for him than her father was; far less, in fact. Oh, he would protect her as his wife, give her children, but she would never matter any more to him than any other woman he might have chosen to fill the position. She could expect consideration but not caring, physical attention but never love, protection but not devotion.

But if she refused him, she would likely die without ever marrying and having her own family, and her woman's heart cried out for children.

"I've changed my mind about visiting Patience," Honora Millican said in her soft voice.

Olivia looked up, startled. Her mother had been looking forward to visiting her sister in San Francisco in the summer, and Olivia couldn't think of anything that would have changed her mind. Truth to tell, she'd been as eager for the trip as her mother. They seldom saw Aunt Patience. It had been almost five years since their last visit, and other than visiting her favorite relative she had also been eager to visit the glorious shops in San Francisco again. "But we've been planning it for over a year now!"

"I know, dear, but I really don't think we should leave town for several months just now." Honora smiled sweetly at her daughter, the smile that Olivia had inherited.

Olivia was both confused and disappointed. "Why ever not?"

"With the attention Mr. Cochran has been paying you? It wouldn't do to be gone so long and let some other young woman gain his attention."

Olivia bent her head over the embroidery to hide her expression, which she knew must reveal the leap of panic she felt. Had she also been hoping against hope that this time she would meet someone special in San Francisco? "You talk as if it's a foregone conclusion that he intends to propose," she said, though she thought it was herself.

Honora said placidly, "Of course he does. Why, everyone can see it in the way he looks at you."

"He isn't in love with me," Olivia said, raising troubled eyes to her mother.

But Honora didn't look in the least disturbed. "I admit Mr. Cochran isn't one to wear his heart on his sleeve. But why else would he pay such attention to you?"

"Because I'm the banker's daughter," she replied. "I'm presentable, and I was schooled back East."

Honora put down her needle and frowned, her interest now wholly engaged. "That's a remarkably cynical outlook, dear. What makes you think Mr. Cochran isn't interested in you for yourself? You're a beautiful young woman, even if I do say so myself."

Olivia bit her lip, knowing that she didn't have any solid reasons she could put forth for her statement, only intuition. She didn't want to cause Honora any worry. Her mother tended to fret to excess if any ill wind of health or humours blew on the two people she loved most in the world, her husband and daughter. It was both a source of security, knowing herself so well loved, and a sense of responsibility that she should do whatever she could to keep Honora from being upset.

So she made herself smile at her mother and say, "All the same, I'm not certain it wouldn't do Mr. Cochran some good to think about me meeting so many good-looking men in San Francisco."

Honora's face cleared, and she began to chuckle. "I see. You don't want him to feel too sure of himself. Wonderful idea! But all the same, I don't think we should go off for the entire summer this early in the relationship."

Olivia stifled a sigh. She had hoped that Honora would think it such a good idea that the decision not to go to San Francisco would be reconsidered. Now she knew that she would have to tell her mother all of her fears and uncertainties in order to change her mind, and Olivia wasn't willing to do that. For one thing, she wasn't certain that she wasn't simply being foolish, fretting over "love." No other young woman in town would hesitate a minute if given the opportunity to marry Lucas Cochran—well, except for Dee, but Dee was different. Another reason was that Olivia was a naturally reserved person, respectful of the privacy of others simply because she needed it so much herself. Not even to her mother could she reveal her inner fears, because Honora would then find it necessary to confide in Olivia's father and perhaps even in certain of her friends in town; in short, it would soon become common knowledge.

Both of her parents would become so upset and make such a fuss that she simply couldn't face it. She was their only child, having been born after Honora had miscarried twice, and they had showered her with all of the devotion that should have been shared with a houseful of children. They wanted only the best for her; nothing else, in their eyes, was good enough. She would do anything to keep them from knowing how unhappy she was.

So she bent her head over the embroidery and said nothing else on the subject, pushing her unhappiness to the back of her mind as she listened to Honora's placid chatter about the upcoming social. Prosper had a rather active social life for a town its size, with various small parties and entertainments arranged throughout the year. Late each spring the women of the town put on a large picnic and dance, and everyone in the area was invited. The women in town took turns organizing the affair, and this spring was Honora's turn. The older woman was in her element, planning and organizing, delegating, double-checking and triple-checking each detail. For weeks her conversation had consisted of how well or ill things were going, and today was no exception. Olivia listened patiently, offering advice whenever asked but for the most part providing only an audience, which was really all Honora wanted.

As often as not, when Honora began reviewing her plans and accomplishments she eventually remembered some little detail that had to be taken care of immediately, and that day was no exception. She abruptly dropped the embroidery hoop to her lap and said, "Oh, dear."

The moment of crisis was so predictable that Olivia smiled with gentle amusement even as she asked, "Is something wrong?"

"I completely forgot to arrange with Beatrice Padgett for us to use her punch set! I can't believe it slipped my mind like that."

"I'm sure she takes it for granted that her punch set will be needed," Olivia comforted. "After all, she's the only person in town who owns over three hundred punch cups."

"Still, it would be terribly rude not to *ask* her, just to *assume* that her possessions are available for our use. I'll write her a note right now," Honora said, putting the hoop aside and rising to cross to her writing desk. "Do you have a moment to spare to take it to her, dear? I simply have too much to do this afternoon, though I'd love to visit with Beatrice, but you know how she talks. It's practically impossible to get away from her once she gets started."

"Of course," Olivia said, gladly putting her own embroidery hoop aside. She was very good at needlework, but that didn't mean she enjoyed it. "I think I'll go for a ride while I'm out." She wanted to be alone for a while; maybe a brisk ride would banish her melancholy, which lingered as a hollow feeling deep inside despite her efforts to push it away. Or maybe she would visit Dee. As soon as she had the thought she realized that was exactly what she needed. Dee's implacable logic always went straight to the heart of a matter, and she always said exactly what she thought. Olivia needed that kind of clear thinking right now.

She went upstairs to change into her riding habit while Honora set about writing. By the time she came back down the stairs Honora was folding the note.

"There," she said, tucking the paper into Olivia's pocket. "Take your time, dear, and do tell Beatrice that I'm sorry I couldn't come myself, but I promise to visit her soon to go over all the plans for the social."

The Millicans kept their two horses in the livery, so Olivia walked first to the Padgett house, which took only five minutes. But it was the truth that Beatrice Padgett liked to talk, and it was over an hour before Olivia was able to leave. Beatrice insisted that she come in for tea to the point that continued refusal would have been embarrassing, so Olivia found herself once again sitting and listening, with nothing more required of her than an occasional nod or comment.

It was an enjoyable hour, though, because Beatrice was a genuinely likable woman, friendly and without malice. Olivia had often thought that Beatrice and Ezekiel Padgett were something of a mismatch. Beatrice, in her late forties, still retained enough beauty for one to see that she had once been quite something. She was a warm woman given to hugs and pats, freely affectionate and exuding a soft, rather voluptuous sensuality. Ezekiel, on the other hand, was tall and dour, seldom smiling, his face too rawboned for handsomeness. Olivia had wondered how they could live together in any sort of harmony, though she had once seen Ezekiel look down at his wife's face when he thought them unobserved, and his expression had softened almost to tenderness.

So love did grow even in unlikely marriages, perhaps had been there from the beginning, at least on Beatrice's part, for why else would such an affectionate woman have married such a dour man? It was plain to anyone why Ezekiel would have married

Beatrice, even without love, so Olivia didn't consider that.

Perhaps she was foolish to worry about marrying Lucas. Maybe they would grow to love each other as much as Beatrice and Ezekiel did, as much as her own parents did.

But no matter how she tried, she simply couldn't imagine such a look on Lucas's face as she had seen on Ezekiel's.

Dee looked out the window when she heard someone riding up and smiled when she saw it was Olivia. It had been too long since they'd had a chance to chat, but now that the weather was better Olivia would come to visit more often. She poured two cups of coffee and walked out on the porch to greet her friend.

Olivia dismounted and took the coffee with a smile of thanks as they sat down on the porch. "I thought winter was never going to end," she sighed. "I've wanted to come out several times, but the weather never cooperated."

"From what I heard in Winches's store, Lucas Cochran's courting you."

That was Dee, going right to the point. Olivia's tension eased a little. It was a relief to talk to Dee because there were no social inanities with her, no need for a polite social mask or worry that Dee might be shocked at anything she said. Not that she was likely to say anything shocking, Olivia admitted ruefully to herself. It was just that it was nice to know one *could*.

"It seems so," she said.

"Seems? He either is or he isn't."

"Well, he hasn't actually said anything. It's just that he's paid attention to me."

"Enough attention for people to start talking about a wedding?"

"Yes," Olivia admitted, unable to hide the misery in her eyes.

"Do you love him?"

"No."

"Then don't marry him," Dee said with a finality that suggested the matter was closed.

"But what if he's my last chance?" Olivia asked softly.

"For what?"

"To get married."

Dee sipped her coffee. "Do you really think you'll never meet anyone else?"

"It isn't that. It's just that no one has ever fallen in love with me, and maybe no one ever will. If I can't have love, I'd still like to have a family. He truly may be my last chance."

"Well, I'm probably not the best person to come to for advice," Dee said, and she chuckled. "After all, I've already turned down three men. He came out here the other day, by the way. Cochran, that is. He wanted to buy Angel Creek."

The thought of that was interesting. Lucas was accustomed to having things his way. Olivia could just imagine what he'd thought when he'd met Dee, who could be as intractable as a rock wall when she chose.

"What did you think of him?"

Dee grinned. "That he'd make a dangerous enemy.

And that no one tells him 'no' very often. He doesn't take it well."

"And you enjoyed telling him."

"Of course I did." Mischief gleamed in her green eyes as she glanced at Olivia. "He could use taking down a peg or two."

"I don't think he'll give up," Olivia warned.

"No, he won't."

Dee looked as if she positively relished the thought of thwarting Lucas, and not for the first time Olivia wished she could be more like her friend. Dee wasn't intimidated by Lucas, or by anyone. There was a kind of inner strength to her, a surety that most people didn't have. Olivia didn't feel certain of anything, with her longing to have a family at odds with her fear of marrying someone she didn't love. She couldn't imagine Dee ever feeling that kind of uncertainty. Dee would simply make up her mind one way or the other, and that would be that.

"I think Lucas would ride roughshod over me if I married him," Olivia said, and she bit her lip.

Dee thought about it, then nodded. "Probably."

That blunt assessment startled Olivia into a spurt of laughter. "You didn't have to agree!"

"Oh, you aren't weak," Dee explained, smiling a little. "It's just that you're too gentle to fight him when he needs to be fought. But cheer up. Maybe you'll meet someone in San Francisco you really want to marry."

"Mother's canceled the trip. She didn't think it would be smart to leave Lucas for such a long time while he's showing so much interest. Of course, Lucas may not have any plans to marry at all, and I could be worrying over nothing." The thought popped into her head that Dee would make Lucas a much better wife than she herself would, and she almost blurted it out but stopped herself in time. Dee would look at her as if she were crazy if she said such a thing.

But it was true. In both temperament and character Dee was a fair match for Lucas; both of them were so strong that they would completely overshadow anyone who wasn't just as strong. The only thing was, Dee wasn't the least interested in getting married.

Nevertheless, the idea lingered.

On the way home Olivia detoured by the bank to tell her father hello. Just as she stepped up on the sidewalk the door to the bank opened, and Kyle Bellamy came out, flanked by two of his men. He removed his hat as soon as he saw her.

"Miss Millican, how are you today?"

"Fine, thank you, Mr. Bellamy. And you?"

"Couldn't be better." He looked down at her, giving her his self-confident smile. No doubt about it, Kyle Bellamy was a good-looking man, and he knew it. His dark hair was thick and curly, his eyes light brown beneath black brows, his smile white and straight. Moreover, he was tall and muscular, and his ranch, though nowhere near the size of the Double C, was prosperous and growing. For all that, something about the man made her uneasy.

He made no move to continue on his way, and Olivia's innate good manners came to the fore. "I hope you're making plans to attend the spring social. It won't be long," she said.

"I wouldn't miss it." He gave her his white, wolfish grin. "Especially if you're going to be there."

"Just about everyone in town will be there," Olivia replied, neatly sidestepping his comment, which was personal enough to make her feel uncomfortable.

"I'll look forward to claiming a dance with you." He tipped his hat again and stepped past her, followed by both of his men.

As the second hired hand passed he, too, tipped his hat, surprising Olivia into darting a quick look at his face. She had only a fast impression of black hair, darkly tanned skin, and black eyes warm with admiration before he was past her, but the impact was strong enough to freeze her in her tracks, a little stunned.

Surely she had mistaken his expression. After all, her glance had been so quick. No, surely the man hadn't looked at her with *tenderness,* the way Ezekiel looked at Beatrice. How could he, when he didn't even know her? But the fact remained that his look, imagined or not, had made her heart beat a little faster and her skin feel a little warm.

She entered the bank, smiling politely and returning the greetings of those who spoke to her on her way into her father's office. Wilson Millican rose on her entrance, beaming his welcome. "Your mother's had you running another errand, at a guess," he said, and he laughed as their gazes met in perfect understanding. "She's enjoying this as much as if she were sixteen again and this was her first party."

"She'll swear she never wants to be involved in the planning again, but by the time next February rolls around she'll be fretting to get started."

They chatted for a few minutes, with Olivia telling

him about her visit with Beatrice. She didn't want to take up too much of his time, so she kept her visit short. She was rising to her feet when her curiosity got the better of her, and she said, "I stopped outside to talk with Mr. Bellamy for a few moments. Who were those two men with him?"

"Two of his cowhands, Pierce and Fronteras, though from the looks of them I'd say they were handier with a pistol than a rope."

"Gunmen?" she asked, startled. "Why would he need gunmen?"

"Now, I didn't say they were gunmen. I said they looked like they'd be handy with their pistols, and maybe they are, but then a good many men around here are good hands with a firearm. As far as I know, Bellamy's cowhands are just that, cowhands." He patted her arm in reassurance, though he wasn't too certain of his own words, especially when they concerned the two men that had been with Bellamy. One thing was certain, though, and that was that he wouldn't want either of those two men anywhere near Olivia. She was too fine a person to associate with that type of man. None of the ranch hands caused any trouble in town other than the normal drinking and fighting sometimes, but as a father he couldn't be too careful of his daughter's well-being.

"Which one was which?" Olivia asked, still driven by her curiosity.

"What?"

"Which man was Pierce, and which was Fronteras?"

"Pierce has been with Bellamy for a couple of years now. He's a quiet man, never says much. The dark,

Mexican-looking man is Fronteras. Guess he is Mexican at that, though he's tall for one. Must be mostly Spanish."

He was a Mexican. She felt a little surprised at herself for not having realized that at a glance, though he *was* tall, as her father had noted. Then she was even more surprised by her own curiosity about a man whom she had never even met, because passing on the sidewalk certainly didn't constitute an introduction. It wasn't her usual behavior, but then she was upset by her increasing sensation of being caught in a trap. She didn't know what she could do to escape, or even if she wanted to escape. All she knew was that she felt on the verge of panic.

"A man could do worse than marrying a banker's daughter," Kyle Bellamy mused. "Especially one who looks like Olivia Millican."

Pierce grunted in reply. Luis Fronteras didn't say anything.

"She's his only child. When he dies she'll get everything. Or rather her husband will."

"I heard Cochran was courting her," Fronteras murmured.

Kyle shrugged his shoulders. "That doesn't mean I can't pay attention to the lady, too."

He sipped his whiskey, thinking about Olivia Millican. Why not? He had as much chance with her as anyone else, maybe more. Women had always seemed to like him. He liked a bit more spunk in his women than Olivia seemed to have, but she was pretty and rich, and in Kyle's experience money made up for a lot of shortcomings. He was doing all right with money right now, but he had learned the hard way not to count on everything staying all right. Having Wilson Millican's money would make his life a whole lot more comfortable. He'd start his own courting of Olivia and give Cochran something to think about.

He was on his second whiskey, savoring both the biting, smoky taste of the liquor and his mental image of marrying Olivia Millican, when Tillie sauntered over to him. He leaned back against the bar and enjoyed the sight, because Tillie had a walk that could make a man's privates stand at attention even if he had a lot more than two whiskeys in him.

Tillie was something, all right. He'd met her for the first time about ten years back, in New Orleans. She'd been all of fifteen then, he guessed, remembering how fresh and wild she'd looked. He grinned, thinking that he was probably the only person in town who knew that her name was Mathilde. He called her that sometimes, when they were in bed together, always earning a long warning look from those heavy-lidded eyes of hers. It was all right with him if she chose to be Tillie the saloon girl; he just didn't want her to forget that he knew where she came from.

Of course, she knew more about him than anyone else, too, but he didn't worry about it. Tillie had never tried to use the information to get money out of him. She was oddly accepting of her life in a two-bit saloon in a small town, her rich brown eyes full of a half-weary, half-accepting worldliness. A man never felt as if Tillie was judging him; she simply took him as he was and expected nothing else.

A lot of the men in Prosper, including the married ones, had found their way into Tillie's embrace. She was generous even when her time was paid for, giving at least the appearance of affection and sometimes even her passion.

Kyle never expected anything less than full participation from her and never let her give less. Sometimes she wanted to hold back from him, but he'd known her a long time, knew exactly how to make her squirm and buck beneath him, and in the end she would always give him what he wanted.

She looked more like twenty than twenty-five, he thought, admiring her creamy skin and dark mahogany hair. She was still slim, still supple, her breasts full and upright.

She leaned against the bar, her mouth voluptuous with invitation. "Kyle," she murmured in greeting.

He didn't need much encouragement. His name in that soft drawl was enough. He set his glass down and took her arm. "Upstairs."

She blinked at him in mocking surprise. "Well, hello to you, too. Nice day, isn't it?"

He ignored her light sarcasm and continued propelling her toward the stairs. He gave an abrupt flick of his hand to Pierce and Fronteras, letting them know that he'd be a while and they could do whatever they wanted.

Luis Fronteras watched Bellamy disappear up the stairs with his arm around Tillie's waist before returning his attention to the beer in front of him. Pierce sat down at a table with him, silently nursing his own beer. That was normal for Pierce, who seldom said more than three words in a row.

Luis was irritated by the small pang of jealousy he'd felt watching Bellamy and Tillie go upstairs together.

Not because of Tillie, though God knows she was a head-turning woman, but just because of the simple fact there was a bond between the two of them, even if it was comprised mainly of plain sex. It had been a long time since he had felt kinship of any sort with anyone. Ten years, in fact. Ten years of drifting, of occasionally relieving his sexual urges with a willing woman but never giving her any more of himself than the use of his body. At first he had needed the mental and emotional solitude, then it had become habit, and now it felt impossible to change even though he sometimes wanted more. More . . . what?

More women? He could have a woman anytime he wanted. Luis had a gift for pleasing women, and he knew it. Mainly it was that he liked everything about women, even their tempers and jealousies and plain contrariness, and what woman could resist being so frankly appreciated? To Luis it was simple: He was a man, therefore he loved the ladies. They were the most delicious creatures he could imagine. Women had flocked to him from the time his voice first began to deepen.

But he wasn't interested in a multitude of women. Right now he was interested in one woman: the blonde Bellamy had spoken to outside the bank. Miss Millican, the banker's daughter. Olivia. He had liked her quiet composure and pretty face as well as the shape of her bosom beneath the prim cut of her riding habit.

He hadn't liked the idea of Bellamy courting her, using her just to get his hands on her father's money. A woman deserved more than that, especially one who looked as sweet as Olivia. It wouldn't bother

Bellamy at all to use her, but Luis had unerring instincts when it came to women, and something told him that such callousness would destroy her.

There was already sadness in those pretty blue eyes. He had caught only a glimpse of it, but it had been there. Something was making her unhappy. Bellamy would only make her even more unhappy.

He'd like to kiss those sad shadows out of her eyes, hold her and pet her and tell her how very lovely she was. A woman always needed to know that she was appreciated.

He smiled cynically to himself. He was a drifter and a Mexican, too handy with a gun for his own good. She was the banker's daughter, and it looked like she would have her choice between the two richest ranchers in the area. There wasn't much chance Miss Olivia Millican would ever even know his name, let alone let him hold her.

4

SOMEHOW DEE WASN'T SURPRISED TO SEE LUCAS Cochran riding toward her three days later. It was still early in the morning; she was outside with a pan of chicken feed, scattering it to the clucking fowl grouped around her skirts. "Mr. Cochran," she said in greeting when he was close enough to hear her.

He didn't dismount but leaned down to prop his forearm on the saddle horn as he watched her strew the feed. "Good morning," he said. "I was on my way into town and thought I'd ride over to check on you."

Her eyes were bright in the strong morning sun, and greener than any he'd ever seen before. "I don't remember saying anything that would give you the impression I needed to be checked on, Mr. Cochran," she said with more than a little sharpness. She had painstakingly taught herself how to be independent and resented his implication that she wasn't capable of taking care of herself.

"Call me Lucas," he said. "Or Luke."

"Why?"

"Because I'd like for us to be friends."

"Not likely."

He grinned, enjoying her starchiness. It was refreshing to be around a woman who didn't cater to him and defer to his every opinion. "Why not? Looks to me like we could both use a friend."

"I like being alone," she replied, tilting the pan upside down and slapping it lightly on the sides to knock loose the last few grains of feed. She crossed to the small back stoop and hung the pan on a nail driven into the wall. Lucas walked his horse behind her as she strode swiftly to the barn, her skirts kicking up with each step. She wore only one petticoat, he decided, eyeing the brisk sway of that blue skirt. And a thin one at that.

He ducked his head down to enter the barn, automatically closing his eyes for a second so they could adjust to the dimness, and watched as she efficiently ladled feed to the single horse and two cows.

She was damn good at ignoring him, he saw, and he began to get a little irate at her manner. Then he remembered that it was her farm, and she hadn't invited him. His horse stamped a hoof restively as she fetched a stool and positioned a milk bucket under one of the cows. Lucas sighed and dismounted, looping his reins over a rail. The other cow needed milking, too. "Got another bucket?" he asked.

Streams of milk were already hissing into the bucket in time with the motions of her hands as she turned her head to him. Those green eyes had a dangerous look to them now. "I don't need any help."

"I can see that." His irritation was growing, and it echoed in his voice. "But did you ever think about accepting an offer of help, not because you couldn't handle it just fine yourself but because the chore would get done faster with two people working at it instead of just one?"

She considered that, then gave a brief nod. "All right. There's another clean bucket in the tack room there, to the right. But I don't have another stool. You'll have to squat."

He fetched the bucket and patted the cow on her fat sides, letting her know he was there before he slid the bucket under her. He squatted down and wrapped his strong fingers around the long teats, then pulled with the rhythmic motion that, once learned, was never forgotten. Hot milk splashed into the bucket. His mouth moved in a wry grin as he thought how glad he was none of his men could see him now.

"Have you always been such a hedgehog?" he asked in a tone of casual interest.

"I reckon," she replied in the same manner, and he grinned again.

"Any particular reason for it?"

"Men."

He snorted. "Yeah, we can be real bastards."

He wasn't certain, but he thought he heard a chuckle. "I wouldn't dream of disagreeing."

"Those lovesick swains of yours must have been persistent," he said, hazarding a guess.

"Some of them. But it wasn't love they had on their minds, and we both know it. It seems like men just naturally see a woman alone as fair game."

There wasn't another woman in town who would have said that to him, but then he had already realized at their first meeting that Dee was blunt in her speech and frank in her opinions. He felt a slow burn of anger at the thought of other men trying to seduce her, or maybe even just catch her alone when they wouldn't bother with pretense of seduction. The knowledge that he was determined to seduce her himself didn't moderate his temper. For one thing, he didn't intend to dishonor her; no one but the two of them would ever know what went on between them. He wasn't a raw kid who felt the need to boast about his women in order to impress others with his masculinity. For another thing, damn if he didn't respect her for what she had accomplished out there. It had taken a lot of hard work, but she hadn't flinched from it, rather had risen to the challenge and gloried in it. The pristine condition of the farm was a true measure of her fierce spirit.

His voice was tight with that possessive anger when he said, "If anyone else bothers you, let me know."

"I appreciate the offer, but it's something I have to take care of for myself. You might not always be around; they have to know I can defend myself, that I don't need to rely on anyone else."

Her logic was unassailable, but he didn't like it. "I can make certain they never come back."

"The shotgun tends to be persuasive," she said with humor in her voice. "There's nothing like buckshot in his backside to make a man reconsider an idea. Besides, I'm not sure I can afford to have you as a protector."

He didn't pause in his milking, but his brows drew together and his head came up. "Why not?" he demanded sharply.

"Folks would think we were sleeping together." When he didn't reply to that, Dee continued to explain. "The men around here pretty much leave me alone now because I've convinced them I don't want *any* man. But if they thought I'd let one man in my bed, then they would think I was available, and they'd take even less kindly to being turned down than they did before. It would get nasty, and I'd probably have to kill some of them."

His strong hands had emptied the cow's udder, and he lifted the bucket away, rising to his feet just as Dee finished milking. Her cheeks were flushed with her exertions as she slid the bucket away and stood, stretching her back. Lucas leaned down, picked up the other bucket, and walked out of the barn toward the house, leaving her to follow. Her brows rose at the way he made himself so at home on her place. It was obvious he was used to being the boss. Then she shrugged; he was being helpful, so it would be petty of her to complain that he was too self-confident about it.

He waited on the back stoop for her to open the door. "What do you do with this much milk?"

"Most of it goes back to the animals in their feed," she admitted. "I churn it for butter, drink some of it, use it in cooking."

"One cow would do."

"With two cows I get two calves a year that are butchered as yearlings. You had some of the beef in the soup you ate the other day. And this way, if one of the cows dies, I still have milk." She wrestled the churn out and tied the straining cloth over it. "I don't guess one cow more or less matters much to you."

"Not when I have a couple thousand heads of beef on the range." He tipped one of the buckets and slowly poured the milk through the straining cloth, then emptied the other bucket.

Dee picked up the coffeepot and shook it. "There's more coffee left. Would you like a cup?"

Lucas was too smart to push her this early in their acquaintance, but being around her was fraying his patience, and he decided not to linger. "Not today. I need to get on to town, then back to the ranch. Thanks for the offer, though."

"You're welcome," she replied gravely. "And thank you for your help. I promise not to tell anyone you milked my cow."

He looked sharply at her, and though her expression was bland he could see a gleam of laughter in her eyes. "You'd better not."

She actually smiled then, and his body responded immediately. Damn, she was something when she smiled!

She walked out on the porch with him and leaned against a post while he returned to the barn, then walked out leading his horse. She watched him mount, noting the play of muscles in his arms and shoulders and the way his pants pulled tight on his buttocks and thighs. The brim of his hat shadowed his face, but she could still see the intense blue of his eyes.

"See you," he said, and he rode off without looking back.

She tried, but she couldn't stop thinking about him as she went about the rest of her morning chores. She knew plain enough why he'd come over the first time, since he'd been honest about wanting to buy the land, but why had he ridden so far out of his way this morning? At first she had been expecting him to make a grab for her, but he hadn't said or done anything the least suggestive, and she admitted to herself that she was just a tad disappointed.

Not that she would have let him kiss her. After all, the man was intending to marry Olivia. But Olivia didn't want him. Dee knew how much her friend wanted to fall in love and have a family, that she was worried she would never have the chance. And Olivia wasn't even certain Lucas had any intentions of marrying her. After meeting him the second time Dee was certain that he wasn't the man for her gentle friend.

It had been nothing less than the truth that she couldn't afford for anyone to think she was available, and it was likewise true that she wasn't interested in marrying anyone. None of that, however, negated a third truth: She was human, and she was a woman. She had liked talking to him this morning, liked his company. He talked to her as an equal, giving her a subtle but delicious sense of freedom because she didn't have to censor her words or behavior for him. Most men would have strongly disapproved of the things she had said, but Lucas had seemed to enjoy the frankness of their conversation. And despite herself she had responded to him as a woman, her skin growing warmer, her breath coming quicker. If he *had* reached for her, would she truly have pushed him away? She was honest enough with herself to admit that the temptation was there.

She was a bit embarrassed by her own duplicity. No matter that she had told him she wasn't interested in men, no matter that she told herself she neither needed nor wanted his admiration of her as a woman; she was very much aware of him as a man, and it hurt her ego a bit that he didn't seem the least bit attracted to her. Then again, why should he? He was Lucas Cochran; he could have any single woman in town, and probably quite a few of the married ones. He was not only very good-looking, he was almost over-whelmingly male, tough and strong and sure of himself, mentally as well as physically. She could read plainly in his eyes that he could be ruthless, and that a person had to be either reckless or a fool to stand in his way.

She, on the other hand, wasn't anything special. She saw it in her mirror every morning when she washed her face. She was a woman who worked hard, and who was more inclined to spend any extra money on books than to buy clothes or luxuries for herself. There was nothing refined or delicate about her, though she did suppose she was fairly intelligent and better educated than most, the latter point due to her mother having been a teacher and instilling a love of books in her early in life. They were two characteristics that equipped her well to manage her own life but made her particularly ill-suited to be content under anyone else's rule.

There was nothing in her for a man like Cochran to

desire, and it was foolish of her to wish it were different.

Lucas never deliberately sought out Olivia except at social functions where they would have met anyway, for he saw no reason to solidify any relationship between them when it would be at least a year before he had any real time to devote to courting and marriage. Nor did he ever feel any great need for her company; she was pretty and pleasant, but she didn't fire his senses. As he rode into town that morning after leaving Dee, however, he not only made no effort to see Olivia, he was downright reluctant to meet her even by accident.

He liked Olivia; she was sweet and kind, a true lady. He could even imagine taking a great deal of pleasure in bedding her. What he couldn't imagine, however, was ever feeling aroused to the point of madness with her. When he thought of heated sex, of sweat and twisted sheets and fingernails digging into his back while he reveled in a female body beneath him, that body was Dee's, the face was Dee's, and it was long black hair that lay tangled on his pillow. Dee would never docilely accept him; she would fight against his domination, her hips thrusting back at him. She would claw and twist and fiercely seize her own pleasure. And afterward, lying exhausted, she would watch him with those enigmatic green eyes, daring him to take her again.

He couldn't even think of Olivia with those images of Dee burning in his mind. He wanted her with an urgency that surprised him. He had desired women before, some passionately, but the mere thought of a woman had never made him feel as if he were on fire. And he hadn't even so much as touched her hand yet! But he would, and soon. He couldn't wait months to have her, or even very many weeks.

He gritted his teeth against a hard surge of arousal. The way he felt now, the time remaining to Dee's chastity could be measured in days, and even that was too long. He wanted her now; he was as hard and fractious as a stallion ready to mount a mare in heat.

Instinctively he knew that Dee was a virgin, even though she had lived alone for five years. Her innocence both hindered and helped. She would not immediately recognize the seriousness of his seduction and wouldn't know how to control her responses to him, which certainly gave him an advantage. But her innocence also meant he would have to restrain himself, to make certain she had been pleasured even before he entered her, and his control was already under a great deal of strain. Once he had her naked in his arms he would be near madness with the need to penetrate and find his ease within her. If he lost control and gave her only pain, she would fight like a wildcat the next time he tried to touch her.

No, no one in his right mind would ever categorize Dee as docile. She was a wildfire, while Olivia was as cool and contained as a mountain lake.

He stopped in at the saloon even though it was earlier than he liked to drink; maybe a beer would dull the ache in his groin. At that hour the saloon was almost empty, with only one other customer, who sat slumped sipping a whiskey with his back to the batwing doors as if the light hurt his eyes. Lucas recognized the signs of a hangover and left the man alone.

The bartender was polishing glasses, not paying any attention to him after serving him a beer. The two saloon girls were playing cards together in a half-bored, half-lazy fashion, spending more time talking than playing.

After a while Tillie, the red-haired one, got up and sauntered over to Lucas. Though his senses were too focused on black hair and green eyes for him to react to Tillie's lush beauty, he admired the sensuousness of her walk. She didn't just walk; she swayed, she glided, she undulated. It was a movement so completely female that even the man with the hangover followed her with his bloodshot eyes.

"Good morning," she drawled, sitting down at his table. Her accent was distinctly Southern, lazy and soft-sounding. She tilted her head at the other man. "He's got a reason for drinking, but you don't look like you're having a hard morning."

He was having a hard morning, all right, in one sense of the word. "Just passing the time."

"Or maybe you came in here for another reason." Now her voice was even softer, slower, more inviting.

"I'm not in the mood for a woman," he said abruptly.

Tillie gave a warm laugh, sitting back in her chair. "Oh, I think you are, sugar, but I'm not the woman, and that's exactly what your problem is. You've got that angry, hot-and-bothered look that a man gets when a woman doesn't lie down for him the minute he thinks he wants her."

"A man never gets that look around you, does he?" Lucas countered.

"Not often, sugar, not often. Well, if you're not in here to drink, and you don't want to go upstairs, why don't you join Verna and me in a poker game? We get bored just playing each other."

But he wasn't interested in a card game either, and he shook his head. Tillie sighed sympathetically. "Then there's nothing I can do for you, Mr. Cochran, other than wish you luck."

"I don't need luck," he growled, getting up from the table. "What I need is patience."

Tillie's soft laughter followed him out of the saloon.

Olivia lingered in the dry goods store until she saw Lucas exit the saloon and head back in the direction of the Double C. It was cowardly of her to hide from him when he had never been anything but polite, but the possibility of meeting him in the street with innumerable eyes looking on had made her feel slightly ill. She wouldn't have been able to say a coherent word to the man, what with wondering about the whispering and conjecturing going on behind all the storefront doors. Nor had he looked to be in a particularly good mood. Even from a distance she had been able to see the dark scowl on his face. If Lucas was overwhelming when he was in a good mood, how much more intimidating would he be in a temper? She didn't want to find out.

5

Maybe if Dee hadn't been so tired it wouldn't have happened, but she had spent the morning replowing the garden, breaking up the huge clods of dirt into smoother soil, suitable for planting. The first few days of garden work were always the hardest on her, for her muscles had grown softer over the comparatively lax winter months. So when she climbed into the barn loft to fork down more hay for the livestock perhaps she wasn't as alert as she normally would have been, and maybe her reflexes weren't as fast. For whatever reason she didn't see the cat, and she stepped on its paw. The cat squalled; startled by the noise, Dee lurched backwards and misjudged her step. She hurtled out of the loft to land flat on her back on the ground, her head hitting with a soft thud.

For a long, agonizing moment that seemed like an eternity she couldn't draw air into her lungs, and she lay as if paralyzed, stunned with pain, her sight growing dim. Then her insides decided to work properly, and she inhaled greedily despite her aching rib cage.

It was another several moments before she felt able to take stock of herself. Her arms and legs moved without undue pain, and her sore ribs felt more bruised than broken. Her head was throbbing dully. If the ground hadn't been covered with a thin cushion of straw, she had no doubt she would be in much worse shape than she was.

The cat leapt out of the loft and meowed at her in rebuke, then disappeared around the corner.

She staggered to her feet and managed to finish feeding the animals, but when she went back to the house she could barely climb the steps. Cooking seemed too much of a bother, so she didn't. She merely cleaned herself up with a sponge bath and gingerly brushed out her hair. Her head ached too much for her to be able to tolerate the tight braid she usually put her hair in for sleeping; she winced at the thought. It was all she could do to pull on her nightgown and crawl into bed.

She didn't sleep well because every time she moved in her sleep her aching muscles protested and woke her up; but when dawn came, and she opened her eyes for good, she was relieved to find that the headache was gone. She would have been in a fine mess if she had sustained a concussion, but thankfully that didn't seem to be the case.

Still, when she tried to get out of bed she sank back with a stifled cry as a sharp pain laced around her ribs.

She lay there panting for a few minutes before gathering herself and trying again. The second attempt was no more successful than the first.

She was loath to try again, but she knew she couldn't simply lie in bed all day. For one thing, she had natural needs that had to be attended to.

The third time she didn't try to sit up but rather rolled off the bed and landed on her knees, which probably added to her collection of bruises. She leaned against the side of the bed with her eyes closed, trying to summon the strength and determination to stand. Fortunately, getting to her feet was less painful than sitting up had been, but the effort still made her turn pale.

She managed to take care of her more urgent needs and gulp down several dippersful of water, for she was very thirsty, but the simple act of removing her nightgown defeated her. She could not raise her arms to lift it over her head. Even if she could, she wasn't at all certain she would be able to dress herself properly.

But the animals needed caring for, and it wasn't their fault she had been so stupid and clumsy as to fall out of the loft.

She had been lucky that in the six years she had been alone she had never before been ill or hurt. Knowing that she had no one else to rely on, she had always been extremely careful, even to the point of holding a nail with a long pair of tongs rather than risking hitting herself on the hand with a hammer. She had done everything she could think of to make her surroundings and her habits safe, but none of her precautions had kept her from stepping on that cat.

Even if she managed to get down the steps and wore

her nightgown to the barn, how would she feed the animals? She couldn't lift her arms, much less heavy buckets of feed.

She was so furious at herself for having been careless that she could barely think. It didn't help that each movement brought a renewed onslaught of pain.

Her legs were stiff and sore, but she rather thought that was from the unaccustomed exertion of plowing. Her back, however, seemed to be one massive bruise from shoulders to hips, and her ribs ached with every breath she took. She tried to sit and found that she couldn't. She considered simply falling onto the bed, but the thought of what she would have to endure when she tried to get up again kept her from doing that. Standing seemed to be her only recourse.

But the spring morning was chilly, and she was growing cold standing there barefoot, wearing nothing but a nightgown. The coals in the fireplace would catch if she could place a fresh log on them, but that, too, was beyond her. It looked as if she would have to go back to bed to keep warm, regardless of the pain it would cost her to get up.

When she heard the drumming of hoofbeats her first thought was that she had to get the shotgun, and she moved too quickly. The resulting pain shut off her breath, and she froze with a stifled moan.

"Dee!"

The shout made her almost weak with relief. It was Lucas. She would swallow her pride and ask him to take care of the animals today; surely by tomorrow she would be able to do it herself. Painfully she moved to the window just in time to see Lucas heading toward the barn to look for her.

"Lucas," she called, but he didn't hear her.

She went to the door, holding her breath against the jarring of each step, then stared in frustration at the bar she had automatically dropped across the door when she had come in the night before. She tried to lift her arms but found that even if she forced herself to bear the pain there was a point beyond which her muscles simply wouldn't work. That point, unfortunately, came before she could get the bar raised out of the braces.

"Dee? Where are you?"

He came out of the barn and headed toward the back of the house. Panting, Dee bent her knees and wedged her shoulder under one end of the bar, then straightened. The heavy bar bore down onto her sore flesh like an axe cutting into her, but she couldn't think of any other way of getting the door open, so she ground her teeth together and ignored the tears of pain that burned her eyes. The bar slid out and hit the floor with a thunderous clatter.

Lucas heard the noise and paused, then turned back toward the house, certain that the sound had come from there. Caution made him put his hand on the butt of his pistol.

She managed to pull the door open and stood wavering with one hand gripping the frame for support. "Lucas," she called. "I'm in front."

He came around the side of the cabin and took the steps with two long strides, dropping his hand from his pistol when he saw her. "Why didn't you answer?" he asked in irritation, then he stopped as he got a good look at her.

She was swaying slightly as she stood in the doorway, while her right hand, held down at her side, clutched the frame so tightly her fingers were bloodless. She was barefoot and wore only a plain white nightgown, long-sleeved and high-necked, as demure as a nun's habit except for the fact that he could see the darkness of her nipples beneath the cloth. Her heavy mane of hair was loose and tousled, hanging down her back in a black tide. At first glance she seemed perfectly all right, and his body was already responding to her improper attire, but almost immediately he realized that her face was white and that she was holding herself stiff and motionless.

"What's wrong?" he asked, reaching for her because she looked as if she would collapse at his feet. Alarm made his tone rough.

"No, don't touch me!" she cried in panic, shrinking away from his hand. The movement brought more pain, and though she bit her lips to keep from crying out, a moan sounded low in her throat. When she had control of herself again she said, "I fell out of the barn loft. I'm too sore to do anything."

"Come back inside and let me shut the door," he said. He didn't make the mistake of trying to help her, even though she could barely move. He suppressed a strong urge to yell at her because if she didn't insist on living by herself and doing a man's work she wouldn't be hurt, but that would wait. He entered behind her and closed the door, then crossed to the fireplace and quickly added a couple of logs, using the poker to stir up the coals.

"When did you fall?" he asked curtly, turning back to her.

"Late yesterday afternoon."

At least she hadn't been lying helpless for days. It had been a week since he had seen her, so she could easily have been injured all of that time.

He tossed his hat aside and knelt on one knee beside her. "This will hurt, but I'm going to check for any broken bones. Just stand there as still as you can so I can get it over with."

"I don't think there's anything broken," she protested. "But I'd be grateful if you'd take care of the animals today. I'm just bruised, so I'll be able to take care of them tomorrow after I get the soreness worked out."

"Don't worry about the animals. And I'll see for myself if any bones are broken or not."

His mutter was rough, his face grim. He had decided what he was going to do, and she knew she wasn't in any shape to stop him. Dee clenched her fists as he put his hands under her nightgown and ran them up her legs as briskly and efficiently as if she had been a horse. His probing fingers were necessarily less than gentle, and she sucked in her breath as her sore muscles protested. He looked up, blue eyes narrowed, at her intake of breath.

"My legs are just sore from work," she gasped in explanation.

His hands went higher, to her thighs. The hem of her nightgown bunched over his arms. His touch was hot, his callus-roughened palms and fingers hard on her silky skin. She was acutely aware of her nakedness beneath the thin cotton, and of the heat of his big body as he crouched so close to her that her thigh was practically nestled into the curve of his broad shoul-

74

der, and his face was almost against her belly. "Stop," she whispered.

He looked up, and she saw that he was enraged. His eyes looked like blue fire. "Stop, hell," he snapped. "You can forget about your modesty, because this damn nightgown is going to have to come off."

"No."

He rose to his feet with savage grace. "That's what you think."

She lifted her chin in a stubborn movement. "I can't take it off. I've tried, but I can't raise my arms."

He glared down at her, then abruptly pulled his knife from his belt. She couldn't move fast enough even to begin to evade him. He grasped a fistful of cloth in the front of the gown, pulled it out from her body, inserted the knife point, and sliced upward. The garment gaped open.

Dee made a futile effort to grab the edges together again, but in her present condition she was no match for him. He simply brushed her hands aside, then pulled the nightgown off of her shoulders and down her arms. The material caught for a moment on the curve of her hips, then slid downward of its own accord to pool around her feet.

Panic and humiliation combined to engulf her in an enormous flood. A strange gray mist obscured her vision, and her ears began to ring.

"Goddammit, don't faint," Lucas barked, putting his hands on her waist to catch her in case she did. "Take a deep breath. Breathe, goddammit!"

She did, because pride refused to allow her to faint like a ninny. The sickening gray mist faded, and she focused on his face, set in lines of pure rage. A strange sort of relief spread through her, because his anger gave her something to concentrate on.

"Don't swear at me, you bastard! You cut my clothes off of me!"

His hard fingers clenched her waist as he fought the urge to shake her. Only the knowledge that she really would faint if he did kept him under control. Damn her, didn't she know when to quit fighting? She was hurt, and someone had to take care of her because she couldn't do it herself.

But color had rushed back into her white face, and that curious panic was gone from her eyes, which had darkened to emerald with her anger. Despite his own temper he almost grinned, because if she were well enough to be angry she probably wasn't hurt too seriously. Besides, Dee's anger was exhilarating, intensifying her color and reassuring him of her strength. If he had cut a nightgown off of any other woman he knew, he'd have been faced with screaming hysterics. But Dee had sworn back at him and matched his anger with her own even though she was as helpless as a kitten.

"Shut up and let me see what other damage you've done to yourself," he said, thrusting his face close to hers.

Dee swayed on her feet, painfully aware of her bareness as the cool air brushed over her skin, but she couldn't fight him, couldn't run from him, couldn't even manage to wrap herself in a blanket. She loathed being helpless, but reality made her admit that she was. He was looking her over good, and she moved her hands in an automatic attempt to shield herself. A flush pinkened her torso and face.

"For God's sake, I've seen naked women before," he snapped, putting his hands on her rib cage and forcing his attention to the tracing of each rib, probing for breaks.

"I don't care what you've seen," she snapped back, carefully not looking at him. If she didn't watch him examining her, she might be able to preserve some small mental distance. "*I've* never been naked in front of a man before."

"I'll pull off my own clothes if it'll make you feel better."

"Lucas!"

"Dee!" he mocked in the same tone of voice, then he brushed her hair back over her shoulders. The thick mane had veiled her breasts, which were now revealed to be high and creamy, conical in shape, lushly rounded and tipped by small pink nipples. His stomach muscles contracted, and a rush of blood to his groin made his shaft thicken. Damn, she was pretty, all slim and firm and rounded in exactly the right places. He grimly tightened his control, but his nostrils flared at the sweet warm scent of her, and his fingers ached to slide into the notch between her legs. If she hadn't been hurt . . .

He fought for sanity. If she hadn't been hurt, she wouldn't be standing naked under his hands now. She would be outside doing her chores, encased in clothing, her wild tumble of hair sternly twisted into a knot. But she *was* hurt, and he had to remember that. Her collarbones were straight, without any telltale lumps to signal breaks, and she didn't flinch at his firm touch even though he carefully watched her face for any sign of pain. He felt her neck and told her to turn her head from side to side, which she did with some care but no great difficulty. Then he walked around behind her, gathered the great mass of hair which fell to her hips, and looped it over her shoulder.

He swore softly between his teeth.

"I figure I'm bruised," Dee said, staring into the fire. "I landed on my back."

Her shoulders appeared to have taken the brunt of the fall, because a great black and purple welt stretched from shoulder blade to shoulder blade. Her lower back was also bruised, the discoloration extending down to the twin dimples of her buttocks.

Gently he checked her ribs and found them sore but not broken, as was the case with her arms. All things considered, she was lucky to have escaped with such minor injuries.

He began thinking of all the things that needed to be done. "I'll fix you some breakfast," he said. "Do you want to go back to bed or sit here by the fire?"

She turned her head and gave him a baleful look. "I can't sit around like this."

"I don't object. The scenery looks good from my view, except for the strange colors." He lightly patted her bottom, taking care not to touch her bruises.

She moved jerkily, painfully away from him, and he was briefly ashamed of himself for teasing her when she couldn't fight back. He went into the bedroom and pulled a blanket off the bed—a double bed, he noted —then returned to her and folded it snugly around her. She hugged it to her with a look of intense gratefulness and relief, and he realized how difficult it had been for her to be unclothed in front of him. He wanted to kiss her and tell her that it would be all right, that soon she would be accustomed to him, but it was never good tactics to let your adversary know your plans in advance.

He helped her to the big, well upholstered chair before the fire, but sitting down was something she had to do at her own rate. When at last she was as comfortable as she could get he turned his attention to the wood stove.

Cooking was something he had learned by necessity, and he was competent with the basics. He put on a pot of coffee, deftly made a pan of biscuits, and sliced bacon to put on to fry. After satisfying himself that the stove wasn't too hot, he went outside and gathered enough eggs for breakfast. He had eaten some biscuits and cold beef before riding over, but now his stomach was demanding more.

When he returned to the house Dee was still in exactly the same position she'd been in before he'd gone outside. The blanket had slipped away from her bare feet. He went over and knelt down to cover them, wrapping them more securely in the folds.

"Thank you," she said. Her frustration with herself was plain in her eyes.

He patted her knee. He knew how being sick or hurt grated on the nerves. The few times in his life that he had been confined to bed, even as a child, he had raised such hell that everyone around him had breathed a sigh of relief when he began to mend.

He finished breakfast, put everything on the table, and returned to her chair. "I'm going to pick you up," he said. "I'll put my arm around the middle of your back, where you aren't so sore."

"I have to get dressed," she said irritably. "I can't eat with this blanket wrapped around me."

He slipped his arms around her, one across her back and the other under her thighs, and lifted her easily. His muscled back and arms barely felt the strain. "I'll take care of the blanket. Don't worry."

By the time he had her settled her cheeks were hot again, because by necessity the repositioning of the blanket had caused her breasts to be exposed. When he finished she was wrapped in a roughly fashioned toga, with her right arm and shoulder completely bare. She found that if she moved carefully, she could feed herself by moving her arm only from the elbow down. It was movement from the shoulder that was excruciating.

"Do you have a bathtub?" he asked, taking generous portions for himself.

"I use a washtub."

The washtub would have to do, Lucas thought. It wouldn't be as comfortable for her as a bathtub that she could recline in, but he would manage.

As soon as they had finished eating he redeposited Dee in her chair before the fire, then cleaned up the dishes and hauled in buckets of water to begin heating on the stove. "I'm going to feed the animals while the water's getting hot," he said, and he left the cabin.

Dee tried to find a more comfortable position. Tears of frustration prickled her eyelids, and angrily she blinked them back. She refused to let herself bawl like a baby despite her predicament.

Only part of it was because of the pain and helplessness, which was galling enough. Her nakedness in front of Lucas was more distressing to her, assaulting her modesty and adding to her sense of vulnerability. It would have been bad enough with any man, but when Lucas looked at her she felt as if he were stroking her in all of her private places.

It was an hour later when he returned to the house. He replenished the fire, then dragged the big washtub inside and positioned it in front of the fireplace. Dee watched as he carried in more water and began filling the tub, then dumped in the hot water until steam was rising.

"All right, in you get," he said, rolling up his sleeves.

She clutched the blanket tight with her fist, gazing longingly at the steaming tub. A long hot soak would be heaven for her sore muscles, just what she needed, but her nerves had been stretched almost to the limit by her nudity before him that morning. "I think I can manage on my own," she said. It would hurt, but she would bear the pain for the pleasure of that wonderful hot water.

For an answer Lucas tugged the blanket free and pushed it aside.

"Damn you," she said between clenched teeth as he lifted her.

"For once, would you just shut up and let me help you?" Her stubborn independence made him angry all over again, but he handled her carefully as he knelt and lowered her into the water. She sucked in her breath at the heat of it but made no more protest. Her common sense told her that at this point it would be a wasted effort.

He left her sitting in the water while he found two strips of toweling. He folded them and placed one on the edge of the tub behind her head. "Lie back and let your head rest on this," he ordered. "Get your shoulders underwater."

Gingerly she did as he said, wincing at each movement. He placed the other towel across the rim at her feet and lifted her legs out of the water, resting them across the towel. Then he brought more hot water and slowly poured it in until the water level rose almost to the edge.

Dee closed her eyes against the picture she knew she must make, lying there in the clear water, completely nude like a wanton.

The sight of her was making it difficult for Lucas either to move or to sit, with his hardened shaft cramped beneath his pants as it was. Her breasts bobbed gently in the water, making him think about sliding an arm under her back and lifting her up so that he could take those sweet nipples in his mouth.

Though her eyes were closed and he couldn't read her expression, he knew that the redness of her cheeks wasn't due entirely to the heat of the water. He ran his fingers through the length of hair hanging down the side of the tub to pool on the floor. "Don't be embarrassed," he murmured. "You're too pretty to be ashamed of being naked."

Dee swallowed but didn't open her eyes. "You shouldn't see me like this."

"Even though you're hurt? Don't be silly. If I were shot in the leg, do you think you wouldn't have to take my pants off so you could tend to me?" He continued to gently stroke her hair. "You're just damn lucky I came by today. What would you have done on your own? What about the animals?"

"I don't know," she admitted, then honesty prodded her. "I'm grateful to you, truly, but this is—it's scandalous."

"If anyone knew about it," he agreed. "But it's between us, and no one else is going to know. I suppose I could have gone into town and tried to get some woman to come out here and take care of you, but I'm strong enough to pick you up without hurting you. And I like looking at you," he admitted quietly. "If you weren't hurt, I'd be trying to get between your legs." He paused. "Are you afraid I might force you while you're helpless?"

She did open her eyes then, her look somber and searching. "No. You wouldn't force me. You aren't that type of man."

His mouth twisted wryly. "Sweetheart, don't put it to the test when you're in good shape again. I'm so hard right now my guts are hurting."

No man had ever talked to her like that before, but she had seen the animals mating and knew what he meant. And when it came down to it, she felt more comfortable with his bluntness than if he had pretended to scruples she couldn't trust.

He kept her in the tub for almost an hour, dipping out water when it cooled and replacing it with hot water fresh from the stove. Her skin was red and wrinkled when he finally lifted her out and stood her, dripping, on the rug. She found that some of the soreness had eased, and she could move her arms a bit more. He dried her with one of the towels, his hands moving over her bare body with excruciating attention. Then he carried her back to the bed and placed her face down on it.

Dee bit her lip and kept her cries locked inside while he firmly rubbed a strong-smelling liniment on her aching muscles. The resulting heat was almost worse than the original pain, but again she held back her protests.

Sweat beaded Lucas's forehead when he was finished. He asked, "Do you have any of your pa's shirts left?" He had had almost all he could endure. If he didn't get her covered up, he might end up on that bed with her despite his best intentions. Her soft round buttocks, creamy white and perfect, would feel wonderful against his lower belly, or cupped in his big hands.

"No, I got rid of all of his things."

Damn. He stood and pulled his own shirt free of his pants, then unbuttoned it. Like most shirts, it only buttoned halfway down, and he pulled it off over his head. "You should be able to get into this," he said, straightening the garment and placing it on the bed before helping her to her feet again. Then he knelt and held the shirt for her to step into, and he worked it up her hips. The position brought his face very close to her soft body, and his breathing grew quicker.

He guided her arms into the sleeves and eased the cloth into place. The shirt engulfed her, hanging almost to her knees, the sleeves dangling past her hands. He buttoned it, then rolled the sleeves back until her hands emerged. "There, you're decent again," he said with a strained look on his face.

Not quite, since her lower legs were still bare, but she was painfully grateful to him for the covering. The shirt was warm from his body and carried his scent. She felt surrounded by him, and the sensation was remarkably pleasant.

She found herself staring at his chest. It was broad and muscled and hairy, the dark curls crisp-looking against his tanned skin. He evidently spent a good bit of time working without his shirt. "How will you explain going home without your shirt?" she whispered, not raising her eyes.

"I don't reckon I have to explain," he drawled. He was the boss. He could wear a shirt or not, as he damn well pleased.

She was still looking at his bare torso with helpless fascination. "Look at me," he said, putting a finger under her chin and tilting it upward. Her lashes swept open, and those deep green eyes fastened on him. He moved closer, bent down, and closed his mouth over hers, forcing her lips to part and using his tongue. He didn't trust himself and quickly released her, stepping away from the enticement of her firm body beneath the thin shirt, but the kiss was enough to make her eyes go dark with shock.

"You're safe for now," he said. "But when you're healed, things will change. I'll be coming after you, and it won't take me long to get you."

6

Dᴇᴇ ꜰᴇʟᴛ ᴍᴜᴄʜ ʙᴇᴛᴛᴇʀ ᴛʜᴇ ɴᴇxᴛ ᴅᴀʏ, ᴛʜᴏᴜɢʜ ꜱᴛɪʟʟ
not able to lift her arms more than a few inches. Lucas
showed up again shortly past dawn, and they went
through the same routine, with him cooking for her
and taking care of her chores. Afterward he insisted
that she soak in hot water again, and this time was far
more embarrassing than it had been before. She
wasn't in as much pain and therefore was even more
acutely aware of her nakedness. So was Lucas. She
could see it in his clenched jaw and the sweat glisten-
ing on his brow.

She had lain awake a good bit of the night, going
over and over what he had said. As accustomed as she
was to defending her virtue with a shotgun, it had still
rattled her to find that Lucas had the same intentions
as all those others who had come slipping around.
What made him far more dangerous to her was the
fact that knowing it didn't rouse her to contemptuous

anger, as was the case with the others, but rather made her heart beat a little faster. It frightened her to admit that she *wanted* Lucas to want her, but it was the truth.

So what was she going to do about it? Let a man into her life after fighting so hard to achieve independence? Have an affair with him, when it would destroy her respectability if anyone found out about it? *Betray Olivia?*

Nor could she ignore the possibility that what he really wanted was Angel Creek. He no doubt planned to exploit her vulnerability to him to convince her to sell out. After all, buying the land had been the reason he had first sought her out.

What she knew about sex was only what she had seen in the barnyard, when the bull mounted one of the cows. She knew what happened but had had no idea of the fierce physical attraction between a man and a woman until Lucas had come riding up. His kiss, as brief and hard as it had been, had shown her that there was a great deal more to mating than she had suspected. She had foolishly thought she would be able to keep him from kissing her, but she had not only let him, she had wanted more. She had felt the burn of physical desire for the first time, and it tormented her, for her body had felt out of her control.

If Lucas wanted the land, he also wanted her. She wasn't so naïve that she didn't realize the significance of the bulge in the crotch of his pants, even if he hadn't so bluntly admitted his intentions. It weakened her to know that the torment was mutual.

After he had dried her and clothed her in another of

his shirts, brought specifically for that purpose, he silently put her back in bed and left the cabin, his boot heels thudding on the porch. When he returned half an hour later he was back in control of himself, but his blue eyes still held signs of his bad temper.

"I don't think you should come by tomorrow," Dee said, pulling the sheet to her chin. "I'm much better today, and the soreness will leave faster if I work it out."

"Trying to get rid of me?" he asked. "It won't work."

She turned her face away from him. "What about Olivia?" she asked quietly. "She's my friend."

She couldn't see him, but she could feel his fierce gaze fasten on her. He didn't show surprise at her words. He just said, "What about her?"

"The talk is that you're going to marry her."

"I'd thought about it," he admitted, his temper fraying. Did she think he would be there if he had committed himself to another woman? "But not lately. We certainly as hell don't have any sort of understanding between us. I'm a free man."

She plucked at the sheet, still not looking at him. "It would probably be better if you didn't come by tomorrow anyway."

"If you weren't such a damn idiot, you wouldn't need for me to come by," he growled, glad that she had provided him with an excuse to release his temper. Being around her, with her either naked or only partly clothed, had strained his control to the limit. He felt half-mad with the need to have her.

"I know," she said, readily accepting the blame,

which only made him angrier. "I try to be so careful, but that time I wasn't."

"You shouldn't be pitching down hay in the beginning!" he yelled. "You shouldn't be working this farm by yourself! Why can't you move to town and be a normal woman, instead of trying to prove that you can make it all on your own when it's pure insanity that you'd even want to?"

Dee looked at him then, her eyes narrowing in a dangerous, catlike way. It wasn't in her to simply take his attack in silence, so she didn't. "What I want to know is why you think it's any of your business," she said in an even tone. "I appreciate your help, but that doesn't give you the right to tell me how to live."

"You know what gives me the right." He walked over to stand by the bed, glaring down at her. "You know it's going to end only one way."

"I believe that's still my decision."

"When the time comes, you're going to lie down and open your legs for me," he said savagely. "Don't try to fool yourself."

She tried to lift herself up on an elbow, but her shoulders and arms were still too sore, and she fell back with a stifled moan. This further evidence of her own physical helplessness, however, didn't mean that she thought he was right. "Then I see only one solution: Don't come back here, because you aren't welcome."

"Are you going to use the shotgun on me?" he taunted, leaning down so close that she could see the glittering depths of his eyes. "Then take your best shot, sweetheart, because I'll be back."

She lashed out in retaliation. "You overestimate your charm. I'd always wonder what you really wanted, me or Angel Creek."

"Both, sweetheart," he said, and he crashed his mouth down onto hers. It was a rough kiss, and she tried to bite him, but he jerked his head back, then returned to kiss her even harder. His fingers clamped on her chin and held it down so he could enter her mouth with his tongue. Dee clawed at his arms, but with her limited range of movement it was a wasted effort. He held her down and ruthlessly kissed her until she felt the coppery taste of blood in her mouth. He tasted it, too, and the pressure eased. He sucked her lower lip into his mouth and stroked it with his tongue, soothing the hurt.

He unbuttoned the shirt she wore and opened it, baring her breasts. Her breath caught in her throat as his hard, warm hand closed over one of the soft mounds.

"This is what it would be like between us," he muttered. "Hot and wild. Think about it, damn you." His thumb rubbed her nipple into a tight peak, and her entire body clenched from the pleasure and pain of it. He cupped both breasts, holding them high and together, and buried his face against them. His hot breath washed over her, then he took one nipple between his teeth, drawing it into his mouth with a strong sucking motion. Incredible heat shot through her, and she whimpered, her hips writhing a little.

As if that were a signal he released her breast and stood, his face dark and taut with both anger and physical need. "I can make you go wild," he said.

"Remember that when you think about using the shotgun on me."

He walked out, leaving her lying on the bed with her shirt unbuttoned and spread open, her bare breasts heaving with the violence of the response he had stirred in her. A moment later she heard him ride away. "Damn you," she whispered, and she would have shouted it if she thought he might hear her. She was shaking with anger—or was it from the empty torment he had aroused in her body? Perhaps it was both, though the whys didn't really matter.

She had never before been vulnerable to a man, but she was to him. That was the most frightening thing she had ever faced in her life, far more frightening than being left alone to fend for herself. She had never doubted her ability to survive, but she was terrified of what Lucas could do to her.

Losing first one parent and then the other had shaken her to the core. She had been afraid, so horribly afraid, but she had had to go on. She had been forced to recognize, with brutal swiftness, how fragile life was, how easily it could be taken. She had pulled deep inside herself, unwilling to trust her emotions to anyone else because she simply couldn't bear any more pain and couldn't take the risk of losing someone else she loved. Devoting herself to the garden had saved her sanity, given her a sense of life again, because the earth was so giving. It, at least, was eternal. It would be there long after she herself had died. She could trust the warm soil, the cycles of the seasons, the renewal of life each spring. Except for Olivia, she hadn't even been tempted to let anyone close to her again.

And now Lucas was shattering her mental wall of remoteness. He could destroy not only the life she had built for herself but her very self-respect. If she let him mean too much to her, he could reduce her to someone she would despise, without will or spirit, willing to do anything to keep him happy. Wanting him hadn't blinded her to his nature; Lucas was strong and arrogant, ruthless when it came to getting what he wanted. He wanted her, and he wouldn't listen to any of her refusals. It wasn't that she feared he would force her, for his own ego wouldn't let him do that, but rather that she would lose her own will to tell him no.

He had demonstrated to her very aptly how weak she could be when he wanted to make love to her. And he hadn't even done that much—kissed her, and touched and kissed her breast—but she had been on the verge of pleading with him for more. It was humiliating to realize he could handle her so easily.

Though anger had motivated her to tell him not to come back, now that she had calmed down she realized it was only common sense, and the best thing for her. The question, though, was if Lucas would obey.

She had her answer early the next morning when she heard hoofbeats approaching. She looked at the shotgun but admitted that it was a futile threat, right now at least. Though she had managed to dress herself in a fashion, she still wasn't capable of lifting the heavy weapon and firing it with any sort of aim.

Without knocking he opened the front door, which had been left unbarred for the past two days. Dee turned from the stove to look at him, a stinging rebuke on her lips that she forced herself to swallow; after all, the door had been left unbarred for that precise reason.

It gave her no small measure of satisfaction to see his black eyebrows snap downward in a scowl when he saw her standing at the stove turning bacon with a fork.

"You shouldn't be doing that."

"I told you, I'm feeling better. I can manage this."

"But not putting on your shoes," he observed, looking down at her bare feet.

She had tried but hadn't been able to bend down far enough to pull on her stockings or shoes. It was also true that she still wore his shirt, but it served well enough as a blouse. She had struggled until she had donned her underdrawers, a petticoat, and her skirt and tucked the shirt in. After two days of being bare or almost so, the heavy clothes had given her a certain sense of comfort.

He tossed a small package on the table. She looked at it, then lifted her brows inquiringly at him. "It's a nightgown. To replace the one I cut off of you."

She was glad that he had thought of it, for she only owned two. "I'll wash your shirts and return them."

"No hurry." He was watching her so intensely that she began to feel uncomfortable and had to resist the urge to check if all of her buttons were buttoned. But he only reached out to take the fork from her hand and said, "Sit. I'll finish this."

Lucas was very aware of the short pause before she did as he said, and he didn't relax until she was safely sitting down. He had ridden up to the cabin with every nerve alert, waiting for a shotgun blast at any second. He had pushed her too hard and too far the day before, and he knew it. With most women—hell, any other woman—he would have expected nothing more than a temper tantrum at worst, and more likely tears or sulking. But Dee was likely to do just as she said and greet him with buckshot. Which was, he thought grimly, just what he deserved for having been so stupid. He had been thinking with his gonads, not his brain. Just because he had been hot and hard and frustrated he'd let his temper get the best of him.

After breakfast he knelt and slipped plain white stockings on her feet, smoothing them up her legs and tying the garters just above her knees. After the past two days such a service didn't even bring a blush to her face. Then he laced her into her sturdy work shoes, and his face became grim again as he thought of the dainty cloth slippers she could wear if she didn't insist on working like a horse. This time, however, he had sense enough to keep his mouth shut.

He took her outside to walk around, her first trip past the cabin door since the morning after she had fallen. She insisted on inspecting the garden plot she had plowed, and she told him what she planned to plant. "Corn, of course, and peas. I had good luck selling squash last year, so I'll add another row of it this time. Here I'll make the beds for the onions and carrots, and a few pepper plants. And I think I'll try potatoes this year. Mr. Winches always has them, but I imagine he pays a pretty penny having them shipped in."

Her eyes were shining as she looked at the plot of raw earth; she saw green food-bearing plants, plants that fed her through the winter and gave her a means of living. Lucas looked at the same earth and thought of the work she would have to do, first planting, then the daily battle with weeds and insects, and finally the harvesting days, when she would have to work the hardest, for she would not only be doing her normal chores but working in the kitchen to put up in canning jars the vegetables she would need over the winter. A farm woman didn't have it easy at the best of times; a farm woman on her own was likely to work herself into an early grave. Unless she had sense enough to sell out.

Dee was strong, her slim body lithe and well muscled, but eventually the work would get to be too much for her. Lucas looked down at her, with her hip-length hair flowing down her back and her exotic face lifted to the morning sun, and he swore to himself right then that he would get her off the farm before it killed her or made her old before her time. He'd have to fight her every inch of the way, but that would keep him on his toes.

Before he thought, he bent his head and kissed her, his hands on her waist to pull her close against him. Her green eyes widened with surprise, then slowly fluttered shut as her mouth opened gently for him. Her lips were soft and full, the lower one still slightly swollen from his roughness the day before. He treated her with more care now, keeping the pressure light even though his tongue probed sensually. This time she tilted her head and met his advance with first a hesitant touch, then a tender searching with her own tongue that made his senses reel. His hands tightened momentarily on her waist, then he slid one arm behind her while his other hand moved up to close surely over her breast.

Immediately she tried to pull away, a protest sounding in her throat. Lucas held her, his long fingers kneading the rich flesh, rubbing at her sensitive nipple. "I'm not going to do more than this," he muttered as his mouth moved roughly down her throat. "Just relax and let me make you feel good."

He made her feel too good, Dee thought in despair, and it all happened too fast. One kiss, one touch, and she wanted him to do everything. She even wanted to open her legs to that hard length she could feel pressed against her belly, and that would never do, because it would be such an enormous error to give Lucas that sort of hold over her.

She couldn't push at him, but she found enough strength, enough sanity, to turn her head away and say, "No, Lucas. No. I don't want you to do this."

"Liar," he said, but he raised his head. His lips were shiny from kissing her, the set of them a little cruel. She was totally at his mercy and she knew it, but she wasn't certain he had any mercy. If he chose to continue making love to her, she would not only give in, she would join in, even beg him if necessary.

"I'm not lying," she insisted before he could kiss her again. Honesty impelled her to add, "I didn't say that I don't want you. I said that I don't want you to treat me like this."

"Even in that, you're lying." But he slowly let her go, and that was what she had intended.

She felt as if all of her clothes were awry; it was disturbing to look down and find that nothing was disturbed after all. All of the turbulence had been inside.

"You wouldn't do this if I were anyone else." Her voice was low as she made the charge. "You wouldn't treat Olivia like this." She remembered the day she had first seen him since his return, how civil he had been to Olivia and the giggling young women grouped around her. He would never handle any of them the way he had been touching her.

Lucas's gaze sharpened. "Like a woman, you mean? Maybe you're right. But don't accuse me of treating you like a whore, damn you, because we both know different."

"A whore is what people would call me."

"How would anyone know? What's between us is private."

There was nothing more to be said, it seemed. She turned to go back to the house, and he fell into step beside her, his strong hands helping her up the steps when her back muscles protested. He kissed her again, then left her to attend to the chores.

She was alone that night when, more out of curiosity than for any practical reason, she opened the package that contained the nightgown, as she was still confined to sleeping in his shirt. The garment that was revealed had nothing in common with her practical white sleepwear, not even intent, for surely this wasn't meant to be worn *in* bed, merely *to* bed, where a lover's eager hands would remove it.

She trailed her fingertips over the sheer silk, noting the exquisite workmanship. The part of her that appreciated the luxuries of life marveled at the beauty of it, and at how well the pale, shimmering pink would complement her coloring, but the practical part of her was furious with him for depriving her of something she had needed, and trying to replace it with this highly impractical gown. Of course there was no mistaking his intention—that she would wear the gown for him.

He would have made her less angry, she thought, if he had bought *two* gowns, one to replace the gown he had destroyed and this bit of froth for his own amusement. Let him think what he liked, but she truly needed another warm nightgown.

She said as much to him the next day, starchily adding that she might as well continue wearing his shirts, which at least had sleeves. He grinned at her, a devilish glint in his blue eyes. "I like you in either one," he said.

It was two more days before she was well enough to dress herself completely and do the chores, albeit with much less dexterity and speed than normal. The last day, having made a deliberate effort to be up and about early, she was already milking one of the cows when Lucas arrived. He said nothing, merely helped her finish with the milking, then carried the milk inside for her. Both of his shirts had been washed and neatly ironed and were folded on the table for him.

He went outside and came back in with another package. "Just to keep you warm when I can't," he said, grinning as he tossed it to her.

She opened the package, half afraid this choice would be even more inappropriate than the other. But the soft white cotton gown was all she could have asked for, long-sleeved and high-necked. The bosom was set with tiny tucks, and the buttons extended down almost to the waist. She would be able to step into it, she realized, and she gave him a truly warm smile for his consideration. Her shoulders and arms still protested if she pulled anything on over her head.

"I wonder what Mrs. Worley thinks about you buying so many nightgowns," she mused, trying to picture that stern lady's face when Lucas purchased the silk confection. Come to think of it, where *had* he bought the silk nightgown? She couldn't think of any merchant in Prosper who carried such goods. He would have had to special order it from the East, or from San Francisco, and certainly he hadn't had enough time for that.

"Mrs. Worley doesn't think anything about it," he replied maddeningly. "The cotton gown was my mother's."

He didn't say where he had gotten the silk, she noticed.

He had been ignoring his own work to attend to her, and now that she was on her feet again he would have to spend the next several days seeing to business. "I won't be able to check on you for a while," he warned. "For God's sake, be careful."

"I am careful. After all, that's the first accident I've had."

"And it could have been your last, if it had broken your neck."

"What? And deprive you of a reason to complain?" she said sweetly. "I'd never do that."

"The spring picnic and dance is next week," he said, thinking ahead and ignoring her jab. It was such a busy time at the ranch, with all the spring branding

99

and castrating to be done, that the picnic would probably be the next time he'd see her. "If I don't get by before then, I'll see you there."

"I doubt it," she said. "I don't go to the spring dances."

He stopped and gave her one of those grim looks of his. "Why not?"

"Why should I?"

"To socialize with your neighbors."

"If I did that, someone"—meaning some man—"would assume that I wanted to be friendlier than I have been in the past. It seems easier not to encourage anyone."

"You could spend your time with the women."

She laughed out loud at that. "What poor woman wants me to monopolize her time? People go to have fun with their friends, or to flirt, and I don't qualify for either. Besides, this is a busy time for me, and I really can't afford to waste an entire day doing nothing, especially since I've lost so much time this past week."

He scowled down at her, angered that she allowed herself so little in life. He had been looking forward to dancing with her, to feeling her long, strong legs brushing against his. In the hurlyburly of the day, no one would be paying any attention to them. "I want you to go," he said. "Put on your best dress and for once forget about the damn farm."

"No," she said. No more excuses, no reasons, just no.

Lucas didn't take rejection well. "If you aren't at the picnic," he said, "I'll come looking for you."

7

THE DAY OF THE PICNIC DAWNED WITH PERFECT WEATHER, the sun rising in a glorious display of cream and gold on the snow-capped peaks of the far mountains. Olivia was awake to see it, for it seemed there were a hundred last-minute details that needed to be seen to. That was always the case, but in the past she had enjoyed the excitement of preparation; this year it was all she could do to present a serene face to her parents and friends. She dreaded the day, without having any one solid reason for doing so. Perhaps, she thought, it was that she had given up hope. Always before the future had loomed before her with its great golden promise, but in the past months she had lost her faith in that promise.

It wasn't that a proposal from Lucas seemed imminent; in fact, in the last few weeks she had begun to wonder if she had only been imagining his intentions.

In some indefinable way she no longer felt that intense will focused on her. It was silly, because when they had met, which was seldom, he had been exactly the same: courteous, protective, occasionally even flirting a little, but taking care not to overwhelm her.

Though she couldn't help feeling relieved, she was saddened almost beyond bearing at the very real possibility that she would never have her own family. She could just picture herself ten, even twenty years in the future, quietly sitting beside Honora with their heads bent over tiny embroidery stitches, while her hair grayed and wrinkles appeared at her eyes and throat, and her body lost its firmness. Her parents would be sad, too, because there would be no grand-children for them to cherish.

It was as if her life had slipped by while she wasn't looking, and now she was left with empty hands. And empty arms, she thought, mourning the tiny babies she had wanted but seemed destined never to have.

So she went through the motions, sheer determination keeping a smile pasted on her face, and by midmorning the Millican carriage had joined a parade of buggies, wagons, carts, people on horseback, and a great many even walking, all making their way to the large meadow just outside of town where the picnic was always held.

It was a truly perfect spot, with enough trees to provide shade for those who sought it, yet plenty of open space for the youngsters to play. A good many people were already there, and by lunch all but a few people from within a fifty-mile radius would be wandering over the meadow, with nothing more serious on their minds than seeing friends and enjoying the picnic, an entire day with nothing to do.

Except the women always had plenty to do, Olivia thought. There was the food to be seen to, the children to be watched, games to be organized. The men, of course, stood about in groups talking and laughing or perhaps organizing their own contests of strength or skill. An impromptu horse race wasn't unknown. The women soothed the normal array of wounds and tempers from both children and men, until sometimes Olivia wondered if there was much difference between the two groups.

Practically the first person she saw was Lucas, his tall, powerful form easily spotted in the crowd. He was wearing brown pants and a white silk shirt, his brown hat shading his eyes from the bright morning sun, and he caught her attention more easily than those men who had dressed in their best suits. As he approached she noticed how his dark hair curled down over his collar. He reached them with a murmured greeting and began helping to unload the small mountain of food they had brought in the carriage.

She wondered uncertainly if she had been wrong about his intentions after all and thought she would go mad with this seesawing back and forth. All of it was in her own mind, of course, so she had no one but herself to blame. Was he interested or not? If he was, did she want him to be, or not? If he asked, which would be worse, to accept or to refuse?

When all of the food was safely arranged on a quilt spread beneath one of the trees Lucas tucked her hand in the crook of his arm. "Do you want to walk around and see everyone?" he asked.

She could scarcely refuse with her mother beaming at them, and she tried to make herself relax as they strolled slowly about.

When he returned her to the same spot an hour later it was without anything personal having been said between them. To her relief, he had treated her as an undemanding friend.

Lucas truly liked Olivia, but during the long walk his attention had kept slipping to the knots of people they passed, and he'd been aware that he was looking for a small, queenly head with a wealth of black hair, or a woman who moved with a long, free-swinging stride that made her skirts kick up in a way that definitely wasn't ladylike. He was sure all of those excuses she had given for not attending had been just that—excuses—and he fully expected her to be there. What woman could resist the chance to flirt and have fun?

"Have you seen Dee Swann?" he asked Olivia absently, still surveying the constantly moving throng of people.

Olivia lifted her brows a little at the casual way he said Dee's name, and her eyes sparkled with quickly veiled interest. "No, I haven't. I doubt she'll be here. She never comes."

"I told her to come. I mean, I think she needs to get away from that farm. . . . I heard she fell out of the loft and hurt herself week before last."

"Oh, no," Olivia cried. "How bad was she hurt?"

Lucas didn't stop to think that Olivia sounded more distressed than such news would merit from a casual acquaintance. "Heard she was bruised up pretty bad. But she's back in fighting form now."

Olivia's interest heightened. Even though she was worried about Dee, she realized how uncomfortable Lucas was, as if he'd accidentally said more than he should have. Indeed, from whom would he have heard that Dee was injured? Olivia knew perfectly well how isolated Dee was. It was obvious to her that if Lucas knew her friend was injured, it was because he had seen her himself, visited her, maybe even tended to her. She remembered the stray thought she had had about how well Lucas and Dee would suit. Perhaps . . .

"She should be here," he said again, and he was scowling.

Lucas didn't accept that Dee really wasn't going to show up until lunchtime. He kept expecting to spot her in the mingling crowd until finally he realized that she wouldn't be with a crowd of people even if she did attend the picnic; she would be on the outskirts watching, her deep green eyes as enigmatic as a cat's. He couldn't imagine her enjoying a cozy gossip or giggling with a group of girls.

On the other hand, he wouldn't have been the least surprised if she had come sauntering up at the last minute, knowing he'd been getting angrier and angrier with every passing second, wearing her most arrogant expression and daring him to say anything.

But finally he realized that she wouldn't be there, and his anger continued to build in him. He kept it tightly controlled and forced himself to act as if he enjoyed the food he ate, when in truth he hardly knew what he put in his mouth. *Damn* her, why hadn't she come? He knew now that she wouldn't attend the dance either.

He also knew he wasn't going to let her ignore him.

Dee was nearby, for she had broken the hoe handle and had driven the wagon into town to purchase a new one, only to find the general store closed for the day.

She felt like a fool. Of course the Winches family, like everyone else, was at the picnic.

She shouldn't have expected anything else. The streets were deserted. Everyone in town seized the opportunity to relax and enjoy the day.

It would mean another trip to town to replace the hoe handle, but there was no help for it, and she was too practical to stand around fretting. Weeds could be pulled up by hand as well as chopped down by hoe. So she turned the wagon around and headed back home. The only other people in town, she noticed, were the two saloon girls, who of course weren't welcome at the town's social events. Both of the women sat outside on the sidewalk, something they would never have done if the town hadn't been temporarily deserted.

One of them, the redhead named Tillie, waved to her, and Dee waved back. "Good day," she said.

What must their lives be like? Dee wondered. They had to be painfully lonely, though they were almost never alone. Her own situation was the opposite, for she was often alone and enjoyed it.

"May I walk with you?"

An air of heavy content had settled over the crowd as the huge quantities of food mingled with the afternoon heat to make everyone drowsy. More than a few were actually dozing on the quilts brought from home. Olivia had been strolling aimlessly about, smiling at friends but not stopping to talk. Lucas had left soon after eating, and since then Kyle Bellamy seemed to have been everywhere she turned. He had been very polite, but she just couldn't warm to the man. His eyes were too bold, and he was too persistent. She had finally been driven to keep walking, for if she stopped he soon appeared at her side.

She was startled by the soft, deep voice behind her and turned to find the Mexican, Fronteras, watching her with a smile in his black eyes.

She hesitated, remembering that he worked for Bellamy, and that she didn't know him.

"Of course, if you don't want to, I understand," he said.

She was stricken as she realized he expected his invitation to be refused because he was a Mexican. Her sympathetic heart squeezed a little, and she found herself saying, "Of course I'll walk with you." At least Kyle wasn't likely to catch her as long as she kept moving.

He fell into step with her. For once her impeccable manners seemed to desert her, and she could find nothing to say. They had walked for perhaps a minute when he said, "My name is Luis Fronteras."

"I'm Olivia Millican." Silence fell again. Finally in desperation she blurted, "Are you Mexican?" Immediately color flooded her face. Of all the things she could have said, why had she said that? She wanted to bite her own tongue.

"I was born in Mexico," he said with a lazy smile, not the least bothered by the question. "I suppose that makes me Mexican, though I haven't been there since I was a child."

Indeed, he spoke just like everyone else she knew, without a trace of an accent. "Have you lived in the area for long?" She wouldn't necessarily have met him even if he had, for the banker's daughter didn't move in the same social circles as a cowhand.

"Do you mean in Colorado itself, or here around Prosper?"

"Both," she said, interested. It sounded as if he had traveled a great deal, and she had always wondered about how it would be to live a nomadic life.

"I've wandered through Colorado several times over the years. I spent several years down in New Mexico Territory, and some time up in Montana and further west, around the Snake River." He looked thoughtful. "I've been to California a time or two, so with all the crisscrossing I guess I've been in about every part of the country west of the Missouri."

"You can't have spent very long in any one place." He was tall, as tall as Lucas, she noted. It made her feel small to walk beside him, and protected. She darted a look at the big revolver in the holster tied down to his right thigh. He wore the weapon casually, as if he was never without it. Was he more of a gunman after all, rather than a cowhand?

"I've drifted a bit." For a while he had thought New Mexico would be his home, but that dream had died under a stallion's murderous hooves. He had been so empty after burying Celia, as if part of him had gone into the grave with her. After a long time he had realized that he still lived, but it wasn't the same. Life had a way of going on regardless; he didn't know when the mourning had ceased, only that it had. He remembered Celia now as a bright smile and almost piercing sweetness, but he couldn't quite form her features in his mind. Ten years had passed, and in those ten years he had traveled a lot of ground, held a lot of other women in his arms.

"I've often thought I'd like to travel," Olivia said, looking up at the sun through the shifting pattern of leaves overhead as light breezes stirred the limbs. "To not see the sun set in the same place two days in a row."

She could scarcely have said anything more unexpected. Luis looked down at the delicate oval face and tried to imagine her going days, weeks without bathing, with a thick layer of dirt and grime coating that white skin, and found it utterly ridiculous. And who would ever expect her to sleep rolled in a blanket on the ground?

"You wouldn't like it," he stated positively. "Insects, dirt, bad food, not enough water, and never able to get a sound sleep. That's what it's like to live on the trail."

Her lips moved into a smile. "Ah, but there are other ways to travel. Imagine going by train from city to city, letting the rails rock you to sleep at night. Perhaps I wouldn't want to do it forever, but I would like to try it."

There was a little of the adventuress in that ladylike soul, he thought with appreciation. He'd like to travel the country by train with her. They would have a sleeping compartment, and at night he would enter her and let the train rock them to completion, rather than to sleep.

Some children were chasing a ball, shrieking with laughter as they shoved and slipped across the field. Luis stopped, his hand on her arm, until the children tumbled safely by, then slowly they resumed their walk.

Olivia felt oddly at ease with him, and she couldn't really say why, because they had only just met and hadn't really talked of anything, but there was something about him that made her relax. Perhaps it was the small things, the way he adjusted his long stride to match hers, or the care he had taken not to let the children collide with her, but she felt safe. Of course, most men were courteous in those ways, but with this man it felt like more than mere courtesy, as if it were his very nature to protect her.

"Do you have family nearby?" she asked.

"I don't have any family at all, or at least none that I remember. I guess that's why I've drifted the way I have."

"And you've never been married?" She immediately said, "I'm sorry, I shouldn't pry."

"I don't mind answering. I was planning on marriage once, but she died. That was ten years ago."

"Do you still love her?" *Why* couldn't she control her unruly tongue? She had no business at all asking him such personal questions, but she couldn't seem to stop herself. She felt her face heat at her rudeness, but he treated the question as easily as if it were about the weather.

"In a way." Thoughtfully he continued, "Celia was a wonderful person, truly worth loving, and I still love the person she was. But I'm not still *in* love with her, if you understand the difference."

"Yes, I do." Olivia was astonished at the relief she felt.

They came to a small stream and walked along it until they reached a log that had been placed across it. Olivia looked back at the picnic, blinking in surprise at how far they were from the others. Only a few people were visible from where they were, most of the townsfolk hidden by trees and brush and the curve of the meadow.

"Perhaps we should go back," she said a little nervously.

Luis stepped up on the log and held his hand out to her. "And perhaps we shouldn't. The explorers would have taken forever if they had never ventured out of the sight of the crowd."

She bit her lip, then cautiously placed her hand in his and let him help her up onto the log. She couldn't believe she was doing this. Olivia Millican had never done anything as outrageous as wandering off with a strange man; but then, she thought a little rebelliously, Olivia Millican had always longed to travel. Perhaps it was time to start paying attention to the secret Olivia. After all, she felt perfectly safe with Luis.

The log rolled unsteadily as they made their way across it, but fortunately they needed only a few steps to cross, and then Luis was clasping her waist in his strong hands and lifting her the rest of the way. She felt as if they had crossed a huge obstacle to their explorations, rather than a small stream. She didn't think she had ever been in this area before.

They walked beneath the trees, and Luis pointed out different kinds of birds to her. She was enthralled, for she had lived all of her life in towns, and the limit

111

of her knowledge about birds was that she could tell a robin from a crow. Behind them the sounds of the picnic faded completely away, and she could hear only the birds and the wind rustling in the trees, their quiet steps, and their voices. He was holding her hand, his strong fingers wrapped securely around hers, the heat and roughness strangely reassuring. She ought not to let him hold her hand, she thought, but she didn't do anything to stop him. They should return to the picnic. She said nothing.

They were as alone as if miles from town, wandering deeper and deeper into the forest. She wondered if her parents were worried but knew they would simply think she was with friends.

The rich smell of the forest satisfied something deep inside her. The contentment shone out of her face as she looked up at him with a luminous smile, and without thought Luis reacted to that sweet femininity, pulling her into his arms and bending to her mouth.

Instinctively he kept the contact light, feeling the softness of her lips and letting her respond at her own rate. Olivia did so by degrees, beguiled by the tenderness of the touch and the hard warmth of his body. Her forearms, which had been resting on his chest while she subconsciously decided if she should push him away or not, slid up, and her hands laced around his neck as her body made its own decision. It felt so good to be held by him like that, so she snuggled closer. His taste was intriguing, so she instinctively parted her lips to taste him more, and that was all the encouragement Luis needed. He put his hand on the back of her head and held her while he deepened the kiss, first gliding his tongue over her lips, then slipping it inside when she didn't protest. He felt the little start of surprise she gave, but it was followed immediately by sweet yielding.

Olivia was dizzy from the pleasure of kissing him. She had been kissed a few times before—she was, after all, twenty-five years old—but no one else had ever kissed her with an open mouth, inviting her to part her own lips. She shivered with delight at the sensation of his tongue first touching lightly, then moving deep inside her mouth. She jerked at the unexpected invasion, expecting it to be awful, but the swift rise of intense, heated pleasure instead had her pressing closer to him.

"You're so sweet," Luis murmured against her mouth as he slanted his head and returned for more of those hungry, invading kisses.

She had never felt passion before, never suspected that any man could make her feel that way. She had never before let any man hold her fully against him, her breasts crushed into his chest. It felt wonderful, she thought dimly. Her breasts ached, and that hard pressure seemed to ease them. Another ache was growing in her, deep in her belly, and she couldn't understand it or find ease for it.

He raised his head, staring down into her dazed blue eyes. His own eyes were hot with need. He was breathing hard, but so was she, her soft breasts heaving. Luis recognized all the signs of an aroused woman, but he also plainly saw the innocent bewilderment behind the passion.

He hadn't brought her out here for this, he told himself. He had watched her for a long time, noticed how she kept trying to evade Bellamy, and had impulsively asked her to walk with him. But now they were alone, and he hadn't been able to resist that sweet mouth.

He could have her now. He could lower her to the moss-covered ground and have her skirt up before she fully comprehended what she was doing. As inexperienced as she was, she wouldn't have an inkling how to control her own desires. But a hasty seduction would likely be the only time he would ever have her; he knew women well enough to know that afterward she would go to any lengths to avoid him. That wasn't what he wanted. She was so sweet he wanted to lose himself in her time and again, and the only way to do that was to be patient and truly win her.

He realized all of that but couldn't bring himself to let her go without tasting even more of her. He began kissing her again, tightening his arms around her and positioning his hardness against her soft mound. He felt the gasp she gave, took it into his mouth, and kissed her beyond her alarm. Slowly he sank down to his knees, taking her with him.

Boldly he put his hand on her breast, squeezing it through the cloth, but that wasn't enough. He wanted to feel her warm, naked flesh. Olivia arched away from the touch, her eyes flying open.

"Don't be frightened," he crooned, lulling her with more kisses, stroking her breast and ribs.

"You—you shouldn't do that."

"This is part of making love. Does it feel good?" Some women found it painful rather than pleasurable, so he was always careful to ask.

"Y-yes," she stammered. "But that isn't the point."

"What is the point, then?" He continued kneading her breast, and he found her tight little nipple with his thumb. She gasped again as he rubbed it, and hot color tinted her cheeks.

"That—that we shouldn't be doing this." She closed her eyes, involuntarily concentrating on the wonderful sensations.

"Do you want me to stop?"

"No," she moaned. Then her nails dug into his shoulders. "Yes. We have to."

"Not quite yet," he whispered, and he slipped his hand inside her bodice. Olivia gave a pleasured cry at the searing heat of his palm on her naked breast. Her nipple was very hard, thrusting eagerly forward. Swiftly he opened her dress so that both breasts were bare, then bent her back over his arm and took one of the succulent little buds into his mouth, circling it with his tongue before pulling at it with a hard sucking motion.

She shook and shuddered, straining against him, soft little cries coming from her open mouth. The ache low in her body had grown beyond her control, and she writhed with it, her hips moving, asking for something she couldn't identify. Luis felt the movement and knew exactly what she needed, but now wasn't the time. He forced himself to be content with teaching her just part of the pleasure he could give her.

Her breasts were small and milky white, the nipples pink and delicate. She quivered every time he rubbed them, luring him to complete what he had started. It took all of his willpower to resist, to bring her down gently by pulling the edges of her dress together again and holding her close, kissing her and murmuring to her, telling her how much he wanted her and how he ached, knowing it would make her feel better if she knew that he wasn't unaffected by this.

Still, her pale face flamed with embarrassment when her senses returned. She pushed his hands away and began fumbling with her dress, trying to restore it to decency.

"Don't be ashamed," he said. "You're beautiful."

"How can I not be ashamed?" she asked in a strangled voice. "You're a stranger, and I've let you—" She broke off, unable to put into words the depth of her disgrace.

"We aren't strangers now," he said in a quiet voice. "Olivia, look at me, darling."

She shook her head, so he caught her chin and firmly tilted it upward. "Do you think I can't respect you or I wouldn't have touched you like that?"

The distress in her eyes was his answer. He leaned forward and gently kissed her. "I touched you, darling, because I want you so much I couldn't help myself. I stopped because I *do* respect you and want to see you again."

She surged to her feet, her face red. "Oh, no!" she cried involuntarily.

He caught her hands when she would have run from him. "Because you think this will happen again?"

Olivia could barely stand still, so great was her distress. Tears swam in her eyes. "We must never—"

"Don't expect me to stay away from you, because I can't. And I'll kiss you again every chance I get.

Eventually we'll make love, Olivia—yes, we will," he said sternly when she began shaking her head. "Forget that I'm just a drifter and you're the banker's daughter, and remember how it felt with my mouth on you, because it will be much better than that, darling. Much better."

8

Dee was drawing a bucket of water when Lucas rode up that afternoon. Her heart slammed against her breastbone at the sight of him; it had been over a week since she had seen him, and it was alarming how much she had missed his high-handedness. The battles with him made her feel more alive than she ever had before because she could be herself while she was fighting him, and nothing she said would shock him.

He swung down from the horse and looped the reins around the rail. "I told you I'd come after you," he said grimly, walking toward her.

Dee hefted the bucket of water with a warning glint in her eyes. "And I told you I wouldn't go to the picnic. I have my reasons, and I'm not going to ruin things just to satisfy one of your whims."

His eyes glittered with an unholy blue light, and he kept on coming. "I've been wet before," he said.

Maybe the water wasn't much of a deterrent, but the

bucket was heavy. Dee swung it at his head, soaking both of them as the water sloshed out. He ducked, and she quickly shifted position, drawing back for another swing.

"You leave me alone," she warned.

"There's no way in hell," he retorted, and he grabbed for her.

Dee ducked, and the wooden bucket caught him on the shoulder. He stopped, swearing while he rubbed the place she had hit. Those blue eyes narrowed on her. "You'd better knock me out this time," he said, and he lunged.

She took him at his word and tried her best to knock him in the head, but this time he didn't let the heavy bucket stop him. It banged against his back as he dived under her swing, and before she could dodge away he jammed his broad shoulder into her midsection, then lifted her. He straightened with her dangling over his shoulder and strode purposefully toward the house.

Furiously she discovered that she was helpless in that position. Her kicking legs were anchored by his left arm, and the only target she had for her fists were his legs and buttocks. Since it was the only thing she could do, she bit him.

He roared with mingled pain and rage and slapped her bottom with all his strength, which was considerable. Dee cried out at the burning impact, then tried to bite him again. He twisted, dumping her off of his shoulder onto the back stoop, then immediately grabbed the back of her collar and used it to drag her into the house.

As soon as he released her she jumped to her feet

and sprang at him. "You little bitch," he said admiringly, and he laughed as he evaded her fists, taking hold of her arms and instead forcing her back against the wall.

Dee fought with the intent to win, and that meant using whatever means she could. She was severely hampered by the way he held her arms, so she resorted to kicking, trying for his crotch. His laughter stopped abruptly when her foot landed on his thigh, far too close for comfort, and he solved the problem by crushing her up against the wall with his body.

"Now fight me," he panted.

She tried, twisting and heaving, but with the wall behind her and his heavy body pressing her from the front she had no room to do anything more. She kicked, and he used the moment of motion to force his legs inside hers. With another quick move he had her lifted off her feet, his muscled thighs holding hers apart while he ground his pelvis against her.

She stopped fighting, because it was useless and would only increase the heavy pressure of his erection between her legs. She leaned her head back against the wall, panting. "Damn you, let me go."

Instead he lifted her higher and hungrily closed his mouth over her breast. The wet heat penetrated her layers of clothing, and she felt her nipple tighten, pebbling under the onslaught of his tongue. Desire mingled sharply with anger until she wondered if they weren't the same thing after all.

He released her arms so he could pull at her blouse, and without that support her weight dragged downward, pressing her even harder against his groin. A heavy surge of pure need shook her, making her cry out, and she clenched her hands in his hair rather than using her new freedom to fight him off. Her blouse ripped under his savage hands, then his fingers locked in the top of her shift and jerked, subjecting it to the same fate. He cupped her naked breasts in his hands and pushed them together, his beard scraping her soft skin as he sucked at first one breast and then the other.

She twisted, crying out again. Lucas drank in the sound, roughly kissing her while he continued massaging her breasts. There was no stopping this time; he had to have her, had to satisfy the burning, untamed hunger in both of them. He worked his hand under her skirt and untied her drawers, dragging them down over her buttocks.

Dee stilled as she felt her underwear slipping down; her head turned away, and her eyes closed. She had been totally naked in front of him before but had not felt so bare as she did now, so vulnerable. He moved back a little from her and let her legs come together, and the cotton drawers slithered down her legs to pool around her ankles. "Step out of them," he whispered, and mindlessly she did.

The heavy weight of his body returned to lie against her, holding her to the wall. His hands were still under her skirt, on her naked flesh, kneading her buttocks and stroking her thighs, and finally covering her mound.

She held her breath, not even daring to breathe in her agony of anticipation and need. His hand moved slowly, one long finger sliding down into the slit of her soft folds. The lash of pleasure was almost cruel, and so strong that she bucked in his arms. He held her, that one finger moving mercilessly back and forth. He sank it a little way into her, and she almost screamed from the shock, yet her legs opened wider to allow him to do whatever he wanted. She squirmed, her nails digging into his shoulders as his wet finger returned to find the small nub at the top of her sex and roll it back and forth, this time shattering her control and making her scream.

"God, you're beautiful," he muttered, watching her skin flush with desire. She was unutterably wild and glorious, with her head tilted back and her bare breasts heaving from the force of her breathing. She had blazed up like wildfire, burning beyond her control, just as he had known she would.

She was wet silk between her legs, so soft and hot he thought he might explode just touching her. He held her securely and eased his finger into her again, probing deeper, using his thumb to rub her and keep her hot so she wouldn't object to his penetration. She jerked, whimpering, and her internal muscles tightened on his finger to hold it so snugly he almost groaned aloud, thinking how tight she would be on his shaft. He couldn't enter her very far before he met the surprisingly firm resistance of her maidenhead, and he knew that this initial act wouldn't be very easy for either of them.

His hand had brought her close to orgasm, and she squirmed wildly against him, seeking release from the terrible, exquisite tension. "Easy, easy," Lucas whispered against her mouth as he pushed his thigh between her legs, shoving it high and hard against her.

The heat of her burned him even through his pants. "Let me show you how."

He put both hands on her hips and began rocking her against his thigh. She shuddered and moaned and couldn't stop, the low gasping sounds growing louder as the aching need intensified. The hard thigh between her legs both eased the ache and made it worse, so that she didn't know what to do. She began sobbing and beat at him with her fists, but he merely pushed her higher so that her toes were off the ground and she forked his leg. His hard hands kept her hips moving in that maddening rhythm, and she couldn't take it any longer, she couldn't, until it felt as if every muscle in her lower body clamped down and convulsed and her senses exploded in a storm of sensation. The great waves of ecstasy washed over her one after the other and finally passed to leave her as weak as a kitten, barely coherent and limp in his hands.

Lucas lowered her to the floor and stretched her out, his face hard with his own passion as he tore his pants open. If he took the time to carry her into the bedroom she might recover enough to begin fighting him again, and he had to be inside of her or go mad. Nothing was easy with Dee, and certainly not her denouement; having tested the strength of her maidenhead, he knew it would hurt her, and Dee didn't take kindly to being hurt.

He shoved her skirt to her waist and spread her legs, then settled between them. She made a low sound deep in her throat, and her slim legs came up to clasp his hips. Lucas set his mouth on hers, feeling the sleepy parting of her lips and the slow glide of her arms around his neck. He drank in the sweetness of her response even as he reached down and guided his shaft to the small, soft opening and pushed inside. He did it with a strong, even stroke, not pausing at the internal resistance but not being rough with her either. He could almost feel the shock reverberate through her body as it absorbed his penetration, the virginal walls tightening about him as if to prevent him from going deeper, and it felt even better than he had imagined. She was hot and wet and impossibly tight, the sensation racing along his nerves.

Then she screamed. It was a sound of mingled pain and fury, and just what he had expected. Some women would lie docile beneath a dominating man, but not Dee. She exploded into movement, her entire body heaving and bucking in an effort to dislodge him from inside her. Everything about it maddened her: the burning pain as he forced his way into her, his weight as he held her down, the very penetration of her body. She couldn't accept it; she mindlessly struggled against that domination, against the invasion of herself.

Lucas held her down with all of his weight and the iron strength of his arms and legs, letting her fight it out until she became accustomed to his length inside her. Her fierce struggle moved her on him almost as if he were thrusting, and he ground his teeth as he held himself as still as possible. Sweat sheened his skin as he waited for her to tire, for the pain to lessen, for her to begin to feel the pleasure of a man's fullness stretching her and probing deep. She was naturally voluptuous, and he had already shown her the heights of physical enjoyment; she wouldn't be able to deny herself for long. He hoped.

That point came gradually. She was already tired from both their previous struggle and her climax; he could feel her muscles relax, against her will, for she would almost immediately tighten them for renewed rejection, but the pauses between struggles grew longer until the struggles finally ceased. She lay still beneath him, breathing hard, her eyes closed against the naked triumph in his.

He kissed her forehead and smoothed the tangle of hair back from her face. "Is it still hurting?" he murmured against her temple.

She moved restlessly, and her hands settled on his sides as if she couldn't decide whether to embrace him or push him away. "Yes. I don't like it." Then honesty compelled her to add, "But it doesn't hurt as much as it did at first."

"Just lie still for a little longer, sweetheart. If it still hurts then, I'll stop."

She was silent, and her breath continued to slow. Lucas shifted against her, luxuriating in the feel of her enveloping him. Sweat trickled down his back.

"Damn you, you knew it would be like this, didn't you?" Experimentally she flexed her inner muscles around the burning shaft that had invaded her, relaxing a bit when it didn't result in pain.

Lucas tensed and groaned. "Jesus. Sweetheart, please, don't move."

"You're crushing me," she said in a low voice. "Couldn't you at least have put me on the bed?"

"We'll get to the bed," he promised, brushing her

lips with his. For now, he thought, the floor was just fine.

She opened her eyes. Her gaze was solemn and questioning. "What you made me feel before—doing this will make me feel the same?"

"If I do it right. If you want me enough."

She gave a little laugh and lifted her knees alongside his hips. "Oh, I want you."

"Enough?"

She knew what he was asking, and her somber green eyes met his intense blue ones. "Yes. Enough."

He moved slowly, thrusting inward until his entire length stretched her. Dee gasped, her body arching upward, and just as slowly he withdrew. "You don't want me to stop?" he asked, just to make sure.

Her hands clutched at his sides. "No." Her voice sounded strangled. "Oh, no."

"I don't know if I can hold back long enough to satisfy you this time," he said with grim honesty as he began moving in a strong rhythm.

For answer she locked her strong legs around his hips and lifted herself up to him, offering her body, as generous as he had been in first taking care of her. That was all it took. He began moving into her with a powerful rhythm, and she accepted him, welcomed him. With a stifled shout he went rigid, then shuddered violently and convulsed with the force of his seed spurting from his body.

An hour later they lay naked in the bed, exhausted and almost asleep. Scarcely had they recovered from the first lovemaking than he had grown erect once again, and that time he had carried her to the bed and finished stripping their clothes off. She had found that making love could be a slow tangle of bodies, hot and languorous, that carried them to the same conclusion.

He had drawn it out, building her arousal so high that when the crest finally broke she had been wild with it, so that she had inevitably carried him to the same heights. He had made love to his share of women, but none of them had ever engrossed him the way Dee did. He was fascinated by the changes passion wrought in her body, from the hardening of her nipples to the moistening of her sweet little female channel. She was a she-cat in bed as well as out, giving just as fiercely as she took. He had known making love to her would be a challenge, but he hadn't known it would be both tiring and exhilarating, like riding and conquering a tidal wave until it subsided into gentle breakers on a beach.

He felt a cold twinge of panic as he lay there. Making love to anyone else after having had Dee would be like giving up the bite of whiskey for the sedative effects of heated milk. Because he didn't want to think she had ruined him for anyone else he willed the idea and the panic away, but it kept returning.

There was no way he could be satisfied with Olivia now. Before meeting Dee he had been certain in his mind that Olivia was the wife he wanted, a gently bred woman who knew how to hostess a large dinner, who would be at ease with politicians and millionaires. He had planned to acquire her just as he had planned to acquire more land, but in one short afternoon those plans had been turned to ashes. Thank God he had held back and hadn't actually asked Olivia to marry him; she deserved a lot more than a husband who couldn't get another woman out of his mind.

He thought of Denver and the political maze he would have to negotiate to build the power base necessary to influence decisions the way he wanted. There would be receptions and dinners, endless maneuvering taking place with the socializing. He was willing to do that to build the Double C into an empire, maybe to pave the way for one of his own sons to be governor, but he had pictured Olivia at his side during the endless social functions, her cool, polished manner perfect for the situation.

Now when he brought up the image he found that the woman didn't have a face. No matter how hard he tried, he couldn't imagine Dee there. He couldn't see her catering to the comfort of a self-important politician; she would be more likely to skewer him with that rapier tongue of hers. No, she didn't fit in at all with the life he had planned for himself, even supposing she would be willing to try, which she wasn't. She had made it plenty clear that she liked her life the way it was, thank you, without anyone to tell her what to do. Sometimes—hell, most of the time—he wanted to grab her and shake some sense into her, but at the same time he grudgingly gave her the respect she deserved. It took a strong-willed woman to accomplish what she had, and she wasn't likely to submit that will to any man's.

So where did that leave him? Right where he was, he thought, and he didn't like the idea. He had learned not to make assumptions where Dee was concerned. Just because he had made love to her twice didn't mean she would regard him as her lover, that she wouldn't fight him next time. And even if she didn't put up a fight about that, she would still resist with every stubborn inch of her against allowing him into any part of her life beyond that.

But for now she was sleeping in his arms, and he was exhausted from a physical satisfaction that went bone deep. He held her closer, made utterly content by the feel of her warm, sleek body lying naked against him, and he drifted off to sleep himself.

The sun was going down when Dee woke. For a moment she was totally disoriented, without any sense of what time or what day it was. She never slept during the day, but from the angle of the sun she knew it wasn't dawn. She was too groggy to make sense of it until she woke up enough to realize that she wasn't alone in the bed. That in itself was startling, for she had never before shared her bed with anyone, but then full reality hit her with stunning force. She was in bed with Lucas, and they were both naked because he had made love to her.

She didn't feel ashamed; her nature was too elemental for her not to be aware of the naturalness of the act. But she did feel a strong need to retrench her position, to reestablish herself as an individual after the mindless giving of her body. It was as if he had taken over control of her when he thrust his thick shaft inside her. She had fought against the natural domination of it even as her traitorous flesh had begun shivering with delight around him.

She shifted cautiously, feeling the unaccustomed soreness in her thighs and loins, and the movement made her aware of the stickiness between her legs. Another wave of reality hit her full in the face. Twice Lucas had emptied his seed deep inside her. He might have made her pregnant.

As women had done for thousands of years, she counted the days until her next monthly flow. It would be over two weeks until she knew, two weeks of fear and worry, because her life would be impossible if she were to have a baby.

Lucas pulled her closer and lazily cupped her breast, his big hand possessive. She hadn't realized he was awake until he did so, and she quickly looked up but immediately lowered her gaze from the hard, gleaming triumph in his eyes.

"What are you thinking?" he asked, his voice a deep, lazy rumble against her hair.

"That we can't do this anymore." She looked up at him again, her expression a little haunted.

That look on her face stilled his automatic rise of anger. "Why not, sweetheart? You liked it, didn't you?" He stroked her hair back from her face.

"You know I did," she said steadily. "But now I might have a baby."

He paused, a slight frown gathering his brows. A baby. In the savage delight of possession he hadn't given a thought to the possible consequences.

"When will you know?"

"About two weeks. A little more."

He stroked her breast, enthralled by the satiny texture of it. She was his now, damn it, and he wasn't going to give her up. "There are ways to keep you from getting pregnant."

"I know," she said tartly. "All I have to do is stay away from you."

He smiled and kissed her, his mouth rough on hers. "Other than that. I'll get a sponge for you."

She was instantly curious. "What do you mean? How can a sponge keep me from having a baby?"

"I don't know how it works, I just know it does. It's just a little sponge, and you soak it in vinegar and put it up inside you."

Her cheeks flamed, and she jerked upright, away from his exploring hands. He laughed and grabbed for her, wrestling her back down on the bed. She wasn't fighting in earnest, only huffy and embarrassed by the notion, and he grinned as he subdued her.

"How did you learn about anything like that?" she snapped, glaring at him. "It's a whore's trick, isn't it?"

"I imagine whores would know about it, but other women use it, too." He didn't answer her question about how he knew about it. He'd had some wild times in New Orleans and other places, but she didn't need to know about them.

Dee turned her head away from him because she knew full well he had learned about such a thing from other women. Part of her was relieved that there was a solution, but part of her, like a child, wanted to retreat to the way things had been before this afternoon, when she had been unaware of the way her body could respond to his, before she had felt his hard length plunging into her. Things had changed, and she couldn't change them back.

The question, of course, was if she really wanted to change them. She felt as if she had leapt headlong over a cliff in the dark. It was frightening, taking her to places she hadn't known before. If she truly wished the changes undone she would have to wish Lucas out of her life, wish he had never ridden up to her door, and she couldn't do that. As infuriating as he was, as determined to have his way, he made her feel more than she had ever imagined possible.

She was very much afraid she had fallen in love with him.

9

OLIVIA HAD TO FORCE HERSELF TO ATTEND THE DANCE
that night. Lucas was absent, and she knew people
were whispering about it, but his absence was the only
bit of relief she could find. Because of their strange
talk about Dee, Olivia suspected he had gone out to
the farm. She mentally crossed her fingers, for if Dee
were ever to marry it would have to be to a man like
Lucas, someone as strong as she was. Dee would
totally cow most men; she could never be happy with
someone who didn't match her in strength. Olivia
wondered if perhaps she was wishing away her own
last chance to be married, but at least she wouldn't be
faced with the nerve-racking decision of whether or
not to accept Lucas if he proposed. Now it looked as if
he wouldn't, and she was glad.

But Lucas wasn't her real concern. All she could
think about was what had happened in the woods. She
didn't know how she had gotten through the day. Her

nerves felt so frayed she thought she would scream if she had to smile at one more person. She couldn't look her mother in the face. Honora had raised her to be a good, decent woman, yet at the first opportunity she had let a strange man lead her into the woods and take liberties with her. Not just kisses; she had once supposed a kiss to be a daring thing, but now she knew the respectful pecks on the lips she had received before had been as chaste as a brother's. She had not only accepted Luis's tongue into her mouth, she had delighted in it, actually participated. No wonder he had thought he could touch her breasts! He must suppose her to be as immoral as the saloon girls, for she certainly hadn't conducted herself as a lady ought.

She could barely attend to any of the conversation around her, so she became even quieter than usual, her face pale with distress. Everyone was having such a good time that no one noticed, except for Luis, standing on the edge of the crowd, watching her.

It so unnerved her that when Kyle Bellamy approached and asked her to dance Olivia had placed her hand in his before she realized what she was doing.

His hand on her waist drew her closer to him than she wished to be; after this afternoon she was acutely aware of a man's body. She wondered with sudden horror if Luis had bragged to his boss about his success with her. Would that be why Kyle assumed he could hold her so close?

She stiffened in his arms. "Mr. Bellamy, please."

"I'll please you in any way I can."

She couldn't decide if the remark was suggestive or

merely flirtatious, and at the moment she didn't care. "You're holding me far too close."

He immediately loosened his grip and let her move back. "I apologize," he murmured, but his smile made her suspect he wasn't sorry at all.

Kyle danced well, his movements strong and sure. Under any other circumstances she might have put aside her instinctive uneasiness about him and enjoyed the dance, but tonight it was impossible. She could only pray it would be over soon.

"Would you like to walk outside with me?" he asked. "It's a pleasant night, and the air is stuffy in here. I confess I've been wanting a chance to talk to you, to get to know you better."

"Thank you for the offer, Mr. Bellamy, but I'm tired from this afternoon and would rather sit in here."

"Then perhaps I may sit with you?"

She didn't know what to say. She couldn't be rude to the man, but she had no desire at all for his company.

"I plan to go home soon," she said, desperately improvising.

"Then may I sit with you until then?"

God, he was persistent! What else could she do but say yes?

When they were sitting down he kept brushing his leg against hers, and Olivia twisted a bit to the side to prevent the contact.

"I'd like to call on you tomorrow," he told her.

Her guilty conscience made her feel certain now that Luis had told him, and he obviously expected to enjoy the same liberties! She could think of only one excuse, and she hastily used it. "I don't think that would be proper, Mr. Bellamy. I have an—an unspoken agreement with Mr. Cochran. I'm sure you understand."

"If it's unspoken, then I assume you're still a free woman," Kyle said boldly. "And I don't see Cochran here tonight."

"No. He—he had business elsewhere."

"A man who would desert a lovely woman like you doesn't deserve her."

Luis watched the byplay from across the room and could easily imagine the conversation he couldn't hear. He didn't like the way Bellamy was leaning so close to Olivia, and from the frozen expression on her face she didn't care for it either but didn't know how to stop him.

Olivia glanced in his direction and froze. She couldn't help looking his way, and every time she did she found him watching her. Her distress grew, because she imagined his black eyes held disdain. After all, what else could he think after the way she had behaved?

What Luis was thinking was that he should have known she would suffer under a massive load of guilt, and he ached to comfort her. Poor darling, she really had no idea about the physical side of life. Olivia had been raised too conventionally and was herself too ladylike by nature for it to be any other way. She didn't even know how to rid herself of Bellamy's unwanted attentions.

Luis looked around, and his gaze settled on two of the Bar B's ranch hands, men he knew to be hot-tempered. They were almost always contesting each other in one thing or another, and tonight was no exception. The object of their competition tonight was a pretty little farm girl whose face was flushed with pleasure at so much male attention.

Luis eased his way through the crowd. Both men held drinks in their hands, supposedly punch, but he knew the drink was well laced with whiskey. In the jostling crowd it was easy to reach out and bump one man's arm enough to make him spill the contents of the cup all over the farm girl's best dress.

He quickly moved back out of the way, blending into the crowd and listening to the growing sounds of altercation he left behind him. The man who had spilled his punch was accusing the other of deliberately pushing his arm. The disagreement erupted into a full-scale fistfight before he could make his way back across the room.

Kyle scowled with annoyance when he saw that the combatants were two of his own men. He said something to Olivia and left his seat, swiftly crossing the room. It wouldn't do his standing in the community any good if his men were so rowdy, and Luis knew that Bellamy was very proud of his respectability.

Luis looked at Olivia's pinched expression and silently berated himself. He had almost pushed too hard that afternoon, so now she was remembering her shame rather than the pleasure of his kisses. It would take all of his charm to repair the damage.

He made his way through the crowd toward her. She saw him before he could reach her and immediately spun away, retreating from him.

She was afraid of him! Luis was thunderstruck at the realization. No woman had ever before feared him, so why did it have to be this particular woman who ran from him, this woman whom he wanted as he had never before wanted anyone?

Her action angered him. He was a man, instinctive and possessive, and he intended to claim Olivia as his without examining the whys and wherefores of it. He increased his pace and caught up with her before she could reach the safety of her mother's side, stopping her by the simple means of putting his boot down on her skirts. She jerked to a halt and threw him a pleading look over her shoulder, but she had the choice of either staying where she was or having her skirt torn off.

"Dance with me," he said, only for her ears. "Please."

"No!" She gasped the refusal. She was so distraught that she couldn't be in his arms again without somehow betraying herself.

"Then walk outside with me."

"No!" This time the refusal was tinged with horror. Another invitation to do something improper! How *could* he ask her to walk with him again, after what had happened that afternoon? But that was probably the reason he asked, she thought bitterly. He expected to find her as easy again.

Luis put his strong hand on her arm and turned her. "Go outside, Olivia. Now."

She hadn't heard that hard, commanding tone from him before, and it silenced her. Numbly she let him guide her out of the meeting hall where they always held the annual dance, and down the steps.

The cool air washed over her hot face as he led her across the street and into the shadow of a huge tree.

She could still hear the music and the laughter, the cacophony of conversation from a multitude of throats at once, but it was all muted and far away now, overlain by the sounds of the night.

"What do you want?" she whispered almost fearfully. She tried to free her arm, but he tightened his grip.

"I want you to stop looking as if you expect to be stoned to death," he retorted angrily.

Olivia's spine stiffened at his tone. She wasn't given to temper, but that didn't mean she wouldn't stand up for herself if she felt under unjust attack. "I'll look any way I please," she retorted, embarrassed that the best she could think of was such a childish reply. She was at a disadvantage, having had little experience with arguing.

Apparently he noticed it, too, for his grasp eased, and a faint smile teased the corners of his mouth. "Remind me someday to teach you how to fight," he said. "What you should have said was something that would make *me* feel guilty, too."

She bit her lip, immediately reminded of her own lack of decorum. "Why should I?" she asked, the words troubled. "What happened was my fault. I never should have gone with you."

"Ah, darling." He laughed softly and enfolded her hand, carrying it to his mouth. He delicately licked one of her knuckles, and she trembled. "Don't take all the blame on yourself when my shoulders are so much broader. I at least knew what I was doing."

"I'm not a child, Mr. Fronteras." She was irritated that he evidently thought her so stupid she hadn't been aware of the inappropriateness of going off alone with him. "Of course I knew what I was doing."

LINDA HOWARD

He still looked amused. "Did you? I don't think so. If you'd had any experience at all, you wouldn't be so upset now. Has anyone else ever kissed you?"

She knotted her fists. "Of course," she said indignantly.

"Really? How?" He sounded skeptical. "Closed-mouth pecks that didn't even give you a taste?"

Abruptly she realized the absurdity of what she was doing, trying to convince him of experience she didn't have when she had been worried that he would think exactly that of her. She jammed her fingers against her mouth to stifle her laughter, and Luis grinned, too.

"That's better," he said. He gently caressed her cheek. "What happened today is what happens between two people who are attracted to each other. It isn't shameful, though it certainly should always be private. Do you think your friends haven't felt a man's touch on their breasts? I assure you that most of them have."

"Most of my friends are *married,*" she pointed out. "I assume that married people are—are more free with each other," she finished carefully. She could feel her face heating at his bluntness.

"Some more than others," Luis drawled, thinking of the poor souls who probably did no more than ruck up their nightshirts and finish within five minutes. Poor men? Poor ladies! "But you can bet that they made love at least a little even before they married."

"I don't think so," she said, disconcerted at the idea.

A couple of cowboys left the meeting hall just then, their joking voices loud in the still night air. Luis put his arm around her waist and drew her to the other

140

side of the tree, out of their sight. She felt the rough bark against her back and leaned thankfully against the sturdy support.

"Of course they did. It's so enjoyable, after all."

She was finding it difficult to keep the point of the argument in mind. "Enjoyable or not, Mr. Fronteras—"

"Luis."

"—I should never have allowed you such liberties today, and I'm ashamed of myself for such behavior."

"Moralistic little darling," he said tenderly.

"I am *not* your darling! Please don't call me that."

"But you are. You just haven't admitted it yet."

She took a deep breath, trying to compose herself and reorder her thoughts. "Our relationship is far too casual for me to permit such incidences between us, and I won't allow it to happen again—"

He put both hands on the tree, bridging her rib cage and effectively hemming her in. "Don't," he said quietly, interrupting her. "Don't make statements you'll then feel obliged to live up to."

"But I must," she replied just as quietly.

Luis drew a deep breath. He couldn't allow her to turn him away. It wasn't just the protectiveness she stirred in him, or the desire, it was the overwhelming need to have her for himself. He couldn't just seduce her; Olivia would consider herself "ruined" and would never marry, just to keep her sordid secret. She was sweet and honorable and deserved better.

He felt as if he were only slowly beginning to understand his own mind, but suddenly he knew what he wanted. He wanted Olivia, and he would do whatever it took to get her.

He leaned close to her. "No, there's no need. My intentions are honorable. There's nothing to fight against, unless you dislike me so much that you only want me to go away, and I don't think that's the case. Even if it were, I wouldn't go," he finished with iron determination.

Her breath caught. She tilted her head back against the tree, looking up at his lean face revealed by the moonlight spilling down through the gently shifting leaves. She was so stunned that she groped to order her thoughts.

It was almost impossible to comprehend. He wanted to *marry* her? That surely was what he meant by "honorable intentions." Yet how could he? He was a drifter, by his own admission. He had no home. Though she had dreamed of travel, there had always been an image of home in the back of her mind, the center to which she returned. "Home" wasn't her parents' house in those dreams, but a warm, welcoming home she had made with the man she loved. They would have children, so of course there had to be a home. How could she even consider marrying a man who couldn't provide that?

"Nothing to say?" he asked with a wry smile. "You don't love me yet, Olivia Millican, but you will. I won't give up until you do."

Then he leaned down and began kissing her, and her breath caught all over again, for if his kisses had been thrilling that afternoon, they were even more so now that she knew what to expect. She had the brief thought that she should resist, but she ignored it. She didn't want to resist, she didn't want to think about what she should or shouldn't do; she wanted to enjoy, to seize this moment of pure pleasure.

She found that having once traveled a road, it's difficult to keep your feet from turning down it again. His bold hand searched her breasts, burning her with his heat, and she couldn't find the inclination to refuse him. Instead her own hands stroked up his muscled back, kneading the hard flesh with delight as she learned the differences between his body and hers. She found his black hair thick and silky as she ran her fingers along the nape of his neck. He shivered a little, and her heart leapt at the knowledge that her touch excited him.

A thick groan broke from his throat, and he eased away from her, his breath coming loud and heavy. "Go back inside," he said, "or we'll do more than kiss, and this isn't the place for it. Tomorrow is Sunday, so I won't be working. Will you go for a ride with me?"

She couldn't think. What would she tell her parents? They wouldn't approve of her riding with anyone they knew nothing about, much less a Mexican drifter.

He seemed to realize all of that without her saying a word, and he smiled bitterly. "Of course not," he said, answering the question for her. "I understand. I should have thought before asking you such a question."

"Luis," she said hesitantly, "it isn't—" But it so obviously *was* that she broke off in midsentence.

"It is. But when you love me, it won't matter." He kissed her again, lingeringly, then caught her shoulders and turned her back toward the meeting hall, toward music and lights and laughter. "Go on, go back, before your pretty dress gets all mussed up. But if you decide to go riding tomorrow, try the north road. I'll be riding there myself around two o'clock."

He gave her a little push, and her steps carried her automatically back to the meeting hall. She stepped inside and was engulfed in warm air and noise. She was still dazed and couldn't concentrate, but the crushing burden of guilt seemed to have fallen away. She didn't know what to think. It seemed as if in a matter of a few hours the course of her entire life had been re-routed, and she didn't know where she was going.

How odd that she had felt despair at the thought of a marriage proposal from Lucas, who could give her everything in the way of material wealth, yet the thought of marrying Luis, who could give her nothing but adventure, made her feel shivery and excited, even frightened, but never despairing. Luis was right in saying that she didn't love him, for she barely knew him and was too cautious to plunge headlong into anything—wasn't she? Yet she hadn't denied him, hadn't turned him down flat as she was sure she should have. Instead she had let him kiss her and fondle her, after swearing to herself that it would never happen again. And she couldn't get his proposal out of her mind.

He hadn't actually proposed; he had just said that his intentions were honorable, a curiously formal phrase from a drifter.

She saw Kyle Bellamy making his way toward her,

and she quickly reached Honora, who was flushed with pride at how well everything had gone during "her" year.

"I'm going to go home, Mother," she said quietly.

Instantly Honora blinked and frowned, switching her attention from the dance to her only chick. Olivia could almost feel the motherly concern being focused on her.

"Are you feeling ill, darling?"

"I have a headache, and the noise is making it worse." It was the most time-worn excuse in the world, but Olivia wasn't accustomed to lying to her mother and couldn't think of anything more original.

"I'll get your father to walk you home." But right before leaving in search of Wilson Honora gave her daughter such a look of sympathetic concern that Olivia sighed, knowing her mother was thinking the same thing everyone else was. It would be all over town tomorrow that she and Lucas had had a fight, or something else that would explain why he wasn't at the dance and she was leaving early with a headache.

She would have to tell her parents that she had mistaken Lucas's intentions, that he was after all only a good friend. They would be disappointed, but she couldn't let them continue to look on Lucas as her suitor. Not tonight, though. She had far too much on her mind.

Wilson dutifully walked her home, and Olivia went straight upstairs to bed. She lay in the darkness and thought of all that had happened that day. She remembered the way Luis's mouth had closed over her tender breast, and she blushed, clasping her hands

145

over the suddenly throbbing mounds. She should
never have let him—

But she had.

She shouldn't go riding tomorrow, she thought.
Whatever she did, she shouldn't go anywhere near the
north road. She told herself that and knew she
wouldn't listen to her own advice.

10

THE TOWN WAS STILL QUIET FROM THE PICNIC AND dance the day before when Lucas rode in the next afternoon. Church was already out, and people had gone to their homes to rest off the aftereffects. It being a Sunday, when few men could justify stopping by the saloon for a drink, the establishment was occupied only by a few cowhands who had no duties for the day.

Both of the saloon girls were sitting and talking with the drinkers, as that encouraged them to drink more. Tillie looked up and smiled her slow smile at Lucas, and he gave a little jerk of his head. Her eyebrows rose, then she murmured a few words to the cowboy whose table she had been gracing and excused herself.

When she had sashayed close enough Lucas said softly, "Let's go upstairs."

Tillie looked amused. "You still have woman trouble?"

147

"Upstairs," he repeated, not wanting to say anything where they could be overheard.

She walked in front of him, leading him up the narrow stairs. Lucas could feel eyes boring into his back and smiled wryly. If they only knew why he was there!

Tillie's room was small, most of the space taken up by the double bed, though there was a washbasin and a dresser crammed into one of the corners. It was surprisingly clean and sweet-smelling.

She sat down on the bed and crossed her elegant legs. "Do you want anything special?" she asked in that slow, warm voice, and despite himself Lucas couldn't help thinking that her "special" might be almost enough to kill a man.

"A favor," he said.

She laughed aloud. "Somehow I knew my luck wasn't running true today. Well, maybe another time. What can I do for you?"

"Do you have any of the little sponges that keep women from conceiving?"

Those enormous brown eyes twinkled at him, and he grinned back, at ease with the request. Tillie wouldn't ask questions and wouldn't gossip, and her amusement was without malice.

She got up and sauntered over to the dresser. "So your woman troubles are over. You didn't strike me as the kind of man who would let it go on too long anyway, so I'm not surprised." She hummed a little as she opened a door and extracted a handpainted ceramic box. "How many do you need?"

It was his turn to laugh. "I don't know. How many *do* I need? Isn't one enough?"

She giggled, a sound rich and musical. "Here, take three. You know—just in case."

He snorted as she put the three small round sponges in his hand, but the smile still played around his hard mouth.

"Just soak one in vinegar," she instructed. "I suppose you know what to do with it, because it's a sure bet your lucky woman doesn't."

Lucas shook his head in amusement at the thought of the fight he would probably have getting Dee to use these. Then again, he was always surprised by the battles she chose to fight and the ones she ignored, so it was possible she wouldn't say anything at all.

Tillie's dark eyes were suddenly serious. "You take care of that woman, Lucas Cochran," she said sternly. "It wouldn't do at all for folks to find out about you and her, not after all the trouble she's had from some of the men around here."

Lucas's head jerked up, his eyes narrowing dangerously. Tillie held up a placating hand. "Word won't get out from me," she said.

"How did you know?" His voice was silky smooth and deadly. "Did anyone see us?"

"Relax, no one knows but me. I just happen to know who wasn't at the picnic yesterday, and word got around about how you left early. She came into town yesterday morning, to the general store, but it was closed. I was sitting outside and saw her. She waved at me. I've seen her before, and she's never been snooty. She's a straightforward woman, with more grit than just about any two men put together."

"She does have grit," Lucas said.

"There's been lots of talk about you and the banker's daughter," Tillie said. She looked him up and down, then shook her head. "I never could see it. You need someone meaner than that, a woman who can stand up to you without blinking an eye."

Lucas smiled. "Tillie," he said, "you know too damn much about people."

"I've had a lot of time to study them."

He put the little sponges in his pocket. "How much do I owe you?"

"They're on the house. Next time I order some from New Orleans, I'll let you know so you can get a supply."

He leaned down and kissed that exquisite mouth, lazily taking his time about it because she was so damn beautiful. When he straightened she blinked and said, "My, my. I haven't been kissed like that since Charles Dupré—never mind. Are you sure the sponges are all you want?"

He cupped her chin and kissed her again. "I'm sure," he said. "I need to save my strength."

She gave a wonderful, lusty laugh. "I guess you do. This is going to just destroy my reputation, us up here laughing like jackasses and you going back downstairs within five minutes."

He grinned at her as he opened the door. "No, it'll be my reputation that's ruined if I couldn't last more than five minutes."

She fluttered her lashes at him as she passed by. "If I ever got my hands on you, you might *not.*"

Lucas was in a good mood as he rode back to the Double C. The sponges in his pocket provoked a big temptation to swing east and visit Dee, but he resisted it. She would be too sore for making love again, and he wasn't all that certain of his self-control.

Thunder rumbled in the distance, underscoring his decision to go home. He looked upward but saw only deep blue sky. The storm clouds must still be beyond the horizon, he thought. They needed a good rain, since the snowpacks on the mountains weren't as deep as they should have been, but he sure hoped he got to the ranch before the storm arrived.

Luis looked upward at the same rumble of thunder. Olivia kept her attention on the ground before her as her mare carefully picked her way over some rough ground. "I hope it rains and settles the dust," she said.

He hoped it rained for more basic reasons. It had been too long since they had had even a brief spring shower, and the water holes were getting a little low, especially since it was just May. But as much as the rain was needed, he hoped it held off for another couple of hours. He didn't want his time with Olivia cut short.

She had been distinctly nervous when he had ridden up beside her, so he had restricted himself to conversation and the quiet enjoyment of her company. She had slowly relaxed, and now the strain was gone from her face. As much as he wanted to hold her again, he wanted more for her to feel at ease with him. It was time for her to get to know him better. Besides, there were some things he wanted to know about her, too.

"Is there an understanding between you and Lucas Cochran?" he asked quietly, watching her face.

LINDA HOWARD

"No," she replied. "He's never spoken of marriage, and neither have I, though everyone just assumed that he would."

"Don't you want him to? He's a powerful man, and from what I hear he's going to be even bigger than he is now."

"I like Lucas, but he's just a friend." How good it felt to be able to say that! From the way he had acted the day before, she was certain he was fascinated with Dee. "If he *had* asked me, I don't know what I would have said."

"Because he's rich?"

"No. I know I've been raised with luxuries, but I don't think I've ever expected them as my due. But I'm twenty-five, and I'm afraid that if I don't marry soon, I never will, and then I'll never have my own family."

"I'm thirty-two," he said. "I've begun to think that I want to have a family, too."

She gave him a quick look and blushed.

"Why haven't you married before?" He quietly soothed his horse when the animal shied as a blossom blew in front of it. "I know you must have had offers."

"No. No one ever asked. Somehow I just never fell in love with anyone, and evidently no one fell in love with me either."

"I was serious about what I said. About my intentions."

"I know," she whispered. She sighed. "Why have you drifted?"

"It's always seemed the natural thing to do." He looked up at the sky again, but it was still clear. He wondered if he could explain it so she would under-

152

stand. "I've always been good with a gun. I've never hired it out, but when a man is fast with a six-iron it tends to make most people uneasy around him. And sooner or later someone thinks he's faster and wants to prove it. No town wants to have a fast gun settle down there, because it draws other guns. For a while I worked for the Sarratt brothers down in New Mexico, and I could have stayed there, but then Celia died, and so did my reason for staying.

"After a while, moving on seems like the natural thing to do. It has its own lure, to see what's beyond that mountain range, then the next one, then the next one. Always a new place and new faces, and sometimes nothing but a huge empty world with me right in the middle of it, just me and the horse and the sky. I've gone weeks without seeing another human being. And sometimes, when I'm in a town, I miss that."

"But you hired on with Mr. Bellamy. Do you intend to stay?"

"I hired on to rest from the trail for a while and earn some money doing it. I've been here almost two months now, and so far I'm content. I like the town. It's the kind of quiet, sturdy town I like."

She noticed that he hadn't answered her question but didn't feel that she had the right to press him further. What would it take to induce him to settle down? she wondered. Marriage? He hadn't said so, and she would be foolish to assume that such was his intention, perhaps almost as foolish as she would be to consider marrying him at all.

But he fascinated her in a way no one else had ever done. She glanced at his dark, lean face, admiring his wonderfully chiseled features. There was an obvious aura of danger about him, but she never felt threatened. Instead, when his warm, dark gaze touched her, she felt infinitely admired and . . . safe, as if he would forever stand between her and anything that would harm her.

Thunder rumbled again, closer this time. He looked regretful. "We'd better turn back."

Common sense agreed with him, but she felt like shaking her fist at the sky. Why couldn't the rain have held off just another hour or so? The storm might even bypass them completely, but they couldn't depend on that.

Smiling at the disappointment on her face, Luis reined his horse closer to hers and leaned over to kiss her lingeringly. Her lips parted for him without hesitation, so sweetly that it was all he could do to break away. He might not have if his horse hadn't sidestepped nervously, away from such close contact with her mount.

One kiss would have to be enough, he thought, or they would likely get caught by the storm anyway. They reined the horses around and started back.

"I don't know when I'll get back to town," he said after a while, "but I'll see you when I do."

She started to ask him how he would contact her but kept silent when she realized how insulting the question would be, for it would imply that he wasn't good enough simply to come to her house and ask to see her. Yet weren't they going out of their way not to let anyone see them together precisely because they both knew her parents would object?

She should tell them, she thought, and let them know that she . . . what? Was considering marrying

Luis? Without knowing where or how they would live? Honora would make herself ill with worry. Her parents were indulgent rather than dictatorial, so she didn't fear they would forbid her to see Luis; she was twenty-five, not a giddy seventeen-year-old to be locked in her room. But it would upset them, and she didn't want that.

So it seemed as if she could either have them upset or continue to sneak around as if she were doing something wrong, and neither choice appealed to her. The only solution was to stop seeing Luis entirely, which she discarded at once as unacceptable. In one short day he had shattered the pall of gray desolation that had shrouded her for so long, and she felt wondrously alive, her heart pounding with excitement whenever she was with him.

She had always done exactly as a lady ought, living contentedly within the boundaries of convention. This was the only time she had ever stepped outside those boundaries, and she found it exhilarating. If she was condemned for it, then she would simply have to deal with it, for she found that the need for his company was as compelling for her as drifting had been for him.

Dee looked up when she heard the patter of rain on the tin roof, the sound quickly increasing to a soporific drumming that drowned out all other sounds. With the rain came a chill, but she didn't want to light a fire, so she got a quilt from the bed and sat down in her big chair with it wrapped around her. The warmth of the quilt comforted her.

She had been reading, but the book no longer

interested her. She laid her head back and closed her eyes, letting the rain-induced drowsiness wash over her.

Lucas hadn't been back today. She had been jittery all day long, expecting him to come riding up with that intense look in his eyes that she now knew to be desire. He was arrogant enough to expect her to lie down with him whenever he wanted her, but she hadn't made up her mind about the situation.

She loved him. Since she had unwillingly admitted to herself the source of her agitation whenever she was around him, she had analyzed the situation from every angle and accepted that there was no easy solution to it. By loving him she had made herself vulnerable, and she would eventually be hurt by it. He didn't love her, which was the only thing that would have made him equally vulnerable and kept their relationship balanced. Loving him hadn't blinded her to the truth: Lucas was a hard man, one who was ruthless in getting his own way. He wanted her physically, he even cared for her to some extent, but that wasn't at all the same thing as love.

It would be better for her if she stopped the relationship cold, but she didn't know if she could. Lucas wouldn't give up without a fight, and she doubted her own ability to resist him. She wanted him with a deep, primitive strength that frightened her, knowing as she did that it was beyond her control.

There was always the chance that her feelings would lessen over time, as she grew to know him better, but she didn't think so. His character would always challenge her, both infuriating and invigorating, but never boring. She had always been protected from love because she had never met a man whose will was as strong as hers until Lucas. He would fight and laugh and love with her, and she would fall more and more in love with him.

Despite his assurance that there were ways to prevent conception, she knew that she would be at risk every time she made love with him. Bearing an illegitimate child, no matter how beloved, would destroy her standing with the townfolk. She cherished the respect she received now because only she knew how hard she had worked to earn it. Some people might not like her, and probably most of them thought her odd, but no one could say that she wasn't respected.

So she had to consider the possibility of pregnancy, and she ached deep inside in a way she never had before. She was intensely female, vital, and earthy, and thinking about his children shattered her old self-contentment and made her aware that there was something else that she needed in life, something so much a part of herself that she wondered a little numbly how she hadn't known this truth about herself long before this. She wanted children, wanted to feel them growing inside her, wanted to hold greedy little mouths to her breast, wanted to watch them grow and prosper and someday bring their own children to her to be rocked. She wanted Lucas's children.

Perhaps if she became pregnant, he would want her to marry him.

She shied away from the thought as soon as it occurred. She didn't want to be married, not even to Lucas. A woman became a man's property as soon as she became his wife. Dee wasn't afraid that Lucas would ever mistreat her, but she couldn't bear the thought of losing the independence, the acknowledgement of herself as someone to be dealt with, that she had worked so hard to establish. Her land would become his without his having to pay one cent for it.

Thinking about it, she decided that he would be certain to want to marry her if she became pregnant, because Lucas would want his child, would in fact do whatever was necessary to make certain the baby bore his name. And she thought him capable of marrying her in order to get Angel Creek. She couldn't bear it either way, because she wanted to be loved for herself, wanted for herself, not because of a child inside of her or the land she owned.

She sat wrapped in the quilt long after the rain had stopped, long after the sun had gone down, her eyes open and somber as she looked at the various choices she could make. All of them would bring her pain, and because she loved him she would accept that pain in order to have whatever time with him she had been allotted.

11

THE RAIN THE DAY BEFORE HADN'T BEEN ENOUGH TO raise the levels in the streams or watering holes, but the fresh spring grass was vibrantly green and abundant, and the air was washed clean of dust. Lucas was tired and sore after a day of branding calves, but whenever he lifted his head and looked around him he felt a deep sense of peace. All of the land that he saw in every direction was his, and he had never wanted to be anywhere else than right there. He loved it with every particle of his being, and he wouldn't hesitate to kill to protect his home, as he had done before, or to die in the effort. He was willing to spill both blood and sweat on the ground to make it prosper.

When the last calf of the day was branded and had been released to run bawling back to its mother Lucas stood and stretched, turning from side to side to work the kinks out of his back. He eyed the sun; it was only an hour until sundown, not enough time for him to get back to the house and change out of his filthy clothes, then get over the narrow pass leading down to Angel Creek before dark. He could go the long way around, taking the road to Prosper and then cutting back toward the mountains, but the ride alone would take him over two hours, and it was possible someone would see him riding toward Dee's place. He wasn't going to have people whispering about her behind her back, so that option was out. But he needed her with a deep, burning ache that had grown worse as the day passed and wouldn't get any better until he was with her again, sliding deep into her silky body, feeling her wrap those strong, graceful legs around him. He looked again at the sun, thinking of taking his chances over the pass, then finally realized that it would be stupid to try. He would have to get through another night without her.

He had spent only the one afternoon with her, yet he craved her with the ferocity that drove the addicts in the San Francisco opium dens to their pipes. Losing his brother Matt had been hard, and since then he had been essentially alone in spirit because he had taught himself to need no one, to be complete unto himself; but now he had to deal with a nagging sense of incompletion, as if he had left part of himself down at Angel Creek. The notion was ridiculous, and he scoffed silently at himself. No one could mean that much to anyone else. It was just that Dee wasn't like other women he had known, and her differences were what intrigued him. He wanted her, that was all. It was a challenge to get past all of those thorns to the wild-honey sweetness of her.

He wondered with disgust when he had taken up lying to himself.

Thunder boomed, and he looked at the sky for the third time. His foreman, William Tobias, evidently thought he was looking for signs of rain and said, "I don't think that one's going to come our way. Sounds like it's headed for the mountains." The gangly sun-dried man leaned over to spit. "Sure do wish we'd get a hard spell of rain. We ain't dry, but I'd like to have more water in those holes before summer gets here."

Lucas thought of the pure, never-ending water of Angel Creek and felt the old irritation with his father rise up within him. That land should have belonged to the Double C for a long time, but due to his father's lack of judgment it was now in the hands of a stubborn woman who was likely to work herself to death rather than listen to reason.

But if his father had bought Angel Creek all those years ago, Dee's father wouldn't have settled there, and he would never have met Dee. Lucas frowned, trying to balance the pleasure of owning Angel Creek against the excitement of making love to Dee. The frown changed to a wry smile. Angel Creek wasn't going anywhere; he'd get it eventually. Maybe he was just as glad that it had been unsettled when George Swann had brought his family west.

He and the foreman stood watching the storm clouds low on the horizon as they drifted away toward the mountains. The late afternoon thunderstorms were a frequent occurrence during spring and early summer, so both men expected they would get their share of rain.

Resigned now to the fact that he wouldn't get over

to Dee's after all, Lucas mounted his horse and started back toward the house. If he knew Dee, she had probably decided that he intended to visit only when he needed sex and would have the shotgun in her hands the next time he showed his face.

He realized that he was grinning as he rode home. Damn if getting her wouldn't be worth a load of buckshot in his ass!

Dee stepped outside the next morning just as dawn was turning the sky a glowing, translucent pink. She had reached for the feed pan as soon as she had stepped onto the stoop, but now she withdrew her hand without touching it, her eyes on that wonderful sky arching above her, around her, surrounding her with the glow.

The peace of the morning enfolded her. She turned away from the chores that awaited her and walked silently toward the meadow, her senses drinking in the colors and fragrances of the new day.

The long meadow was filled with graceful spring grass, the morning dew covering it with diamond glitter. A profusion of wildflowers spread before her eyes as far as she could see, a riot of blues and pinks and purples dotted with cheerful yellows and the occasional cluster of crimson clover, the dark red clover heads nodding as if they had to entice the industrious bees who found their sweet scent irresistible. She wandered among them, the dew wetting her faded skirt to the knee, but she didn't notice and wouldn't have cared if she had. Some days were magic and were to be savored. The chores would always be there; this dawn was fleeting and would never be duplicated.

The sky overhead gradually changed from pearly pink to opalescent and finally to a great, shining golden bowl as the sun finally emerged and bathed the meadow in radiance. Birds sang almost deliriously, and the silver rush of water in the creek sounded like a thousand bells.

She walked down to the creek and watched the crystal water dance over the stones. Her blood sang through her veins, and her heart was full. This was her home, and it was paradise.

"Dee."

She heard her name, though it hadn't been loudly spoken, and turned to look at him. Lucas stood some twenty feet away, his glittering eyes narrowed with some unnamed emotion, his face hard and intent. He was perfectly still, his big, muscled body locked in place; he never took his gaze off her, and the force of his lust hit her like a massive wave. Her body reacted automatically to his presence, immediately growing warm and heavy, her skin abruptly becoming too sensitive for the touch of her clothing. Her breasts swelled and ached, and her loins tightened.

She looked like a primitive goddess, and Lucas could hardly catch his breath. She stood next to the creek, surrounded by wildflowers, and the exotic face turned toward him was as serene and dreamy as the dawn itself. He had never seen her like that before, all defenses down, simply a woman exalted by the dawn.

His whole body expanded until he felt as if his skin would burst, and he was dizzy with the rush of his blood. His sex throbbed violently, and he knew he had to be inside of her.

He never remembered crossing the ground between them, only that she didn't move, and then she was within his grasp, her body firm and rich, her mouth inexplicably shy beneath the savagery of his. He carried her down, crushing her into the wildflowers, and shoved her skirt to her waist. The barrier of her drawers maddened him, and he stripped them away with rough hands, her pale thighs naked and vulnerable in the morning sun. He was so swollen with need that he cursed under his breath at the difficulty of unbuttoning his pants. Then he was free. He opened her soft folds with one hand, revealing the small opening, and with his other hand he guided himself to her. He looked down at the broad head of his sex poised against the delicate opening, and his testicles tightened painfully. He thrust into her, groaning aloud with the shattering relief of her tight, silky wet channel clasping his aching length and soothing him with both pleasure and the promise of more.

Dee accepted his heavy weight with slender arms wrapped around those powerful shoulders, accepted the fierce drive of his loins slamming into her, accepted his masculinity and lust and welcomed all of it. She felt almost unbearably stretched and possessed, but there was a bright glory to it, and she reveled in it. Her head rolled slowly back and forth in the dew-fresh grass as her entire body gave itself over to him.

She climaxed abruptly, the sensation exploding in her loins and making her legs tremble around him. Her cries lifted into the crystal air, and her back arched as he reared back on his knees with a guttural roar. His own climax swiftly followed, his head thrown back and his neck corded with the force of his convulsions. He gripped her slender hips and held her tightly locked onto him until the last spasms had eased, until he was emptied of his fever.

Afterward he was silent, and so was she, as he got to his feet and rebuttoned his pants. He bent and picked up her discarded drawers, then lifted her into his arms and carried her back to the cabin. She let her head rest on his shoulder, her eyes closed. There still didn't seem to be anything to say.

Lucas was shaken by the power of the surge of lust that had overtaken him. He had taken her without preliminaries, without gentling her body into arousal, but he hadn't been able to hold back. At that moment nothing had existed in the world but the two of them and his maddened need to have her. By rights, he thought, she should be trying to get to her shotgun rather than lying so still and quiet in his arms.

He sat down in one of the kitchen chairs and cradled her on his lap, his hands stroking her soothingly as if he could give her the consideration now that he hadn't been capable of earlier. Dee sighed with gentle pleasure, her nose turned against him so she could inhale the clean, warm scent of his body.

"Did I hurt you?" he asked, his voice rough-edged.

She stirred a little, then settled in his embrace once more. "No." His intrusion into her body had been shocking, but there hadn't been pain, only primitive joy.

She didn't seem angry, either, but lay in his arms with the sensuous lassitude of a thoroughly loved woman. Of all the reactions he had expected, this voluptuous yielding hadn't been one of them, and it was all the more beguiling because he was taken by surprise. This was one reaction he didn't think he would ever tire of.

"I brought the sponges," he said wryly, his mouth quirking with an ironic smile. He hadn't even given a thought to them, and in any case he couldn't have restrained himself.

She opened her eyes and gave him a heavy-lidded stare. "Did you think they would do a lot of good in your pocket?" she asked. Then she sat up with curiosity on her face. "What do they look like?"

He maneuvered her and stretched out his leg so he could get his hand in his pocket, and he withdrew the small sponges. She looked at them lying in his callused palm, picked one up, and squeezed it between her fingers, then gave it back to him. "They're just regular sponges," she said, visibly disappointed. He grinned a little, knowing that she had been expecting something far more exotic and frankly wicked.

"I know. I expect it's the vinegar that does the job."

"Well, it's too late now."

"But it won't be the next time."

She gave him another of those green, heavy-lidded looks. "Unless you come at me again like the bull on one of the cows."

"Since the next time isn't very far in the future, I think I can promise that," he said.

"I have to do the chores."

"I'll help."

They were back in bed within the hour, their naked bodies twining with the steadily building tension. The small vinegar-soaked sponge sat in a dish next to the bed. When neither of them could wait a minute longer he showed her how to insert the sponge, his long fingers reaching deep inside her and almost carrying her to completion without him. They made love until they were both exhausted, and Lucas pulled the sheet up over them just before he dozed off, his arms wrapped protectively around her slender form. He was contented all the way to his bones.

When they woke up he wanted to make love to her again. He was startled when she tried to squirm away from him. "I don't want to," she said fretfully.

"Damn if you aren't the most contrary woman I've ever seen," he muttered. *"Why* don't you want to?"

She shrugged, her mouth sulky. "I just don't want you holding me down again right now."

He ran his hand through his hair. God, why had he been surprised? The wonder was that she hadn't done something about it before now, but of course she was too inexperienced to know.

"Then you get on top," he said.

Interest sparked in those green eyes. He could see she was intrigued by the idea of controlling their lovemaking, and therefore controlling him. He wanted to laugh out loud but thought she might change her mind if he did. Personally, he loved lying on his back and letting a woman ride him, and his imagination went wild as he pictured Dee's rich breasts swaying over him.

"I don't know how," she said.

His hands were persuasive as they moved over her, enticing her closer. "I'll show you," he said. Just thinking about it had already made him hard and ready.

She loved it, too. By the time she settled astride him, sinking down to envelop his shaft, his hands were locked on the headboard above him as he strained to control himself. He was gasping, his eyes closed from the pleasure she had wrought. She had seduced him that time, her mouth tender on his mouth and chest, her breasts brushing against his stomach and loins as she swayed over him. He thought of other things he would teach her, but right now he had all he could handle. Of course she loved it; she was enthralled by having him at her mercy, if he could call it that. It was more like torment, delicious, searing torment.

Dee moved slowly, rhythmically, her eyes closing as her own hunger built. This was pure ecstasy, she thought, and she knew that she would never regret these moments no matter what happened. It wasn't the physical pleasure that was so precious, but the link between them that was forged by that pleasure. She felt herself dissolving and cried out, unaware that he had reached his peak just ahead of her; then she fell forward onto his chest in exhaustion.

By the time he left late that afternoon she knew that for her, at least, the link between them would never be broken.

12

JUNE CAME IN HOT AND DRY. IT WAS PARTICULARLY frustrating because almost every afternoon thunder would echo from the mountains, and dark clouds would tantalize them with the possibility of rain; but the clouds would slide away, and if they ever released their moisture, it happened on the far side of the mountains, and Prosper got none of the runoff.

Each day dawned as hot and clear as the one preceeding it, and Lucas began to worry, even though the Double C still had good water. There was no telling how long a dry spell would last, and it wasn't just the water holes that were drying up; the grass was getting dry and brittle, with no new growth to replace the grazed areas. The cattle were having to graze farther each day, then returning to the creeks and water holes for water. They were daily growing leaner, and each day they had to cover even more ground. He

169

didn't like it, but there wasn't a damn thing he could do about it. Admitting that didn't sweeten his temper.

After going without Dee for two weeks he rode over to Angel Creek one day, leaving a lot of work undone because another minute without her was one minute too long. He was restless and irritable, not just because of his sexual needs but because he couldn't get her out of his mind. No woman had ever invaded his thoughts like that, getting in the way of his work, interfering with his sleep. His desire for her hadn't cooled; he wanted her more than ever, his hunger all the more intense because it had to be hidden, even from his own men. If the men ever wondered where he went, they never asked. He suspected they all assumed he was seeing Olivia, and of course they would never make joking remarks about a lady the way they would if the woman was less than respectable. It enraged him that anyone would consider Dee less deserving of respect than Olivia, but he couldn't say anything without making Dee a target, so he had to keep his mouth shut.

Dee was sitting on the front porch placidly rocking when he rode up, and she made no effort to get up to welcome him. She was probably mad at him, he thought with a sigh, but then he decided that she wasn't. If Dee had been angry, she would have let him know it. It was more likely that she was just taking it easy in the shade.

He put the horse in the barn where it was cooler, and as he walked back to the house he noticed how green everything was, when everywhere else the grass was turning brown and the tree leaves were limp.

Angel Creek was a lush oasis in comparison. He stopped and looked around. Her garden was thriving, and as far as he could see up the valley the meadow grasses were green and resilient. He could hear the quiet rush of the water in the creek, the sweet, cold, crystal-clear mountain water that fed this little valley and made it thrive.

The valley wasn't big enough to support all of his cattle, but if he owned it, then it would be a safeguard against drought. Enough cattle could survive there to keep him from being wiped out. Indeed, keeping some cattle there would even help those heads left on the Double C, because they would get what grass and water there was to be had.

Dee was still rocking when he stepped up on the porch and sat down beside her. Her eyes were closed, but her foot maintained the slow, steady movement of the chair.

"I'll give you five thousand dollars for Angel Creek," he said.

Those inscrutable green eyes opened and regarded him for a moment before her thick black lashes swept down again. "It isn't for sale."

"Damn it," he said irritably. "That's twice what it's worth."

"Must not be," she reasoned. "Since you offered five thousand, then it's worth five thousand."

"Seven thousand."

"It isn't for sale."

"Would you be sensible about this?"

"I am being sensible," she insisted. "This is my home. I don't want to sell it."

"Ten thousand."

"Stop it."

"What are you going to do when you're too old to work the land? This is hard work, and you won't be able to keep doing it. You're young and strong now, but what about ten years from now?"

"I'll let you know in ten years," she retorted.

"Name any kind of business you'd like to have, and I'll set you up in it. You're not going to get that kind of offer from anyone else."

She stopped rocking and opened her eyes. Lucas watched her intently, his pulse speeding up now that he had finally aggravated her out of her cool demeanor. It was like deliberately prodding a tigress to attack, but he was tired of that blank refusal even to discuss selling Angel Creek. He might not win, but she'd at least listen to him.

"That's not as interesting as the offer Kyle Bellamy made," she said with soft mockery.

He felt a spurt of anger. He could just imagine what Bellamy's offer had been. When he'd first met Dee he hadn't liked it that Bellamy was also interested in buying the land, but now he disliked even more the thought that the man had wanted Dee.

"I can just imagine the offer he made," he said sarcastically.

"I doubt it." She gave him a smile so sweet he was instantly wary. "He asked me to marry him."

This time Lucas didn't feel a spurt of anger, he felt a huge rush of it, so hot that his entire body seemed to expand and burn. His pupils constricted to tiny black points. "Not if I can help it," he said in a voice so flat and toneless she wasn't certain he'd said anything at all.

"It was my decision, not yours. I turned him down, of course."

"When was he here?" Murder was still in his eyes.

She shrugged. "Before you ever came back to town."

Some of the anger faded as he realized that it wasn't a recent event. But if Bellamy ever came back to Angel Creek, it had better be to say good-bye.

"I don't want him here again," he said flatly, just in case she was in any doubt.

"I didn't invite him in the first place." She added thoughtfully, "I didn't invite you, either. Isn't it strange? The poor men who could have used a homestead just wanted me for sex; you and Bellamy have plenty of land, but you want more. I'd have to say that Bellamy wants it more than you do, since he offered marriage."

Lucas tensed, every instinct alert. "Is that what it would take?" he asked, carefully feeling his way. He felt as if he were treading through quicksand, where one misstep would be a disaster. He realized that he was holding his breath, waiting for her answer.

Dee didn't look at him, but out across her land. "Getting married would be even worse than selling out," she said. "I'd lose both my land and my independence. Of the two, selling it would at least let me stay independent."

Sharp disappointment thudded in his chest. Until he felt the force of it he hadn't realized how much he had wanted her to say yes, that she would be interested in a marriage proposal from him. Shock froze him in his chair. He had known since the first time he'd made love to her that she had ruined his plans to marry Olivia, that he couldn't marry Olivia while he still wanted Dee so fiercely. He couldn't imagine Dee consenting to be the mistress of a married man, nor would it be fair to Olivia. And Dee had made her opinion of marriage plain the first time they'd met. Until now he hadn't really thought of marriage to her because she didn't fit in with his plans; he had been prepared to marry her as a necessity if she should become pregnant, but the subject had never come up between them, and it had just been speculation on his part that she would marry him even then. Now he had brought it out into the open, and her refusal had hit him squarely between the eyes. He wanted Dee as his wife, and not because she would fit into his plans. If anything, she would make things harder.

But with her he could laugh and fight and not have to worry about hurting her feelings if he snapped at her. Dee would give back as good as she got. And in bed she was wild and natural, giving him complete freedom of her body without embarrassment and exploring him in the same manner. He would find some way to make her fit into the mold he wanted.

He'd marry her in a minute if she'd have him, but Dee didn't want to marry anyone. Marriage would make her feel caged, and she couldn't tolerate that.

"Then take the money," he said, not looking at her because he was afraid she would read too much in his eyes. "It's enough to invest, so you'll always have enough to live on. That way you'd still be independent, and you wouldn't have to work yourself to death on the land. Hell, you could even buy more land, if that was what you wanted."

"But it wouldn't be Angel Creek," she said softly. "I love it here. I fell in love with it the first day I saw it." And it had given her a reason to live. In exchange for its healing bounty she was its caretaker, its guardian. Sometimes she felt a superstitious fear that she was like a plant that would die if uprooted from the soil of this small valley.

And she would never love any man as much as she loved this damn place, he thought savagely. He would rather have had Kyle Bellamy as a rival than Angel Creek, because he could fight Bellamy, but how could he fight the land? He remembered the look of dreamy ecstasy on her face the morning he had come to her in the dawn and found her out in the meadow, and sharp jealousy pierced him as he realized it had been for the land, for the wash of golden sunlight, for the crystal flow of water, and not for him.

The hell of it was, he loved the Double C just as fiercely. He couldn't condemn her when they were so much alike. That was why he was so relaxed with her, because she matched him strength for strength. But damn it, it wasn't like he'd be asking her to move to another country.

He stood up and held out his hand to her. "Let's go inside," he said abruptly. He needed her. God, how he needed her.

But she didn't take his hand, just gave him another of those cat looks. "If you rode all the way over here just for that, you'll have to be disappointed. I'm having my monthly."

He *was* disappointed but felt no inclination to

leave. Even if he couldn't make love to her, he needed her in other ways. He kept his hand extended. "Then come sit on my lap and drive me crazy," he said.

Her face brightened with interest, and she put her hand in his. She was always willing to drive him crazy.

But as it happened they spent more time talking than snuggling. He had been serious about her sitting on his lap, so that's what she did, both of them in the big chair in front of the fire. He told her about his breeding plans for his herd, about his expansion ideas, how he planned to use the politicians in Denver to further his ambitions. The citizens of Colorado were supposed to vote to ratify the state constitution on the first of July, and it would then go to the federal government for a vote to admit them to the Union. He told her what statehood would mean, and she sat up to frown at him.

"I don't know if I want crowds of people coming out to settle. I like it the way it is now."

"It's progress, honey. With more people we'll get more businesses, and more railroads. Railroads are the key. Colorado can't be completely civilized without them."

"What difference does it make?"

"Money," he said simply. "You can't do anything without money."

"But I don't want things to change." She nestled her head back on his shoulder and said pensively, "I don't like change."

"Everything changes." He combed his fingers through her long hair and pressed a kiss to her temple. She turned her face into his throat, and he held her tighter, as if he could protect her from the changes that were inevitable for them both.

It had become customary for Olivia to go riding every Sunday afternoon. Sometimes she would return without seeing Luis, her disappointment carefully hidden behind her calm demeanor. But most of the time he would join her at some point. She seldom saw him at any other time, for his duties on the ranch kept him busy. The days between those stolen Sunday afternoons crept by at a snail's pace, while the few hours she spent with him were gone almost before she knew it. She was so obsessed with seeing him that she even neglected to ride out to see Dee and felt guilty because she had so much to tell her.

She couldn't seem to think of anything other than Luis. Her heart would begin hammering as soon as he appeared at her side, making her feel as if she would suffocate in the heat. She had already ceased wearing the fitted jacket of her riding habit, but convention insisted that she keep her blouse firmly buttoned all the way up to her throat and the sleeve cuffs fastened at her wrist. The unusually warm weather was uncomfortable, and her physical reaction to Luis made it seem even worse.

She would often look at the open throat of Luis's shirt and envy men the freedom of their clothing, but it wasn't long before the smooth brown skin visible in that open neckline would distract her from the details of clothing, and the heat would intensify.

Luis saw the way her gaze would linger on his open shirt and the flush that would soon climb to her cheeks. Though she didn't realize it, she was becoming more accustomed to the physical desire between them, and as each Sunday passed without anything more than kisses she was becoming hungrier. She was innocent, but she was a woman, with a woman's needs. The day would come, and soon, when her desire and curiosity would grow too strong, and she would reach out for him. He only hoped it would be soon, for the frustration was killing him. He had never waited so long for a woman before, but then no other woman had been Olivia.

As June progressed the heat became even more oppressive, and riding during the afternoon was almost unbearable for both riders and animals. On a Sunday afternoon toward the end of the month Luis found a spot of intense shade under a stand of big trees and reined in his horse, dismounting with the fluid, catlike grace she found so fascinating.

"Let the horses rest," he said, reaching up for her. "We'll start back when it cools down some."

Olivia was more than glad to rest in the shade. She patted her face with her handkerchief and sat down under a tree while Luis gave the horses a little water, then tied them with long lines so they could graze. That done, he sat down beside her and placed his hat on the ground, then wiped his face with his sleeve.

"Do you want some water?" he asked.

She laughed, amused that he had taken care of the horses before offering any water to her. "Is there any left?"

"I brought a full canteen." He plucked a blade of grass and tickled her nose with it. "Always take care of your animals first. They'll keep you alive."

"Since we're less than an hour from town, I think we'll make it before we run out of water," she said gravely, then she laughed again.

He looked up at the blue bowl overhead, and the searing white sun. "If it doesn't rain soon, the water situation could really get desperate. The creeks on the Bar B are almost dry, and I imagine the other ranches are in the same shape."

"I hadn't realized things were that bad," she said, ashamed that she hadn't thought of it. "Are the wells going dry, too?"

"So far, no, but they could."

All of the ranchers, big and small, kept their money in her father's bank. If they went broke, then the merchants would lose money, too. She had always imagined the bank as permanent, but in a flash she saw that it depended on the solvency of the people who used it, which could never be guaranteed. Prosper itself had seemed invulnerable to the vagaries of boomtowns, as firmly rooted as any of the cities back East, yet could it survive if a drought destroyed the ranches? People couldn't stay if there wasn't any way to make a living. Shops and stores would close, neighbors would move away, and Prosper would die.

Everything people built was so fragile, at the mercy of weather or disease or just plain bad luck, and survival was no more than a matter of chance.

She looked up at the sun with both fear and worry in her eyes. Luis was sorry he had mentioned the growing dry spell, for there was nothing that could be done. He was a fatalist; life had taught him to accept what couldn't be changed, and he had learned early that either you survived or you didn't. If a drought destroyed Prosper, then he would roll up his bedroll and saddle his horse, and when he left he would take Olivia with him. Life was too short to fret over changes. He could be just as happy with her sitting at a campfire as he could in a house with a roof over his head.

But she was already fretting about the people she knew who would be hurt by a drought, and he wanted to pull her head down to his shoulder and protect her from those worries. Instead he stretched out on the ground and pillowed his head on her lap, nestling down on the softness of her thighs.

The pressure of his head made her lower body tighten in reaction to his nearness. Olivia held her breath, almost overcome by the sensation flooding her. Her breasts began to throb and swell, yet at the same time she felt oddly protective toward him. Tentatively she touched his damp black hair, then smoothed it away from his forehead. He sighed as if in relief. Once she had touched him there seemed to be no reason why she shouldn't continue, so she began tracing the lines of his face with her fingertips.

His eyes were closed. "Umm, you smell good," he murmured, turning his face toward her. With his head on her lap he could smell the warm, female scents of her body, and he was growing hard.

Olivia smiled, thinking of the perfume she had applied that morning, glad that he liked it. She had even dabbed a bit between her breasts, feeling wicked as she did so. She wondered what he would do if she leaned forward so that her breasts were closer to his face. Would he nuzzle against her in search of the elusive sweet scent?

But she didn't dare, and regretfully she wished that ladies didn't always have to be retiring and genteel, to let the men take the lead. For that matter, ladies weren't even supposed to think of such things!

She looked down and saw that he was watching her and smiling, and she realized that she had heaved a sigh. "It's so hot," she said quickly, by way of explanation.

"Yes, it is. Why don't you unbutton your collar and roll your cuffs back?"

If she did, her immaculate starched blouse would be decidedly rumpled when she returned home, but she was feeling stifled, and baring her arms would bring a small measure of relief. She ignored the first part of his suggestion and briskly unfastened her cuffs, turning them back several times so her forearms were bared.

"That's good," he said, then he lifted his hand to the buttons at her throat.

She stilled, her blue eyes darkening as his strong, lean hand slowly released each tiny button in turn. Her collar loosened, and fresh air seeped in to cool her heated skin. His hand moved down past her collarbone. "That's enough," she said, trying to sound casual.

"Is it?" He didn't stop but unbuttoned the next one, then the next. And the next. The weight of his hand was lying between her breasts now, brushing them with every movement. His eyes held a hooded, sleepy sensuality. His mouth looked full, his lips slightly parted as if he waited for a delicious treat.

The beginning swells of her breasts were exposed, then the lacy edging of her shift. Slowly his fingers moved downward all the way to her waist, leaving her blouse gaping open in their wake. She sat very still, hardly even daring to breathe.

He shifted more onto his side, facing her. Slowly he pulled her blouse free of her waistband, then spread it open. Her lovely breasts were covered only by the thin cotton shift, her nipples clearly peaked beneath it. He traced both of them with a light fingertip, loving the delicacy of her, then moved closer and lifted his head just a bit to close his lips firmly around one of them.

Olivia bit her lip, her eyes closing at the feel of his mouth clamping down on her nipple. His mouth was hot and wet, and his tongue curled around the tip, stroking it through the damp cotton. Then he began to suck, and the rhythmic pulling started a fire that ran straight to her loins.

They were utterly silent. She heard the horses stamping nearby, the chomping of their big teeth on the grass. A small breeze rustled the leaves overhead, and insects droned lazily in the heat. He suckled her with a complete lack of urgency, not caressing her in any other way.

Until Luis, she hadn't known that a man would ever want to put his mouth on her breasts. She had thought of suckling babies but never imagined that such a maternal act could, with a man, be so erotic. The strong mouth working at her breast couldn't be mistaken for an infant's sweetness, nor could the rasp of his beard-roughened cheek against her soft skin. The secret flesh between her legs was throbbing in rhythm with the pull of his mouth, and she leaned helplessly forward to give him better access.

He responded by taking her deeper into his mouth.

Her shift was so wet now that it might as well not have been there, but suddenly it was maddening. Frantically she shrugged her shoulders, letting the straps fall down her arms.

"Be still," he whispered around her nipple.

"No—wait. Here." She whispered, too, lifting her hand to push the loosened shift down over one breast, baring it. She guided the nipple back to his mouth and whimpered softly at the exquisite pleasure of his lips on her nakedness. She cradled his head in her arms and held him to her, suffused with warmth and desire.

Her body delighted in the sensations it was feeling, both subtle and intense. When he finally sat up away from her she made a low sound of regret, but he hushed her with a finger on her lips. "You'll like this, too." And he pulled off his shirt, revealing a broad, muscled chest with a diamond of soft, curly black hair stretching from nipple to nipple.

Olivia reached out to circle her fingertips around the tiny points, marveling at how different they were from hers. They hardened instantly, and she looked up in surprise to see a taut expression of enjoyment on his face. "They aren't so different after all," she murmured, stroking them again.

He put his hands over hers and guided them over his chest. "No, not so different. I love it when you touch me. I want to feel your hands on my bare skin. It feels the same to me as it does to you when I touch you."

His hands left hers, but she didn't move them. She liked it too much, liked the feel of his muscled body under her fingers. She slid them along his rib cage and let them lie there for a minute, enjoying the way his chest expanded and contracted with each breath. His stomach muscles were hard and flat, but the skin on his belly was silky smooth, indicating his vulnerability. Back at his chest again she felt the strong, steady pounding of his heart. His shoulders were wide and sleek and hard, the skin gleaming like satin in the sunlight. He was beautiful. Without thinking Olivia touched her lips to the tender skin just beside the shoulder joint, her tongue lightly tasting the faint saltiness of perspiration. Luis shuddered, and his hands closed hard on her waist, drawing her against him.

Incredibly, she had forgotten that her blouse was open and one breast bare. The warm, hard pressure of his chest against her brought a sharp cry from her, and slowly he turned her from side to side, rubbing her breasts on his hard body.

"Luis. *Luis!*"

"What is it, love?" he asked softly. "Do you want more?"

She dug her fingernails into his upper arms, gasping with the delight of it. "Yes," she said. "Please."

He laughed a little at her impeccable manners even when they were both so aroused it was all he could do to keep from taking her completely. Only his acute instinct about women held him back, for though he could easily seduce her, she wouldn't yet give herself to him out of love. And it was love he wanted from her, not the knowledge that he was skilled enough as a lover to make her body ready before her mind was. When she was truly ready she would let him know. Until then he was prepared to suffer excruciating torment in order for her to discover how much sheer enjoyment she could have with him.

He removed her blouse and let it drop to the ground, then slid the straps of her chemise all the way down and drew her arms free. The soft cotton draped around her waist, leaving her upper torso completely bare. She was blushing a little, her porcelain skin glowing. Shifting to his knees and drawing her up, too, he put his arms around her so that their bodies were together from shoulder to knee and began kissing her. He could feel her shiver with delight as her soft breasts flattened against the hard plains of his chest, feel the instinctive, startled recoil of her hips away from him as soon as she felt his arousal, but then shyly she returned. Her hips sought his, undulating gently as she instinctively searched for the most comfortable position, which was of course the most intimate. He groaned deep in his throat as she finally settled with her soft mound cradling his hardness, her legs parted slightly to make room for him. He thought that she might very well kill him with her own innocent brand of seduction.

"I want to lie naked with you," he murmured. "Every night, love. When you marry me I'll teach you everything a man and a woman can do together, and you'll enjoy every minute of it."

Olivia buried her face against his chest. He hadn't phrased it as a question, thereby relieving her of the necessity of answering. But he had said it so positively, as if he had no doubts she would marry him. Did *she* have any doubts? She didn't know. She was frightened of the sort of life he might expect her to lead, wandering about the country, but at the same time the thought of it excited her. She didn't know if she loved him, but she did know she could barely exist through the week, that she felt truly alive only on the one afternoon a week when she was with him. And she very much wanted him to show her everything about lovemaking.

Since meeting Luis she no longer had any doubts about the bond between Beatrice and Ezekiel Padgett. It was the sweet, hot bond of the flesh, the shared delights when they were together in bed. And would she, Olivia, ever settle for anything less now that she sensed what awaited her?

"I think I love you," she said, lifting her face to his. "But I'm not certain. The thought of marrying you frightens me almost as much as the thought of *not* marrying you. Would we go away from here? Would I have to leave my family?"

"Almost certainly," he replied, not lying to her. His heart was pounding as he realized how close he was to having what he wanted. Her lovely face was troubled as she thought of leaving the secure home she had known all her life. "We would have wonderful adventures together, making love beneath the stars, or taking a train wherever it might happen to go. And we would have babies, love, and a home where they could grow up safe and secure. Do you think your parents would like to keep their grandchildren occasionally while we take to the trail for a while?"

She laughed shakily, her mind whirling with the images he had described, but she couldn't answer the question about her parents. They would be horrified at the thought of their beloved only offspring marrying a drifter. They both wanted so much for her and would be terribly hurt and disappointed. They loved her, and she didn't think they would reject her no matter whom she married, but tears swam in her eyes at the thought of causing them pain. Still, she couldn't go on forever as she had been these past weeks, and neither could Luis.

She looked up at him with tear-wet eyes that held both pain and a promise. "I'll give you my answer soon," she whispered.

Dee walked out on the porch and held out a glass of cool lemonade to Olivia, who sat on the very edge of the rocking chair, keeping it tilted forward on the rockers. She studied Olivia's face, thinking that she had never before seen her friend as edgy as she was now.

"What's wrong?" she asked.

Olivia sipped her drink, then rolled the glass back and forth in her hands. She watched the motion of her own fingers as if fascinated. "I think I'm in love," she blurted. She drew a deep, shaky breath. "With Luis Fronteras. And I'm scared."

"Luis Fronteras?" Dee asked blankly. "Who's he?"

"He works for Kyle Bellamy. He's a Mexican. A drifter."

Dee gave a low whistle of astonishment and slowly took her own seat. This was like a queen taking up with a commoner.

"He wants me to marry him," Olivia continued.

"Are you going to?"

The look Olivia gave her was agonized. "I can't bear the thought of not seeing him again. But it will hurt my parents so, and I don't want that either. I don't know what to do."

Dee wasn't sure what advice to give her. She knew how important family was to Olivia, and she also knew how impossible it was to stay away from the man you loved, even when your common sense told you to.

"What is he like?"

"Gentle," Olivia said, then she frowned. "But I think he can be dangerous, too. It's just that he's always gentle with *me,* even when he's—" She broke off, and her face turned pink.

"Aroused?" Dee suggested helpfully, grinning when Olivia's flush deepened.

"Is Lucas gentle when *he's* aroused?" Olivia retorted with spirit. "And don't tell me you don't know, because I won't believe you. At the picnic he couldn't stop looking for you, and he left right after lunch and never came back. I've thought right from the beginning that he'd be perfect for you," she finished smugly.

"Perfect?" Dee said in disbelief. "He's overbearing and arrogant, and he—" She broke off, because she couldn't lie to either herself or Olivia. "I love him," she finished flatly. "Damn it."

Olivia threw herself back in the rocking chair with a whoop of laughter, sloshing the lemonade over the rim of the glass. "I knew it, I knew it! Well? Has he asked you to marry him?"

"He asked if marriage would be the price for Angel Creek. Not exactly the same thing." Dee managed a crooked smile. "The fact that I love him doesn't mean that he loves me."

"Well, he does," Olivia replied. "If you could have seen him at the picnic! He kept trying not to let it slip that he'd been seeing you, but he couldn't talk about anything else."

Dee went still. "He told other people about me?"

"No, he was just talking to me," Olivia reassured her. "He came here after he left the picnic, didn't he?"

"Yes."

Olivia cleared her throat, good manners wrestling with her curiosity. Curiosity won. "Does he . . . I mean, has he tried to . . . you know?"

"Make love to me?" Dee clarified in her blunt way.

Olivia flushed again but nodded.

"He's a man."

Dee evidently felt that her bald statement was explanation enough. Olivia decided to agree with her. "Do you like it when he touches you?" she asked in a rush. "I mean when he touches your . . ." She stopped, appalled at what she had been about to say. What if Dee hadn't permitted Lucas such intimacies? With her question she had practically admitted that she and Luis . . .

"Stop blushing," Dee ordered, though her own cheeks were growing warm.

"He has, then. Well? Did you like it?"

Confused, Dee wondered just what Olivia was asking and what part of the body she was thinking about. Caresses, or the actual sexual act? Then she shrugged, because the answer was the same regardless of the question. "Yes," she said.

Olivia closed her eyes on a sigh of relief. "I'm so glad," she said. "I thought I was wicked, even though Luis said everyone . . ." She stopped herself again and opened her eyes. She had never before had such an opportunity, and she felt giddy with the freedom. "Does he take your blouse off when he touches you there?"

Dee was beginning to feel harassed. "Yes."

"Has he ever taken the top of your shift down? So that he can see your—er—breasts?"

"Yes."

Though her face was bright red, Olivia wasn't about to stop. "Has he ever kissed you there? Like a baby, I mean, only different. Well, maybe it's the same—"

Dee erupted from her chair. "For God's sake!" she yelled, goaded beyond endurance. "If you must know, he's stripped me naked and done everything there is to do! And I enjoyed every minute of it!" She struggled with herself for control and took a deep breath. In a more moderate voice she said, "Maybe not every minute. It hurt the first time, but it was worth it. Though I do like it better when I'm on top."

Olivia's mouth moved, but no sound emerged. Her eyes were so huge they eclipsed her face. She shut her mouth.

They stared at each other in silence. Dee's lips twitched first. She gulped, then bent double as she shrieked with laughter. Olivia pressed her hand to her mouth in an effort to stifle the unladylike sounds that were bubbling up, but it was a useless effort. She guffawed. That was the only word for it. The lemonade spilled in her lap.

When the hysterical fit of laughter had subsided into giggles they wiped their streaming eyes and struggled for composure. "Come inside and sponge your skirt," Dee said, her voice still shaky with mirth.

Olivia stood and followed her into the cabin. "Don't try to change the subject," she warned, and her shoulders began shaking again. "I want to know *all* about it. If you think I'm going to let a chance like this go by, you're crazy!"

"Ask Luis," Dee replied maddeningly, and it set them both off again.

13

KYLE BELLAMY KICKED AT THE DRY CREEK BED, THEN looked up at the cloudless sky. It hadn't rained in six weeks. It might not rain for another six weeks. They didn't normally get that much rain anyway, but then they didn't usually need it because of the runoff from the snowcaps. But there hadn't been as much snow during the past winter, and now they weren't getting even the normal amount of rain. Who knew how long it would last? Droughts sometimes lasted for years, turning what had been fertile into wasteland. He'd never thought it would happen here, but hell, no one ever settled where they thought there'd be a drought.

He felt an almost sickening sense of panic. He had sworn that he'd make something of himself, something respectable, and he'd been close enough to taste it. Now the damn weather was turning it into dust, literally. The *weather!* Of all the ways he could have been done in, of all the things that could have caught up with him, it was the weather that would bring him to his knees.

There was only one creek left running now on the Bar B. When it dried up his cattle would die. Without the cattle he wouldn't have the ranch, wouldn't have the money to restock, because he'd just spent all of his capital to add to the herd. Damn, why hadn't he waited? But he'd wanted the ranch to expand, and now he was in danger of losing everything. He wouldn't be able to pay his men's wages, would end up as nothing . . . again.

God, he'd been so close. He had thought the years when he'd had to steal food to survive were finished. He had buried his memories of the little boy who lived in the streets of New Orleans and was sold into prostitution at the age of ten. He never let himself think about the man he had killed when he was just twelve, to escape the horror. He had thought he'd never again have to cheat or lie. All he'd wanted was to be like respectable folks everywhere, to be welcomed into people's homes and treated like someone who counted. He'd had that in Prosper. Only Tillie had known him when he had lived with scum, had lived *like* scum, and she would never tell. He and Tillie were alike, two misfits whose backgrounds couldn't bear close scrutiny—for different reasons— but he had chosen the path of respectability, and Tillie had chosen to be as unrespectable as a woman could get.

He had planned to marry, have kids, do all the normal, respectable things and wallow in the doing of them, for that was what he had never before had. His dream had come true for a while, yet now he could see it slipping away from him. Even his plans for Olivia Millican didn't seem to be going anywhere. He called on her, paid all sorts of attention to her, but she still remained maddeningly indifferent to him. Damn it, the banker's money would have made all the difference to him.

Now, unless it rained soon, all of his plans were going to be just like the ground he walked on: dust.

He had racked his brain trying to think of ways to beat the drought. He had thought of building long troughs and filling barrels with water from the well, then hauling the water out to the troughs. But he had too many cattle; they would go mad at the scent of water and trample one another trying to get to it, knocking the troughs over. He couldn't dump the water into the water holes, because the ground was so dry it would just soak it up. Hell, he probably didn't even have enough water in the well to fill more than a couple of barrels anyway. The water table had to be low, too.

Why had he bought more cattle? If the herd was smaller, there would be more graze and water to go around.

Maybe he could sell off part of the herd. They were too thin; he'd lose money if he did, but not as much as he'd lose if they all died. But he was afraid they wouldn't survive the cattle drive to a railhead, either.

He wasn't the only one who was hurting. People in town were getting by fine and would be all right as long as their wells held out. But the other ranchers were all in the same fix he was in; the only creek still running that he knew of was Angel Creek, and he didn't guess it had ever gone dry.

It could have been his. It *should* have been his. He'd never thought the Swann woman would be so stubborn about selling, but she wouldn't even talk about it. He'd even asked her to marry him when it had become obvious she wasn't about to sell, but she'd turned that down, too. The only time in his life he'd asked any woman to marry him, and she hadn't even hesitated before refusing. The funny thing was, by then the land hadn't been his only reason for asking. Dee Swann was a damn fine-looking woman, with those witch-green eyes, and she was respected in town. Maybe not well liked, but they sure respected her. And she was tough enough that she didn't give a damn if they liked her or not.

She was sitting in that rich little valley with all of that water, not doing anything but raising that garden of hers and letting all the rest of the land lie fallow. It was wonderful grazing, the vegetation fed by the creek even when there wasn't any rain, and it was going to waste.

After she had refused to marry him he had followed the creek out of the valley, thinking that maybe he could divert it toward his land. To his surprise the creek bed had veered sharply to the east and dissipated at the foot of the mountains, seeping underground through porous rock to emerge again only God knew where. It came from the mountains and went back to the mountains, detouring only through that little valley and creating some of the best land he had ever seen.

The Bar B had been good land—not as good as Angel Creek, but good ranch land. In the four years he'd been there the rain had come regularly and the water holes had stayed fresh. He'd always worried more about the winters than about the summers, afraid a blizzard would wipe him out, but instead there hadn't been enough snow this past year, and the runoff hadn't been sufficient. Now one rainless summer was destroying a lifetime of dreams.

He mounted his horse, his handsome face drawn as he looked around. Everything still looked green, but it was deceptive. The vegetation was dry and brittle, making a faint crackling sound whenever a breeze stirred. He would have railed at fate if it would have done any good, but he had learned while still a boy in the muddy streets that the only help to be had was what he could provide for himself. Cursing, as well as praying, was a waste of breath.

There was only one person he could talk to about it, only one person who would understand what it meant to him. Not even the other ranchers could know how hard this hit him. Since it was still early afternoon he counted on the saloon being almost empty, and when he got there he found it was. Tillie wasn't in sight, though, and he scowled at the thought that she might be with a customer. Verna, the other saloon girl, was propped against the bar chatting with the bartender. She straightened when she saw Kyle walk in.

"Is Tillie upstairs?" he asked, ignoring the look of disappointment on Verna's face. He imagined she heard that question too often. It couldn't be easy for her, being essentially in competition with Tillie for what business Prosper could provide. Knowing Tillie, though, she probably often sent men Verna's way.

"She went over to the hat shop," Verna replied.

Kyle got a shot glass of whiskey from the bartender

and sat down to wait, but he wasn't a patient man, and it quickly got on his nerves. Hell, what did he care if the townspeople saw him walking with Tillie? He was going to lose the ranch, so what did his carefully cultivated respectability matter? When it came down to it, he'd been born a gutter rat and would die one, no matter how hard he tried to change things.

When he found her Tillie was just leaving the shop, a hatbox held in her hands like an offering. She never gave any indication in public that she knew him, and now she started past him without even glancing in his direction. Kyle stopped her, taking the hatbox from her hands and tucking it under his arm. "I'll walk you back to the saloon."

She lifted her eyebrows in surprise. "You shouldn't be seen with me like this. None of the mamas will want you courting their daughters."

"I don't give a damn," he said under his breath.

She began strolling down the sidewalk. "After all the work you've done to make a place for yourself here?"

He didn't want to talk about it on the street. His emotions were too raw, his disappointment too strong.

Not many people were out stirring around in the heat, but he saw heads swiveling to watch his progress down the street with Tillie. It would be all over town by nightfall that Kyle Bellamy had been parading around town with one of the saloon girls, as brassy as if he didn't know any better. And he simply didn't care. What he cared about was his ranch, and the lack of rain. Let them pass judgment if they wanted. He was sick and tired of the whole charade, pretending to

LINDA HOWARD

be a gentleman when he didn't have a genteel bone in his body.

The saloon was blessedly cool after the harsh glare of the sun. The bartender didn't pay them any mind as they started up the stairs. Verna watched them go with a hint of envy in her expression.

When they were in her room Tillie sat down before her mirrored vanity and slowly began removing hat pins from the delicate froth of velvet and veiling that had been perched on her head. She never visited any of the shops while dressed in the immodest, brightly colored dresses she wore in the saloon. The dress she had on was as demure as any of the dresses the good wives of the town wore to church, but it had probably cost considerably more. Tillie's taste in clothes ran toward the expensive. The bronze fabric was wonderfully flattering to her complexion. He reached out and fingered her sleeve, thinking that her love of good clothes was probably the last remnant of her former life.

"Open that hatbox for me," she said. Her rich brown eyes held a mixture of excitement and satisfaction. Tillie adored hats.

Kyle obeyed, taking the top off and lifting out a small bit of fur and velvet. The hat was a dark burgundy color, the fur was black, and a dashing little black plume curled around the edge. The half veil was attached to the hat with twin cascades of dark red rhinestones. It looked ridiculous in his big hand, but Tillie set it on her head and angled it over one eye, and it was immediately transformed into a masterpiece.

"Miss Wesner does such good work," she purred, turning her head from side to side in sublime satisfac-

198

tion. "I designed the hat, and she made it exactly as I described it."

"And now you have to have a gown made to match it."

"Of course." She met his eyes in the mirror and gave him a slow smile. She must have seen something in his face, because the smile faded and she briskly removed the hat, swiveling to face him. "What's wrong?"

"The drought," he said simply. "I'm losing the ranch."

She was silent. She knew what drought meant, knew that nature was both fickle and merciless.

"I only have one creek still running, and it's low," he said. "When it dries up the cattle will start dying. I tried, but I've lost."

"You've started over before. Do it again."

"Why bother? I'm beginning to think I should have stayed with the cards. At least then I could do something about a run of bad luck."

Tillie shook her head. "You'd have gotten killed. You're a good cheat, but you aren't that good. I could always spot you."

He pinched her chin. "Only because you're so damn good at it yourself, darlin'."

Tillie shrugged, saying nothing. Kyle examined her exquisite face, searching for some sign of the life she had led in either her skin or her expression, but she looked as serene as a nun. She hadn't changed much at all from the days of her girlhood in New Orleans. "Why don't you go back?" he asked suddenly. "You could do it. No one would have to know."

She didn't move but subtly withdrew anyway, her

expression going blank. "Why would I want to go back?"

"Your family is one of the richest in Louisiana. Why would you want to live like this, in one room over a saloon, when you can have a mansion?"

"I couldn't tolerate it when I was a girl," she said gently. "The rules, the restrictions, being treated like a brainless doll. I've been on my own a long time now, making my own decisions, good or bad. How could I go back, even if my father would allow me in the house, knowing that at best it would be just the same? At worst, he would keep me locked up so I couldn't damage the family reputation any more than I already have."

"Does your family know where you are?"

"No. They think I'm dead. I arranged it that way."

"Then your father could be dead by now, and you wouldn't know about it."

"I occasionally get news from New Orleans. He was still alive six months ago. I don't wish him dead," she said, smiling at Kyle. "He's my father. He isn't a wicked man, just very strict, and I couldn't live like that. It's best this way. But why are we talking about me when we should be discussing your plans?"

"I don't have any. I tried, and I lost."

"It isn't like you to give up," she chided.

"I've never wanted anything this much before. I can't imagine working up any interest in anything else."

She touched his cheek in sympathy, her slim fingers cool on his skin. "It could rain tomorrow. Or the day after. And I have money. I can always stake you to get you going again."

He shook his head. "You'll probably need it. If the ranches go under, so will this town. You'll have to set yourself up somewhere else."

"Things haven't gotten that bad yet. I always hope for the best."

"But prepare for the worst." Over the years he had run into her in different places, and at varying degrees of prosperity. He had seen her ragged and hungry, but even then she had always been planning, never wasting what little money she had. They had even thrown in together for a while, living off his winnings at cards, always ready to dodge out of town if anyone spotted his light touch with the pasteboards. They had huddled together under one thin blanket on frigid nights during the worst of their luck and spent three whole days and nights making love in a soft hotel bed once when they had hit a lucky streak.

Then they had gone their separate ways, for some reason he no longer remembered. Likely she had just had her own plans, and he had had his. He hadn't seen her again until they had both wound up, by sheer coincidence, in Prosper. But maybe it wasn't such a big coincidence, for they had both been looking for the same thing: a quiet, steady little town. They had both worked boomtowns and knew it was no way to live. Boomtowns were too violent. Security was better.

"If you change your mind about the money," she said, "all you have to do is ask."

"I know."

He felt a surge of desire for her. He never tired of making love to Tillie. They had known each other for so long, made love so often, that they were entirely comfortable together. He knew just how to touch her and did so, reaching out to fondle her breast with the exact degree of pressure that she liked. She inhaled sharply, her eyes darkening. "Well," she said. "I see your spirits have revived."

He took her hand and placed it on the front of his pants. "That isn't a spirit, but it sure has revived."

"Darling," she purred, "it's never been dead."

They undressed leisurely, pausing often for kisses and unhurried caresses. She started to go down on her knees and take him into her mouth, but he stopped her because, despite his slow pace, he felt that would be more than he could stand, and he wanted it to last longer than that. He put her on the bed and made love to her, using the advantage of his intimate knowledge of her to take her to the peak twice before he allowed himself release.

Afterward, as they lay quietly together, he felt a small measure of contentment. He might lose the ranch, but after all, he still had Tillie. She had always been there when he needed her. He only hoped he had been as good a friend to her as she had been to him.

14

KYLE WAS DRUNK EVEN THOUGH IT WAS ONLY EARLY
afternoon. He seldom allowed himself the excess
because men who drank too much often said too
much, and he wanted to keep his past life just that, in
the past. But there were some occasions that seemed
to call for drink, and watching his ranch die qualified
as one of them.

Besides, he didn't have anything else to do, unless
he wanted to ride out and look at the land drying up.
If he wanted to see water, he'd have to ride all the way
over to Angel Creek.

Now that was an idea, he mused. Maybe if he
offered the Swann woman even more than he had
before, she'd accept this time. Not that he had the
money, but she didn't know that. All he needed was
her signature on a bill of sale. He'd start moving his
cattle in and worry about the money later. Like the
old saying went, possession was nine tenths of the law.

That was what he'd do. He'd offer her so much money she'd have to be stupid to turn it down.

He wasn't so drunk that he couldn't ride, and soon he was on his horse. At least he was doing something, and that was a relief. It was the helpless waiting that drove him crazy, but patience never had been his long suit.

Entering the Angel Creek valley was like traveling to a different part of the country. Where the ground was cracking with dryness on the Bar B and the pastures were turning brown, here the earth was softened by the underground moisture, and the meadow grasses grew tall. It even felt cooler. He reined in, thinking in confusion that it couldn't *actually* be cooler, but then he decided that it really was. He frowned until the slight breeze on his face told the story. The valley acted like a funnel to the breezes coming down from the mountains, sweeping the cooler air downward. It was still hot, but not as hot as it was everywhere else.

The Swann woman came out on the porch when she heard his horse, and she had that damn shotgun in her hands, just the way she had the other times he'd talked to her. She'd never threatened him with it, but he'd never been able to forget it was there, either.

She stood as proud as any of the high-nosed New Orleans ladies of his youth, even though she worked the soil like a man and her clothes were plain and old. Hell, Tillie dressed better than she did. But her head was held high on her slender neck, and those witch-green eyes were rock steady. "Mr. Bellamy," was all she said in greeting.

He didn't dismount. He just leaned forward, resting

his arms on his saddle horn. "I'll double my last offer for this place."

She arched her brows, and he saw the gleam of amusement in her eyes. "Your last offer was marriage. Are you saying you'll marry me twice?"

He wasn't in the mood for sarcasm. "I need this land. I need the water. My cattle are going to die if they don't have water, and you have just about the only good creek for a hundred miles or more."

Dee sighed and looked at the cloudless blue sky. Why couldn't it rain? "I'm sorry, Mr. Bellamy, but I won't sell to you." She did feel sorry for him; she felt sorry for every rancher, big and small, and every farmer. But she couldn't take care of them all, couldn't parcel out the water that ran through her land.

Kyle reined his horse around and rode away without another word. He was so angry he couldn't speak anyway. Damn her! She just wouldn't listen to reason. She was using only a little more than an acre of the land and letting the rest of it go to waste, but still she hung on to every inch as if it would kill her to let it go. For the sake of her piss-ant vegetable garden his cattle were going to die.

No, by God, they weren't.

He was almost sober by the time he got back home, but his anger hadn't abated, and neither had his savage determination.

One of the cowhands was coming out of the barn. "Get Pierce!" Kyle yelled. "And Fronteras!"

The two men were out on the range, so it was late when they finally trudged up to the house where he waited. "We start rounding up the cattle tomorrow," Kyle said. His voice was abrupt and still angry.

Pierce slowly nodded, as if he had to consider the idea before giving it his approval.

Luis was curious. "Where are we taking them?"

"Into the Angel Creek valley."

Pierce said, "That Swann woman's place?"

"I talked to her today," Kyle replied, knowing that they would assume she had given him permission to graze his cattle on her land.

Pierce nodded again. "Valley's small. You want all of the cattle?"

"Yes." The cattle would quickly overgraze, but at least they would have water. His mind was made up. No matter what Dee Swann said or did, his cattle were going into that valley.

Rounding up the cattle wasn't easy. They didn't want to leave what little water they had and tended to stray every chance they got. Everyone on the Bar B worked all the daylight hours the next day and got up before dawn on the second day to start again. The men felt as if they'd grown to their saddles.

It was late morning of the third day before they began moving the herd, and they reached the mouth of the little valley in the middle of the afternoon.

Dee had gotten up early that morning to weed the garden before the heat got bad. She couldn't remember it ever being so hot before, and the plants were beginning to show it. They were growing, but she was afraid the crops were going to be stunted, burned by the sun.

The ranchers had to be in bad shape. She hadn't

been into town for the past few weeks, but the last time she had gone everyone had been talking about how dry it was, and how it was hurting the grazing. Kyle Bellamy had been desperate when he'd ridden out to try to buy her land, and sympathy stirred in her as she remembered his face.

She wondered how Lucas was doing. She had seen him only once since the time he had tried to talk her into selling out; it had been just after the vote to ratify the constitution, and he had been jubilant over that, but tired from work and worried about the lack of water. She had wanted to assure him that everything would be all right, but the words would have been useless. How could she assure rain?

If the drought continued and his cattle died, would he ever forgive her?

She straightened and looked at the sun, already feeling its heat though it was still early in the morning. Her chest felt tight. She had no control over the weather, but she did have Angel Creek.

Lucas wanted her land. Like Kyle Bellamy, he had even offered marriage in an effort to obtain it. Every day since then she had lived with the knowledge that he hadn't wanted her for herself, but for the land. It lay cold and heavy in her breast, and time only seemed to make it grow heavier. It didn't help that she had realized the basis of his attraction to her right from the beginning, because like a fool she had fallen in love with him anyway. She couldn't even let herself attach any importance to their lovemaking, for Lucas was undeniably lusty by nature, and she thought any willing woman would have sufficed for his needs.

Sometimes she thought about riding up to the

Double C and telling him that she had changed her mind, that she was willing to marry him if he was still interested. She would play the scene through in her mind right up to the part where he accepted; then her pride would reject the idea, and she knew she would hate herself if she did it. She had always planned to live alone, enjoyed living alone. She still did enjoy her life, but for the first time she wanted more.

She wanted Lucas. It wasn't just physical, though she yearned for the smell and touch of him, for the release given by his driving possession. She wanted more. She had never had an entire night with him, only a few stolen hours. She had never faced a dawn after sheltering the dark hours in his arms, or watched him shave. She wanted years of thunderous arguments; living with a man like Lucas would keep her on her toes. He would ride roughshod over a woman who didn't stand up to him. It was a kind of strength she had never before seen in a man; she was used to doing the intimidating. Lucas not only matched her, he gave her an unspoken compliment by not holding himself back as if she were a frail flower who would collapse under the storm of his temper.

If he married her in order to get Angel Creek, she would have those years she coveted, but she wouldn't have his love, and she wouldn't have self-respect.

Yet she loved him, and he needed her. Rather, he needed her land.

She looked at her garden. The plants were strong and green, just beginning to bear fruit with the long summer weeks of ripening ahead. Despite the lack of rain they were flourishing, fed by the creek that kept the rich soil moist.

Perhaps Lucas could move some of his cattle into the valley. A fence could be built around the cabin and garden to protect them. He couldn't bring the cattle over the pass, but it would only take a couple of days to bring a herd around the base of the mountain. She saw no reason why he wouldn't agree to the plan; the cattle could even winter there.

If necessary, if he refused to accept the favor, she would sell Angel Creek to him. It would be like selling part of her heart, but she couldn't stand by and let his cattle die when she had the means of preventing it.

Accepting that was a blow that made her eyes sting as she looked around at her home. Saying that she loved it only scratched the surface. Over the years as she had worked the soil, coaxed life out of it, she had found a contentment that went deeper than love. It wasn't just the satisfaction of making things grow, it was everything about Angel Creek, the utter perfection of it. Her soul had taken root there, sinking deep into the earth. She could live in other places, but none would ever be like this, where she so completely, overwhelmingly *fit*.

Yet for Lucas she would give it up.

He had such big dreams, such towering ambitions. He'd achieve them, too, if the Double C survived this drought. Colorado was on the verge of statehood, and he was on the verge of putting his plans into action. He deserved the chance to do it. Men like Lucas were different from other men; he was a leader, a man who got things done.

She had never been to the Double C, never been up to the narrow pass Lucas used to enter the valley. Except for her trips into town she hadn't strayed from

Angel Creek since the day her family had first settled on it. Even if she had been familiar with the way to the Double C she wouldn't have gone, for the mere fact that she had visited Lucas Cochran would be so out of character for her that immediately her relationship with him would have been suspected. Regardless of that, she would go to the ranch and tell him her decision.

After all, it was the way she lived that had necessitated secrecy, for anything less than a spotless reputation would have endangered her. A woman alone couldn't take too many precautions. But if she lived in town, she wouldn't have to be so careful. She and Lucas could be discreet about the extent of their intimacy, but they wouldn't have to conceal their relationship entirely. That was assuming, of course, that they would even have a relationship after Lucas had gotten what he wanted from her, namely Angel Creek.

It was afternoon, and the sun was searing when she finished her chores and went inside to wash off in cool water. Now that she had faced what she had to do in order to live with herself she was restless, filled with impatience to get it over with. Maybe Lucas would accept her offer to graze his cattle in the valley, and she wouldn't have to uproot herself. If he insisted on buying the land, she wanted to get it over and done with, like a dose of bitter medicine.

After washing she changed into clean clothes and stood for a minute looking around. The next couple of hours would decide if she lived here or not, and for a moment the idea of leaving was so hard to bear that she let her head drop forward as she fought tears.

Then a sound made her lift her head, listening. That sounded like cattle bawling. And thunder; she thought she heard thunder. Hope rising, she went to the window and bent to look out. Not a cloud in sight. The bull and both cows were placidly grazing, but she still heard cattle bawling, or something that sounded like it.

She stepped out on the porch, her head tilted to the side as she listened curiously. Her gaze settled on a cloud of dust that was rising above the trees, and she stared at it blankly for a moment before an expression of horror crossed her face. She darted back inside, got the shotgun, and crammed her pockets full of extra shells.

The first of the cattle came into view. Knowing she didn't have a moment to waste, she put the shotgun to her shoulder and fired just over their heads, hoping to spook them the other way.

The cattle milled around in confusion, excited by the smell of water but nervous at the boom of the shotgun. She shot the other barrel and quickly reloaded, her heart pounding so hard in her chest that she felt sick. If the cattle got into the garden, they would destroy it.

"Put the shotgun down," Kyle Bellamy yelled. He rode toward her, a rifle in his hands. "The cattle are going through here."

"Not on my land," she replied fiercely. The valley was narrow, and the cabin was close to the mouth of it; he'd have to herd the cattle right between the cabin and the barn, and the unprotected garden was right behind the cabin. What the cattle didn't trample, they'd eat.

The herd hadn't turned. She fired again, and this time she aimed low enough to hit the cattle. At that distance the buckshot stung without doing a lot of damage, and the cattle bawled in panic, turning sharply away from both the noise and the pain. The leading edge of the herd turned back into the others. She shot a fourth time, and they began bolting.

A rifle cracked, and the wood behind her splintered.

She dodged back into the cabin and slammed the door, hurriedly ramming shells into the shotgun as she did so. With a quick swing of the barrel she knocked the glass out of the window and shot again.

Cursing with every breath, Kyle shot back. "Get the cattle!" he yelled at his men. "Goddammit, turn them around."

Some of the men were already trying. Others had drawn their pistols at the sound of gunfire. They all knew about the Swann woman, knew she tended to greet people with a shotgun. She'd even peppered a few men who'd tried to keep company with her, the bad-tempered bitch. She shouldn't treat people like that. If the boss was intending to give her a taste of her own medicine, that was fine with them. Sporadically at first, then with increasing regularity, they began shooting at the cabin.

Luis reined his horse off to the side, his lean, dark face taut with anger and his hand on his pistol butt. He didn't know what the hell had gotten into Bellamy, but he didn't intend to make war on a lone woman.

He was good with a pistol, but not good enough to take on twenty men in a blood lust. For a split second he considered killing Bellamy, then realized that wouldn't stop it. He didn't have a lot of time to get help before the sons of bitches either killed the woman or overran her cabin and raped her; he'd seen enough blood lust to know that it wouldn't make any difference to them which it was.

The cattle were stampeding wildly, panicked by the gunfire, maddened by the smell of water. A thick cloud of dust billowed over everything, cutting visibility. Luis went with the cattle, yelling to agitate them even more, then finally broke free to turn his horse toward Prosper.

He rode the animal hard even in the heat, and it was white with lather by the time he reined it to a halt in front of the marshal's office. He jumped down, his booted feet thudding on the sidewalk as he shoved the door open. The office was empty.

The most logical place to look was the saloon. If the marshal wasn't there, someone would likely know his whereabouts.

But the marshal was nowhere in sight when he entered the saloon. "Where's Marshal Cobb?" he asked of anyone in the saloon.

"Don't rightly know," a man said. Luis recognized him as a shopkeeper.

"I thought I heard he's visitin' his daughter up Denver way for a few days," another said. "You got trouble?"

"Bellamy's trying to run his cattle into the Swann woman's valley," Luis said curtly. "There's shooting going on, and it'll be either a raping or a killing if it isn't stopped."

Everyone in the saloon was silent. Luis looked around at the men, but none of them were jumping to help. "Since the marshal's gone, are any of you willing to help that woman?"

Eyes shifted away. For the most part the men in the saloon at that time of day were townsfolk, merchants and clerks. They hadn't cleaned their weapons in years. If a bunch of rowdy cowhands had gone wild, they weren't going to stick their noses into it, at least as long as it stayed out of town. It wasn't like Dee Swann was a friend or anything; she always kept to herself.

Ranchers would have had weapons handy and been willing to help, but there weren't any ranchers in the saloon. They were too busy during the day doing what they could to keep their cattle alive. Luis turned away in disgust, his dark eyes going cold.

"Wait," Tillie said, hurrying toward him. She stepped out on the sidewalk, her hand on his arm. She looked pale. "Lucas Cochran on the Double C will help."

"She doesn't have that kind of time," Luis said harshly.

Tillie's brown eyes were huge and anguished. "Then you go back and help her, and I'll ride to the Double C."

Luis gave a brief nod, already turning away. "You'd better hurry."

He cut overland, pushing his tired horse hard and coming in from the side. He could still hear gunfire, which meant that the woman was holding her own. Despite his grimness his mouth twisted in a grin. She must be a real hellcat. A woman like that deserved all the help she could get.

He left his horse and worked his way the last

hundred yards on foot, choosing a thick stand of trees for cover. Bellamy and his men had pretty well settled in their own cover and were taking their time squeezing off shots at the cabin. Some kept trying to work their way around and catch her from behind, but the cabin was in a large clear area, and there wasn't a lot of cover for them to use. The woman was a good shot. She was using a rifle now and was moving from window to window.

Luis considered his strategy. He didn't care about keeping either his identity or his position hidden; his only objective was to help the Swann woman prevent them from overrunning her cabin, or maybe turning the cattle back onto her land. It might even help if Bellamy's men knew he was helping her; though he had lived a calm life in Colorado, his skill with a pistol was well known. It might make some of them reconsider if they knew he was waiting for them.

Time was both their ally and their enemy. If he and the woman could hold off long enough, the Double C men would be able to get there. If aid didn't arrive by nightfall, then Bellamy's men would be able to reach the cabin undetected.

With that in mind, he cooly began choosing his targets. His purpose wasn't to keep them pinned down, but to rebalance the odds in his favor as much as he could. If a man was dead or severely wounded, then you didn't have to worry about him even in the dark. His mouth moved into a thin, cold smile. Hell, he'd spent enough time in Colorado anyway.

Tillie didn't take the time to change into riding clothes or to ask permission to borrow the nearest horse. By the time Luis was galloping out of town in one direction she was galloping in the other. Her garish short skirt made it possible for her to ride astride, though her legs were bared from the knee down. She glimpsed several shocked faces as she raced out of town but didn't spare a thought for the picture she made.

Her heart was pounding as hard as the horse's hooves on the packed earth. Oh, Kyle! she thought. Why had he done it? She would have lent him the money; no one would ever have known, and he could have kept his ranch, kept his dream of being a prosperous, respected rancher. Now he had attacked Dee Swann, and the townspeople would never forget, never accept him. It didn't matter that he had done it out of desperation; he would be condemned. And if Lucas Cochran didn't get there before Dee was raped or murdered, Kyle would be hanged.

The saddle leather rubbed raw patches on the insides of her tender thighs, but she didn't dare slow down, not when every minute counted. It would take Lucas a long time to get to Angel Creek anyway, maybe too long. At least Dee had Fronteras helping her now—unless they were both killed.

The horse began to tire. Panic welled up in her, but she refrained from kicking the poor beast. If she killed it by running it too hard in this heat, she would never reach the Double C in time. But the urge to hurry beat within her like bird wings until her head echoed with the refrain, *Hurry, before it's too late.* Too late for Dee, too late for Kyle . . . too late for herself.

Then she saw the ranch buildings. The Double C

ranch house was two-storied, with a white-columned porch wrapped all the way around it. She didn't pull on the reins until she reached it, and the exhausted horse stumbled clumsily.

"Lucas!" she screamed even as she slid from the saddle. "Lucas!" She ran up on the porch and pounded on the door with her fist.

"Here! Tillie, I'm over here."

She turned and saw him striding up from the barn, his long legs eating up the distance. She ran down the steps and sprinted across the yard toward him, screaming the entire way. "You've got to get down to Angel Creek! They've gone crazy, they're shooting at her, trying to take the land—"

She reached him, and he grabbed her arms to halt her. His blue eyes had turned to ice. If hell had been cold, it would have looked like his eyes. "Who is it?" His fingers bit into her soft arms. She gasped for breath, and he roughly shook her. "Damn it, who is it?"

"It's Kyle," she said, still gulping air. "Kyle Bellamy. He's desperate—the Bar B's water is almost gone."

Lucas turned, roaring for everyone to get their rifles and saddle up. Every man within hearing ran to obey. Lucas sprinted for his own mount. Tillie ran after him, her red taffeta skirts kicking up and showing her petticoats.

"Luis Fronteras is helping her," she yelled. "He rode into town and sent me after you, then he went back."

Lucas gave a brief nod to show that he'd heard. The

tight sense of panic in his chest eased a little as he realized Dee wasn't facing Bellamy and his men all alone.

He swung into the saddle, and Tillie grabbed his leg. "Don't kill Kyle," she begged frantically. "God, Lucas, please don't kill him. I love him. Please, please don't kill him, promise me."

Lucas looked down at her, that icy look still in his eyes. "I can't make any promises," he said. If Bellamy had harmed Dee, he wouldn't see another sunrise.

Lucas put spurs to his horse, riding hard for the pass that would get him to Angel Creek faster than any other way. Tillie stood in the yard and watched the men ride out, and tears slowly tracked down her dusty face.

15

DEE CROUCHED BENEATH ONE OF THE FRONT WINDOWS. She had discarded the shotgun in favor of the rifle, for accuracy, but she was running out of shells. She had prepared for a lot of things, but never for a seige, and that's what this was.

At least they hadn't turned the cattle. Maybe the men hadn't tried but had turned their attention to her. After all, if she were dead, then they could move the cattle in without trouble.

She didn't know how long it had been going on because one of the shots had hit her clock, and she had no idea what time it was. Late afternoon. The sun was red and low in the sky. Come dark, they would approach the cabin, and she wouldn't be able to cover all the windows. She had already blocked the bedroom door so that even if anyone crawled through the bedroom window he wouldn't be able to come up behind her without her knowledge.

She gripped the rifle as she carefully watched for someone to make a careless move and show himself. The wood stock was slippery, and she wiped her hand on her skirt, but it didn't seem to help. She looked down and saw that it wasn't sweat on her hand, but blood. Some of the flying glass had cut her arm.

She was tired, deathly tired, but she didn't dare rest for even a minute. She was thirsty but couldn't even cross the room for a drink of water.

There. A slight movement, a hint of blue. Dee carefully sighted down the barrel and squeezed the trigger, not even hearing the sharp crack as the rifle fired. She saw a brief commotion of movement and knew she'd hit someone.

Immediately another volley of shots struck the little cabin, gouging out long splinters of wood, ricocheting off the wood stove. She flattened herself on the floor as a bullet zinged across the room, gaining herself more cuts from the shattered glass that covered the floor. There wasn't a piece of glass left in any of the windows.

Quickly she sat up, swinging the rifle around. One man darted from cover, and she fired, sending him diving back. Damn, she'd missed him.

It would be dark soon. She had to do something, but there was nothing she could do. If she fired without seeing a target, she would waste her bullets, but if she simply waited, they would win anyway.

She wiped her bloody hands on her skirt again. God, she was bleeding all over from cuts. Her clothes were soaked.

She didn't care. She was thinking with an awful clarity. Those men were in a blood lust, and if they didn't kill her outright, they would each take a turn raping her. And she knew she would rather die. They would not violate her body, the flesh that she had shared only with Lucas—not while she drew breath. Her instinct was to fight, and she supposed it was too late now to start going against her instincts. If she had to die, she intended to take as many of those bastards with her as she could.

She scrambled to her knees, put the rifle to her shoulder, and began firing. The rifle was a repeater, so she shot until it was empty, then hastily reloaded and began firing again. Return fire tore into the cabin.

The window frame splintered, and she fell back with a stifled scream. Her left shoulder burned like fire, and she glanced down to see a long, thin sliver of wood protruding from it. She tried to pull it out, but her fingers were too slippery to hold it. Since there was nothing she could do, she put it and the pain out of her mind.

Luis had attracted a lot of attention once Bellamy and his men had noticed they were being fired on from two positions. He had been hit twice—once a shallow burn on his left bicep that he had ignored, the second time in his right side. The wound hadn't hit any internal organs, but it had bled like a son of a bitch. He had pulled off his bandanna, pressed it over the long gouge, and resumed firing, but soon the blood was streaming down his hip and leg.

He had to have more pressure on the wound. He transferred the pistol to his left hand and pressed his right elbow hard against his side. A wave of dizziness made him shake his head in an effort to clear his vision. If Cochran didn't get there at once, it would be too late. The woman was still shooting, but it would be dark soon, and he was losing too much blood to be able to help her.

Lucas split up his men, sending some of them to circle around behind Bellamy while he and the rest of them approached unseen down the slope, keeping the barn between them and the line of fire. Because of the large clearing around the cabin none of Bellamy's men had been able to work around to the side, and Dee was concentrating all of her fire to the front, where they were using the trees as cover. The surge of relief he felt when he heard her firing steadily made him feel weak. They were in time. Damn, what a woman!

He had to wait until his men who had flanked Bellamy had made their move, then his group began firing from the side. Bellamy didn't have a chance under the savage crossfire of the Double C men. Lucas realized that Dee was still shooting; she didn't know what was happening and was likely to kill some of his own men if she wasn't stopped. "I'm going into the cabin," he yelled. "Keep their heads down."

He ran toward the back stoop under the protection of a hail of bullets, but someone spied him anyway, and a bullet kicked up dust just in front of him. With all the lead flying it wasn't healthy for a man to stand and politely knock at a door; Dee would probably cut him in half with the shotgun anyway before she knew who he was. He leapt up on the back stoop and hit the door at a dead run, driving his muscled shoulder into it and sending it crashing back against the wall. Dee was at one of the front windows, and she scrabbled clumsily around, screaming as she fired the rifle. His heart clenched in pure terror when he saw her covered in blood, but he didn't pause for even a second. He dived to the floor, rolling to the side and coming up to lunge for her. She was still screaming as she swung the rifle at his head.

"Dee!" he yelled, grabbing her. "Goddammit, it's me, Lucas!" He wrested the rifle out of her bloody hands and tossed it aside, then wrapped his arms around her.

She shrieked, trying to throw herself backward even as she pounded at his face with her fists. Her eyes were wild, the pupils shrunk to tiny pinpoints.

"Dee!" he roared again, just trying to hold her still. She was hurt—God, she was hurt, and he didn't want to cause her any more pain, but he had to calm her down. He wrestled her down to the glass-covered floor, pinning her with his heavy weight. "Dee," he repeated, saying her name over and over. "Look at me. It's all right. I'm here, and I'll take care of you. Look at me."

Slowly she stilled, more from exhaustion than comprehension. She was quivering from head to foot, but at least she had quit fighting him. Her wild eyes were fastened on his face as if she were trying to make sense of what was happening. He kept talking to her, his voice low and soothing, and finally she blinked as understanding dawned. "Lucas," she murmured.

He was there. He was really there. She was conscious of relief, not so much because she was safe but because she could rest now. She was tired, so very,

very tired, and oddly cold. The pain that she had held at bay for so long finally caught up with her as she let her tired muscles relax. She heard herself make a strange moaning sound, and her body loosened into total limpness. Her head lolled on the plank flooring.

Lucas could barely breathe. She was drenched in blood, her clothing soaked, even her hair matted with it. For the first time he noticed a long sliver of wood stuck in her shoulder, and he felt sick. As gently as he could he released her and got to his feet. He kicked the furniture she had piled against the bedroom door away and jerked a blanket from the bed, shaking it to make certain it didn't have glass on it, too, then replacing it. Returning to the other room, he lifted Dee as carefully as possible and carried her to the bed.

He looked around for a lamp, but they had all been broken. He examined her as thoroughly as possible in the dim light, his heart pounding as he looked for gunshot wounds. A bullet had creased her left hipbone, and she had that wicked splinter in her shoulder, but all of her other wounds were cuts from the broken glass. She was covered with them—small cuts on her scalp and face, her neck and shoulders and arms. Taken separately, her wounds were not serious, but there were so many of them that she had lost a dangerous amount of blood. Her lips looked blue, and beneath the blood her skin had a chilling translucent quality to it.

He heard his own voice swearing low and savagely as he tried to halt the bleeding, but he wasn't aware of what he was saying. Such minor wounds, and she might yet die.

He heard booted feet crunching on the broken glass, and William Tobias appeared in the doorway. "She all right, boss?"

"No. She's lost a lot of blood. Get the wagon hitched up. We've got to get her into town."

"That Mexican, Fronteras, caught a couple of bullets. He's lost a right smart amount of blood, too, but I reckon he'll be all right. About five of the Bar B men need burying, some more need patching up. There was about thirty of the bastards after her. We hurt 'em the most, I reckon."

Lucas nodded, not taking his attention from Dee. "Hurry up with that wagon."

William left to see to it.

Lucas started to remove the long splinter from her shoulder but decided to leave it. Blood was oozing around it, but if he pulled it out the wound might start bleeding heavily, and she didn't need to lose any more blood than she already had. He carefully wrapped the blanket around her and lifted her.

William pulled the wagon right up to the porch just as Lucas stepped outside with his burden. His men were standing around with their weapons trained on the Bar B men, the look on their faces saying that they wished someone would try to get away. The wounded were sprawled on the ground; the dead had been left where they lay.

"Where's Fronteras?" Lucas asked as he gently placed Dee on the wagon bed. She didn't move.

"Here."

"Put him on the wagon, too."

Two of his men lifted one of the wounded and laid

him on the wagon. Lucas saw the Mexican's dark eyes open. "Is she all right?" he asked huskily.

"She's hurt," Lucas replied, his voice tight. "Fronteras, you have a place on my ranch for the rest of your life if you want it."

Luis managed a semblance of a smile, then his eyes closed again.

"Will, get them to the doc. I'll be along in a few minutes." Lucas stepped back. William nodded and slapped the reins against the horse's back.

Slowly Lucas turned his head to look at the Bar B men. Killing rage was bubbling in his veins, and it was cold, ice cold. Kyle Bellamy stood with his men, his head down and his arms hanging loose at his sides.

Lucas wasn't aware of moving, but suddenly Bellamy's shirt was knotted in his big fist. The man looked up, and Lucas's powerful right arm cocked back, then drove his iron-hard fist into Bellamy's face.

He had never before taken joy in fighting, but he felt savage satisfaction every time his fists thudded into Bellamy. He beat the man to the ground, then pulled him up and beat him some more. He kept seeing Dee's blood-soaked body, and he hit Bellamy even harder, feeling ribs crack as he drove his fists into the man's sides and midsection. Bellamy made no effort to fight back, merely raising his arms to try to block some of the blows. That didn't incline Lucas toward mercy.

Finally Bellamy pitched forward and lay still, and one of the Double C men caught Lucas's arm as he started for him again. "No point in it, boss," the man said. "He can't feel a thing."

Lucas halted and stared down at the motionless

man at his feet. His face was unrecognizable, but Lucas didn't feel the satisfaction of vengeance. His rage was so deep that even killing Bellamy wouldn't ease it.

He hadn't promised Tillie that he wouldn't kill Bellamy, but he owed her. If she hadn't ridden her heart out to reach him, Dee would have died alone in her cabin. He let his hands drop.

"What do we do with them?" one of the men asked.

Lucas growled. There wasn't any use in taking them into town; they hadn't broken any of the laws within the marshal's jurisdiction. Unless he was willing to string them all up right now there was nothing to be done. "Let them go," he said.

He looked at the Bar B men, and his voice was almost a snarl when he said, "Get off this land, you bastards, and take your scum with you. If any of you ever feel brave enough to attack a lone woman again, I swear to God I'll make you think hell is paradise compared to what I'll do to you before you die. Is that clear?"

The Bar B men answered with sullen mutters. Lucas went to his horse and mounted. If he didn't leave, he was likely to kill them all anyway.

It was full dark, and the moon hadn't yet risen, but the light from the countless stars was enough to let him see the road. He rode as fast as he dared and caught up with the wagon just before it got to town.

Doc Pendergrass and his wife, Etta, swiftly went to work on Dee. Luis Fronteras had been put in another room, and he was deemed less critical since he was still conscious and Dee wasn't. Lucas was pushed from the room as soon as he had placed Dee on the table, and he paced back and forth like a caged animal.

Tillie slipped in the door. Though the saloon would be busy now that it was night, she was wearing a dark green dress with long sleeves and a high neckline rather than the short, gaudy outfit she wore when working. Her face was very pale, but her expression was calm. "Did you get there in time?" she asked.

Lucas took off his hat and ran his hand through his hair. "Yeah. I hope. She's cut up pretty bad from the glass where they shot the windows out, and she's lost a lot of blood."

"But they didn't—"

"No. She was still holding them off when we got there."

He hadn't realized how taut she had been until he saw her subtly relax. Her enormous brown eyes never left his face. "Kyle?" she whispered.

"I beat the hell out of him."

She flinched, then controlled herself again. "Thank you, Lucas."

He shook his head. "No. She'd be dead now if it hadn't been for you."

"And Luis Fronteras. Is he all right?"

"He's hurt, but he'll make it."

She stood with her head bent for a minute, then sighed and straightened. She squeezed his arm in a gentle caress before she left.

It was over an hour before Doc Pendergrass came

out, and he firmly shut the door behind him when Lucas started forward. "I got all the bleeding stopped," Doc said. "Etta's cleaning her up now."

"Is she conscious?"

"Not really. She roused up a little a couple of times but drifted out again. Sleep's the best thing for her right now. I'll tell you more after I take care of Fronteras."

Lucas sat down with his elbows propped on his knees and his head hanging forward. He needed to see her, to reassure himself that she was all right.

It didn't take the doctor as long with Luis as it had with Dee. He was out again in fifteen minutes. "Stitched up and sleeping," Doc said tiredly. "He'll be all right, probably up and around in a couple of days."

"What about Dee?" Lucas asked in a hard voice.

Doc sighed and rubbed his eyes. He was a slim, good-looking man in his early forties, but right now weariness made him look ten years older. "There were a lot of cuts. She's had a bad shock to her system. She's going to be a very sick woman for several days, feverish and weak."

"I want to take her to the ranch. Is it safe to move her?"

Doc looked up in surprise, then comprehension showed in his face. Like everyone else in town, he had thought Lucas connected with Olivia Millican. Lucas Cochran and Dee Swann . . . well, well. "No," he finally answered. "Not for a couple of days, maybe longer. It'd be better for her to stay here with Etta to look after her anyway."

Lucas's face was hard. "When she's well enough to travel I'm taking her to the ranch." There was a part of him that wouldn't relax until he had her safe under his roof. Until the day he died he would never forget how he had felt when he had first seen her soaked in her own blood.

16

Luis was hurt. Olivia didn't hear about what had happened until the next morning, when Beatrice Padgett visited and was relating, in shocked tones, the events of the day before to Honora. ". . . and one of Mr. Bellamy's men, a Mr. Fronteras—I believe he must be a Mexican—decided to help Dee hold them off, and he was shot, too."

Olivia made a muffled sound of shock. Honora and Beatrice looked toward her, and Honora quickly got to her feet at the sight of her daughter's white face. "Sit down, dear," she said, urging Olivia toward a chair. "It's horrible, isn't it?"

But Olivia pulled back, her eyes full of anguish. "Where—where is he?" she gasped. "Mr. Fronteras. Where is he?"

"Why, at Dr. Pendergrass's, of course. Mr. Cochran took both him and Dee to the doctor's to be tended," Beatrice answered. "That saloon girl, the one called

Tillie, fetched Mr. Cochran to help. Isn't that the strangest thing? I wonder why she rode all the way out to the Double C."

Olivia whirled and ran from the house, ignoring Honora's alarmed cry.

Luis! Beatrice hadn't said how seriously he was hurt, but it must be bad if he was still at the doctor's. For the first time in her life Olivia forgot about decorum and dignity; she snatched her skirts up and ran, her heart thudding in a sick panic. It was three blocks to Dr. Pendergrass's office. She darted around people on the sidewalks when she could and shoved past them otherwise. By the time she reached the office her hair was falling down and she was gasping for breath, but she had never cared less for her appearance.

She shoved the door open and stumbled inside. The first person she saw was Etta Pendergrass. "Where is he?"

Etta immediately assumed that there was an emergency. "I'll get him, dear. He's just in here checking Mr. Fronteras—"

Olivia bolted past her into the room she had indicated. Dr. Pendergrass looked up at her precipitous entrance and leapt to the same conclusion his wife had. "What's happened, Olivia?" Surely only a serious accident or illness concerning one of her parents could prompt Olivia into such uncharacteristic actions.

But Olivia didn't answer. Her hands flew to her mouth as she stared at Luis, lying on his left side, his upper torso bare. A large white bandage was located at his waist. Tears swam in her eyes, blurring her vision.

"Luis?" she whispered, her voice begging. Let him be all right, she prayed silently. Please let him be all right.

He shifted gingerly onto his back, his dark eyes narrowing at her white face. "Would you let me speak to Miss Millican in private?" he asked the doctor in a tone that commanded rather than requested.

Dr. Pendergrass arched his brows a little and said, "Of course." He left the room, closing the door behind him.

Luis held out his hand, and Olivia ran to him. She touched his face, his chest, his shoulders, whispering incoherently while tears slid down her cheeks. Holding his left hand to the bandage on his side, he struggled to a sitting position. "I'm all right," he soothed, pulling her close to him and kissing her hair. "It's just a flesh wound. I'm stiff and weak, but it isn't serious."

"I just heard," she stammered, clinging to him. "I'd have been here last night if I'd known. Why didn't you have someone send for me? *Why?"*

Using his thumb, he wiped her cheeks. "And let everyone know?" he asked gently.

She struggled to control her breathing. "Well, they know now," she blurted. "I ran through town like a madwoman."

He was silent a minute while his hand rubbed her back in comfort. "I could think of something as an excuse if you want."

Olivia stilled with her head on his shoulder. He wasn't going to take advantage of the situation to force the issue. He had said it was her decision, and he was standing by that. But could she go back to pretending she didn't care about him? Just hearing that he'd been hurt had stripped away the last film of doubt from her mind. Why was she dithering when she felt that way about him? She had never been a silly person, but she had certainly been acting silly the past couple of months. Her greatest dream had come true, and she had been afraid to accept it because Luis Fronteras wasn't a landed gentleman. She was worse than silly; she was a snob.

Slowly she lifted her head, her damp blue eyes locking with his dark ones. A soft smile trembled on her lips. "No, I don't want you to lie for me," she said in as steady a voice as she could muster. "What I want is to marry you, Luis Fronteras."

His dark eyes were piercing, and he held her chin so that she couldn't look away. "Are you sure? Make very certain, Olivia, because once you say yes I won't let you go no matter what happens. I'm not a gentleman. I keep what's mine, and I'll fight as dirty as I have to to keep it."

She framed his face with her hands and leaned forward to kiss him. "Yes," she said. A smile broke like the sun coming up, bathing her face in radiance. "Yes. Yes yes yes yes *yes*. How many times do I have to say it before it's official?"

His dark brows arched, and he locked her in his arms. "It's official," he said. "We'll get married as soon as possible."

"Mother will want me to be married in the church. It'll take at least a month to get everything arranged."

"A month!" he growled. Then he warned, "Don't be surprised if your parents refuse to have anything to do with me."

She felt sad at the possibility but faced it. "If they

do, that's their loss." Nothing would stop her from marrying Luis. Somehow it no longer mattered that she didn't know how they would live, or even where. She would be with him, and that was all that mattered. She loved him. It was a simple truth, and she wondered why it had taken her so long to recognize it.

She had learned in a few horrible moments that morning how swiftly fate could step in and perhaps take him away forever. Before another minute passed she wanted to give him the gift of her love. She said it simply. "I love you."

His pupils flared until his eyes were black and bottomless. "And I love you. We may not live in a big house, but I'll take very good care of you."

"I'm sure you will." A blush rosied her cheeks, but her gaze remained steady. "In all the ways that matter."

He had the most devilish grin she had ever seen, and the power of it almost made her heart stop. "Yes, darling, in that way, too."

He had to kiss her, and it was even more potent than it had been before, because now she felt no need to draw back. She gave him all of her response and the complete freedom of her body. It was only his stifled groan when he moved too abruptly that made them realize where they were and draw back.

Her concern, which had abated when she had seen that he wasn't mortally wounded, returned full force. Now that she had calmed down she could see how drawn and pale he was, and the dark circles beneath his eyes. "Lie back down," she urged, pressing his shoulder with her hand.

He obeyed because he was as weak as a kitten.

Olivia settled the pillow under his head and drew the blanket up to his chest, then sat down beside him with his hand clasped in hers. She couldn't bear to be separated from him just yet. "What happened?" she asked. "Who shot you?"

"In that kind of gunfight it doesn't matter. So many people were shooting there's no way to know."

"But what *happened?* Why did it happen?"

"Bellamy decided to drive his cattle onto Dee Swann's property. The Bar B doesn't have much water left, and I guess he was desperate. Desperate people do stupid things." Luis sighed tiredly. "I thought she'd given him permission, but she hadn't, and she shot to spook the cattle, turn them around. Bellamy seemed to go mad. He started shooting at her, and some of the men joined in."

"And you helped her. Do you even know her?" She was filled with admiration for what he had done.

"No, but she was a woman alone, and it was her land. She was in the right." He decided that it might not be smart to tell his future wife that he had a deep and lasting fondness for women in general, and there was no way he could stand by and let a woman be terrorized. Not that Dee Swann had seemed frightened, he reflected with admiration. She had faced Bellamy like an Amazon.

"Dee's a wonderful friend," Olivia said softly. "Thank you for saving her life. I heard some of the men in town wouldn't try to help her, I think probably because she keeps to herself and doesn't seem to need anyone, but that's just an act. I'm glad you were there when she *did* need someone's help. I only wish you hadn't been hurt."

"I didn't do it by myself. If Tillie hadn't gone after Cochran, and he hadn't got there as fast as he did, Dee and I would both be dead."

Olivia stroked his hand, loving the strength in his lean fingers. "I'll ride out to help her get the cabin straightened up."

Luis's face tightened. "She isn't at the cabin. She's right here. Doc says she's cut up pretty bad and lost too much blood. He's been up with her all night, and now fever is setting in. He's worried about her."

Olivia turned white and jumped to her feet. She hadn't even asked if Dee was hurt! Her mind had emptied of everything but Luis when she'd heard he had been shot. "Oh, my God," she said, and tears slipped down her cheeks. Luis reached out a steadying hand, but she whispered, "I have to go to her." She ran from the room.

Her friend lay silent and motionless except for the faint rise and fall of her chest. The only color in her face was from the livid cuts that marred her skin. Dee had always been so vital that Olivia almost didn't recognize her lying so still. She had never imagined anything could bring Dee down.

Etta was sitting by the bed, keeping a cold cloth on Dee's forehead. Olivia could see the worry plain in her eyes.

"Has she been awake?" Olivia asked, agonized.

Etta shook her head. "She hasn't stirred since Lucas brought her in last night."

Olivia swiped at her wet cheeks. "You must be so tired you can hardly sit up," she said. "I'll sit with her while you rest."

* * *

Tillie rode out to the Bar B. Though there was activity around the ranch house, there was a strangely abandoned feel to it. All of the men looked exhausted, even those who hadn't taken part in the fight, for they had been chasing the scattered cattle for most of the night.

"Where's Mr. Bellamy?" she asked one of them.

"In the house, ma'am."

She knocked, but no one answered, and after knocking a second time she opened the door. "Kyle?"

There was no answer. She walked through the downstairs and found it deserted, then went upstairs. Kyle's bedroom was on the left. She tapped on the door, which was ajar, then stepped inside.

He lay on the bed, fully clothed except for his boots. His shirt bore reddish-brown stains. She walked over and stood beside the bed, looking down at him. Compassion turned her eyes black. He had tried to clean his face, for a stained cloth lay on the floor, but dried blood still caked one of his nostrils and was splotched in his hair and on his neck.

His poor face was so swollen and misshappen she could barely recognize him. Both eyes were blackened and puffy, his nose was broken, and huge knots distorted his cheekbones and jaw.

"Kyle," she said softly.

He shifted a little and groaned. One of his eyes opened a slit.

"I'll get some water and clean you up," she murmured, bending over him so he could see her without turning his head.

He sighed, then muttered, "Ribs." His mouth was so swollen that the word sounded mushy.

"Your ribs are hurt?"

"Yeah."

She touched his arm. "I'll be right back."

She got what she needed from downstairs and returned to his bedroom with her supplies. He didn't look as if he had moved an inch.

She took a pair of scissors and deftly cut his shirt off of him, then probed his ribs. His midsection was mottled with black and purple bruises, testimony to the power of Lucas Cochran's fists. As gently as possible she probed his ribs, searching for breaks. He cried out when she touched a certain place, but she couldn't feel anything out of place and decided they were only cracked.

"Your ribs need to be wrapped," she said. "Kyle, darling, you'll have to sit up. I know it hurts, but I can't do anything with you lying down."

She gently coaxed him into a sitting position, supporting him as much as she was able, but Kyle was a big man, and she didn't have enough strength to give him much aid. When he was sitting unsteadily on the side of the bed she wrapped a wide band of cloth around him, pulling it tight. He groaned but then gave a sigh of relief as the tight wrapping supported his ribs and kept them from moving.

While he was sitting up she washed his face, taking care to use only the lightest touch, then cleaned the blood from his hair and neck.

"Thirsty," he mumbled.

She got him some water. He took a cautious sip and rinsed it around in his mouth, then spat it out into the bowl, turning the water inside an even darker red. Then he slowly drank the rest of the water.

"If you can stand up, I'll undress you," she said, but he couldn't. She helped him to lie down and struggled until she had wrestled the rest of his clothing off, then covered his nude body with a sheet. "Sleep," she said. "I'll stay here with you."

She was as good as her word. She held his hand while he slept, and every time she looked at his face her eyes blurred with tears. She knew she had done the right thing, but that didn't make it easy.

She loved him so much, had loved him for years. He thought it was only coincidence that they had both settled in the same area, but she had found out where he was and left her luxurious house in Denver, where she had been the pampered mistress of a very wealthy man, without a backward look.

He had wanted respectability so much. She knew how he had grown up and knew how he had wanted to put all of that behind him. Kyle wasn't a bad man, though he could easily have been, considering what his life had been like. It was just that the ranch and what it represented had come to mean so much to him; he had lost all perspective when it had been threatened, and now he had destroyed the reputation he had worked so hard to build.

But he was alive, and that was all that mattered to her.

It was late that night before he woke again, and she supported him while he used the chamber pot. He asked for more water but didn't want anything to eat. He went back to sleep.

By morning he was more alert, and Tillie fed him some bread softened in milk. When he indicated he didn't want any more she knew she couldn't put if off any longer.

She had learned to face everything in life without flinching, especially the hardest parts, so now she didn't look away from him. "I couldn't let you kill Dee Swann," she said. "People may never forgive you for what you did, but if she had been killed or raped, you'd have hanged. I'm the one who got Lucas Cochran to stop you."

His left eye was swollen completely shut, and his right eye would open only a slit. Carefully he looked up at her, his gaze devoid of anger. He just looked empty. "I had to do it," he said, the words indistinct. "The water . . . but it didn't work. I didn't mean to hurt her. But I lost. I lost it all."

"No," she said fiercely. "You haven't lost it all. You're still alive, and that's what matters most. Even if this ranch turns to dust, you'll be able to start again. Maybe not here, but there are other places. I have money, and you've always been able to win at the card table. We'll get by."

"We?" he asked. His one good eye didn't move from her.

"Yes, we. We make a good team."

Almost imperceptibly he nodded.

17

Lucas stood beside Dee's bed, looking down at her. Despite her fever her face was deathly pale.

"Has she woke up?" he asked Etta, and his voice was harsh.

The doctor's wife gave him a concerned look and shook her head. "But that isn't surprising. She's very sick, and rest is the best thing for her." She dipped a cloth in cool water, wrung it out, and placed it across Dee's forehead. Dee never stirred.

Lucas wearily rubbed his eyes. It had been almost two full days, and she still hadn't so much as opened her eyes or said a word. After losing so much blood how could she have any strength to fight the fever?

Beneath the nightgown Etta had clothed her in Dee's shoulder was covered by a bulky bandage. He suspected that the shoulder wound was the main source of the fever, but Doc said that he'd cleaned it good and that it was no more inflamed than any of the cuts. It was just that all together her wounds had been a tremendous shock to her system. Added to that, she had exhausted herself trying to fight off the Bar B men. Recovery would take time.

But she was so damn still. Even when she had fallen out of the loft she had still been full of spirit despite the fact that she could barely move. Dee was a fighter, but how could she fight when she wasn't conscious? He was so used to her strength and fierceness that this utter helplessness, this complete absence of her fire made him sick with fear.

In his mind she had always been formidable as both foe and lover. It was a shock to look at her now and realize that she was both smaller and more fragile than he'd ever imagined. He'd always thought of her as a tall woman, even though he knew he could look down on the top of her head; it was the impression that she gave, the way she carried herself, the arrogant tilt of her head, her towering pride—all of these combined made him see her as larger than she truly was. She was of only medium height, if that, and her bones were as slender as a child's. He was stunned at how frail she looked.

He was full of rage at what had happened to her, a rage that burned far deeper and hotter than the anger he'd felt when she had fallen out of the loft. None of it would have happened if she lived like other women. On a rational basis he knew that it wasn't her fault, that accidents happened, that she wasn't to blame for Kyle Bellamy's murderous stupidity. But for as long as she lived out at Angel Creek things like this would happen, her fault or not. The land invited greed with its very perfection, and there would always be someone who thought he could take it away from her. And being herself, Dee would always fight rather than try to protect herself by running.

It was the water that made the Angel Creek valley what it was, and water that was the cause of all this.

He stared down at her, lying there as still as death. If he didn't do something to stop it, the next time really might kill her.

He nodded to Etta and strode out, his face set in lines of grim determination.

The root of it all was the water. Without it the valley would lose its value. Dee wouldn't have any reason for clinging to it, and she would have to live a more reasonable way. There wouldn't be a reason for anyone to shoot at her, or for her to work like a man.

He rode back to the Double C and told William to get ten of the men and some shovels and be ready to ride in fifteen minutes. Then he went to the storeroom and got a couple of sticks of dynamite, in case they were needed.

He already knew how the creek forked up in the mountains, sending most of the water down the east side of the range and into the valley. It had been years since he'd been up there, but he could see in his mind just how the creek beds split. With any luck he'd be able to take away the one thing that made Dee's land so valuable.

God, she'd be mad, but there wouldn't be anything she could do about it. Since it would be his fault that the land had lost its value he would give her the same amount he'd already offered her, and she wouldn't have any choice but to take it and move to town. Eventually she would cool down, and then he'd start courting her again, out in the open this time. He figured by Christmas he'd have her talked around to marrying him, because she couldn't deny the fire between them any more than he could. They'd make love and babies and probably fight like two wildcats tangled up in a pillowcase, and they'd enjoy every minute of it.

They found the gap in the mountain where Angel Creek forked and the lower creek bed cut to the east. "Just look at that water," William said, shaking his head. "Straight from the snowcaps."

Lucas walked the bank, examining the fork. Up there it was big enough to be called a river, and it still flowed strong and clear, deep enough that there was some overflow into the fork that ran down onto his property, though it had been greatly reduced. If he could dig the western creek bed lower at the fork, then the water would divert onto the western side of the mountain.

He pulled off his boots and waded out into the western fork, catching his breath at the icy water. He dug his toes into the soft silt and cursed because just under the thin layer of silt was bedrock. He moved up and down the fork and found the same thing. There was no way they were going to dig through rock, and the dynamite fuse wouldn't burn under water.

He waded out again and stood looking at the water, thinking. The only way to blow that bedrock was to dry out the western fork.

He got a shovel and hefted it in his gloved hand. "Start digging," he told the men. "Pile dirt here at the fork and divert all the water to the east."

"Boss, that'll dry up our water completely," William said, looking at him as if he'd lost all of his senses.

"Temporarily," Lucas said. "When it's dry I'm going to blow the bedrock and lower the creek bed."

William turned back to the river and studied it, then a grin spread across his weathered face. "You're gonna turn that water our way."

"I sure am."

"Dee Swann ain't gonna like it worth a damn."

"I'll handle Dee Swann," Lucas said.

It took them three days. They dug up shovelfuls of dirt and packed the west fork, closing it off. The river swung happily eastward, emptying all of its crystal water into the Angel Creek valley. When the west fork was dry Lucas drilled holes in the bedrock and set the dynamite in it, then strung a long fuse and lit it. He and the men ran like hell for as far as they could before the dynamite blew with a thunderous explosion that shook the ground beneath their feet.

The explosion destroyed the earth dam they had built, and the river split once more, water tumbling down both sides of the mountain. The majority of the flow now went down the west side.

"Close off the east fork," he said. "I want a dam packed so solid that not even a trickle goes down the east side of the mountain. We'll seal it off with clay."

The force of the water would erode the dam, and

he'd have to have it repaired regularly, but that would be a small price to pay for peace of mind. At least he'd be able to sleep at night without worrying about Dee's safety.

By late afternoon of the third day the eastern fork was blocked.

Despite his exhaustion he had been riding into town every night to see Dee. Olivia and Etta had been taking turns sitting with her, and the worry etched on Olivia's face made him break out in a cold sweat every time he thought about it. The night before Dee had awakened briefly for the second time, but the fever still hadn't broken. Four days of a high fever had taken a visible toll on her body, wasting away flesh she hadn't needed to lose. She had recognized him, whispered his name. Lucas had held her hand and talked to her, but she had slipped back into sleep almost immediately. Olivia had touched his shoulder in comfort. "She'll be all right," she said, her voice breaking a little. "She has to be."

He was bone tired, but he couldn't let a day go by without seeing her, whether she knew he was there or not. It was as much for himself as for her that he went into town that night. Every time he saw her he was convinced anew that he had done the right thing, the only thing that would protect her. He didn't delude himself that she would take it well when she found out what he'd done, but by God, he'd never again have to see her lying so deathly still.

This time, however, Olivia looked up with a smile when he entered. She held a finger to her lips and motioned him back out of the room, following him and carefully closing the door behind her. "The fever broke," she said, beaming. "She ate a little bit of soup, then went back to sleep."

Relief washed through him like a flood. He was still exhausted, but he felt a hundred pounds lighter, as if lead weights had dropped from his shoulders. "Did she talk?"

"She asked for water, but if you mean did she carry on a conversation, the answer is no. She's still very sick, Lucas, and weak. She won't get over this in a couple of days. Dr. Pendergrass says it will be three or four weeks before she'll be strong enough to look after herself."

He didn't even have to think about it. He knew exactly what he wanted. "I'm taking her to the Double C tomorrow."

Olivia gaped at him. "You can't do that!"

"Yes, I can. It'll be quieter there than it is here, with people going in and out."

"But she's a woman!"

He lifted his eyebrows at her. "Believe me, I noticed."

"But that's why she can't stay with you."

"She almost died. She's sure not in any shape for what you're thinking," Lucas said bluntly, bringing a blush to Olivia's cheeks. "I'll take care of her, get her back on her feet. And I'm not asking permission, Olivia, I'm telling you what I'm going to do."

Olivia took a deep breath and tried again. "You don't have any women out there on that ranch. Who's going to bathe her, change her clothes? I've already talked with Mother about taking her home with me. Surely you can see that she can't possibly go out to the ranch." Her voice softened. "She's my best friend, Lucas. I know how much she means to you. I'll take good care of her, I promise."

He looked at her sharply. "Dee told me you two were friends, but—"

"Best friends," Olivia repeated. "I feel a bit smug because I thought from the beginning that the two of you were perfectly suited for each other."

Lucas cleared his throat. "I think I owe you an apology, Olivia. I know nothing was ever said between us, but I gave you and everyone else the impression that I intended—"

She put her hand on his sleeve. "No apology is needed. I like you very much as a friend, but I never wanted anything more. You didn't either, really. Besides, I'm very much in love with someone else."

"Do tell." He lifted his eyebrows. "Who's the lucky man?"

"Luis Fronteras."

"Hell!" he said in surprise, then he apologized. "Sorry. He's doing all right, isn't he? I've had so much on my mind I haven't asked."

"He's staying at Lindfor's Hotel now. He's almost recovered."

He gave an approving nod; he couldn't fault Olivia's selection, even if Fronteras wasn't the type of man he'd ever thought would appeal to her. A hard look came into his eyes. "Some folks might have something to say about him, whether it's their business or not. I owe him a debt I won't ever be able to repay, so if you need my help in anything, all you have to do is get in touch."

"Thank you, Lucas." She rose up on tiptoe and

kissed his cheek. "I'll remember that. And I'll take good care of Dee for you."

His face changed, his eyes glittering stubbornly. "I know you would, but I haven't changed my mind. I'm taking her with me."

"You have to consider her reputation," Olivia said in exasperation. "People will talk."

His smile was chilling. "If they're smart, they won't."

"Well, they will. You can't take care of her like that."

Her reasoning gave him pause. He'd intended to do those intimate things for Dee himself, but letting the entire town know was something else. He adjusted his plans but didn't change his mind. "I know you'd take care of her, but I want her with me. I'll hire a woman to help. Sid Acray's oldest girl would be glad of the money." Not only did he want Dee close by, but if she was at the ranch he could control who saw her. That way she wouldn't hear about what he'd done to Angel Creek from anyone else but him, when he decided it was a good time to tell her.

Olivia saw from the expression in those hard blue eyes that he wasn't going to be swayed. He wanted Dee Swann on the Double C, and that's where she'd be. Well, she had wished for Lucas and Dee to get together, and she had gotten her wish. Even with Sid Acray's daughter for a chaperon the townfolk would be scandalized if they didn't get married.

She gave him a stern look. "Do you plan on marrying her?"

"Just as soon as I can talk her around. But don't tell

her," he cautioned. "Maybe I can surprise her into saying yes if she hasn't had time to think about it."

They smiled at each other in perfect accord.

Lucas was back the next morning with a buckboard, the wagon bed padded with quilts. Etta Pendergrass was severely aggravated with her husband for not telling Lucas that Dee was too sick to be moved, but he refused to lie just because his wife was shocked by what she considered a scandalous idea. Dee was very ill, but she would recover just as fast at the Double C as she would in town. Besides, he wasn't fool enough to try to stop Lucas Cochran when he'd made up his mind to do something.

Dee was awake when Lucas entered the room, her eyes dull but aware. "Lucas," she whispered.

He wanted to snatch her up and crush her to his chest, but she was so very frail that he restrained himself. Instead he picked up her hand and stroked her fingers. "I'm taking you home with me," he said.

She nodded and managed a little smile. He wrapped her in one of the quilts he had brought and carried her out to the buckboard. A small knot of people gathered on the sidewalk, murmuring among themselves. The Acray girl, Betsy, climbed into the back to watch over Dee on the trip back to the ranch.

Doc Pendergrass, Etta, and Olivia followed him out. "Just make sure she eats and doesn't try to do too much too soon," Doc told him. "She won't feel like getting out of bed for another week or so at least, but rest is the best thing for her."

"Betsy will take good care of her," Lucas said,

mindful of the people listening. He was filled with satisfaction. The circumstances weren't what he would have liked, and there were some bad storms ahead, but for now Dee would be right where he wanted her—under his roof.

He handled the buckboard carefully on the trip to the ranch, taking twice as long as it would to ride it on a horse, but he tried not to jostle Dee in case her shoulder was more painful than he realized. It was nerve-racking trying to see every rough spot in the road, listening for even a change in her breathing. When at last the ranch house came in sight he heaved a relieved sigh.

He reined in the horse at the porch and stepped over the seat into the wagon bed, going down on one knee beside Dee. "Run inside and turn back the covers on the bed," he told Betsy. "Her bedroom is upstairs, the second door on the right."

Betsy jumped down and scurried to do his bidding. She was only seventeen and thoroughly intimidated by Lucas, though he'd tried to put her at ease. But there was something about him that made some women nervous, so he put it out of his mind.

Dee was awake, though there was still that disturbing lack of expression in her eyes. It was as if she saw and understood but just couldn't muster the strength to care about anything. "Tell me if I hurt you," he said as he slid her on the quilts to the edge of the wagon bed so he could lift her without jostling her any more than necessary. He jumped down and gathered her in his arms, holding her close against his chest. He had carried her before and knew how much lighter she was now. His heart gave a big thud as a remnant of fear lashed him. The loss of blood had come so close to killing her that he didn't think he'd ever recover.

Betsy was standing beside the bed when he carried Dee in. He placed his precious burden down and unwrapped her from the quilt, then settled the covers over her. "Do you want anything to eat?" he asked. "Or to drink?"

"Water," she said.

Lucas glanced at Betsy, who scurried to the water pitcher sitting nearby.

"Whatever you want, just tell Betsy," he said, stroking her cheek. "Sleep as much as you want. All you have to do now is get well."

He dropped his hand and turned to leave, but she said, "Lucas," and he turned back.

"The cattle," she whispered. "My garden—"

Even now she was worried about that damn garden! He controlled his spurt of anger to give her the assurance she needed. "They didn't get in it. You stampeded them all the way back to the Bar B."

A slight smile spread over her colorless lips. Betsy brought the glass of water, and he moved so she could support Dee's head and let her sip. By the time Dee signaled that she had had enough and Betsy let her head rest on the pillow again Dee's eyes were closing with fatigue. Lucas quietly left the room.

He would have only a few weeks until she regained her strength and he'd have to tell her about the water. He meant to make the most of his period of grace to strengthen the bonds between them while he could. As soon as she was well enough to do without Betsy she would be all his.

* * *

It was the custom in the Millican family to spend the evening together after dinner, reading or sewing or just talking. Even when Olivia was a little girl she had been included in that intimate time, her parents always making her feel that her childish contributions to the conversation were as important as theirs. After losing their other children Wilson and Honora had doubly appreciated the preciousness of their daughter and had devoted themselves to making her life as perfect as they possibly could. The harmony of those after-dinner hours had always been a part of her life that Olivia loved, and she feared that she was about to ruin it. Luis had offered to be with her when she told them, but she had declined. If there was any unpleasantness, she didn't want him to hear it. It was ridiculous to protect him, but part of her reasoning was based on diplomacy. It would be easier for him to get along with her parents at a later date if there weren't any memories of harsh words between them.

Strangely enough, there didn't seem to be any gossip. Honora and Beatrice had both been discreet about her behavior when she had learned Luis had been hurt. Etta and Dr. Pendergrass had evidently not said anything either about the way she had flown to Luis's bedside. Olivia almost wished there *had* been gossip so she wouldn't have to introduce the subject so abruptly.

There didn't seem to be any other way to do it, however, so she took a deep breath and said, "Mother, Papa, I have something to tell you." Her mother turned to look at her expectantly, and Wilson put his paper down. "I've fallen in love, and I'm going to be married."

Their eyes rounded with surprise, then Honora clapped her hands and jumped up. "That's wonderful," she cried, laughing excitedly. "I just *knew* Mr. Cochran would propose, though I did wonder when—"

"Mother, no," Olivia interrupted. "It isn't Lucas."

Both their faces had been wreathed in smiles, but now their expressions went blank with surprise. "Not Lucas?" Wilson asked with a perplexed frown. "But he's the only one who's been courting you, except for Bellamy, and of course you'd never have anything to do with him. Everyone in town thought—"

"Everyone but the two people involved," Olivia replied gently. "Lucas is a friend, but we've never been in love."

"But if it isn't Mr. Cochran, then who is it?" Honora recovered from her surprise and was fairly quivering with curiosity.

"Luis Fronteras."

Again their faces went blank. Honora sank into her chair. "Who?" she asked in bewilderment. The name was familiar, but she couldn't place it. And it sounded . . . foreign.

"Luis Fronteras. He worked for Mr. Bellamy. He's the man who helped Dee until the Double C men could get there."

"A gunman?" Wilson was incredulous. "You say you're going to marry a Mexican gunman? Olivia, that's ridiculous. Why, you don't even know him."

"A Mexican!" Honora's eyes rounded with shock.

"On the contrary, I know him well." Olivia met their gazes. "I've been riding with him every Sunday. And I love him."

Wilson folded his paper and tossed it aside. "That's impossible. You have absolutely nothing in common with a man like that. Why, he'll never settle down and provide you with a home."

"Perhaps where I live won't be like this," Olivia admitted. "But this isn't an impulsive decision. I've thought about it for a couple of months. I could marry a man who could give me a big house and a lot of clothes, but I wouldn't be one tenth as happy with him as I would be in a tent with Luis. I want to have a family with him, and I trust him to take care of me and our children. What does it matter if he isn't rich?"

"You'll find it matters a great deal when you have to do without." Wilson shook his head. "We've always done our best to shelter you, so you don't have any real idea of the kind of life you're proposing to lead. Darling, you deserve much more than he can give you. You couldn't survive."

"Of course I can. Don't you see, he *loves* me. And I love him. That's what I need, what I've always wanted more than anything else. Not to marry a rich man, but to marry a man I love."

"Absolutely not," Wilson said sternly. "I forbid it. You're just infatuated with him and have no idea what you're talking about. I realize he's a romantic sort of figure, especially after the way he helped Dee, but you need stability to have a good marriage, not a gun sharp who'll always be looking over his shoulder."

"Oh, Papa," Olivia said sadly. "I'm not asking your permission. I love you and Mother very much, and I want you to be at my wedding, but I'll have it whether you're there or not. I know you're concerned for my safety, and everything you've mentioned has made me think, too. But Luis is more than all those things you've said. He's a good, honorable man. Look at the way he risked his own life to help Dee, to use your own example! None of the fine, upstanding citizens in the saloon could find it in their hearts to give help when he asked for it, but you wouldn't be kicking up such a fuss if I wanted to marry any of them. Please don't turn against Luis because he isn't the type of man you've always thought I would marry. He's exactly the type of man who will make me happy, and I want you to be happy for me."

"You want too much." Wilson's face and voice were both stiff. Honora was quietly weeping.

"I'm sorry you feel that way, but it won't change my mind."

18

OLIVIA LAY SLEEPLESS LONG AFTER THE HOUSE WAS silent that night. The grandfather clock downstairs chimed midnight, but she was wide awake. She had hated the scene with her parents, hated their unhappiness, but it hadn't changed her mind. She had never been as certain of anything in her life as she was of Luis.

At first the scraping noise didn't register, as accustomed as she was to the tree limbs outside her window brushing against the glass. Then she realized that the sound was that of her window being raised, and she leapt from the bed with a scream lodged in her throat.

"Don't run," Luis said in a low voice. "It's just me."

"Just you!" Her knees shook, then buckled a little. She grabbed for the bedpost. "Are you trying to frighten me to death? Don't ever do that again!" But

258

even in her fright she kept her voice to a fierce whisper.

He chuckled. "Yes, ma'am. I hope this is the only time I ever have to climb through your bedroom window."

She was much struck by that fact. "Yes, what *are* you doing climbing trees so soon after being shot? What if you opened the wound again?"

"I didn't. It was just a little wound, after all. I feel fine." He put his hand on the back of her head and kissed her. "I couldn't wait until morning to find out if I have to wait a month for a fancy church wedding, or if we can do it a lot faster."

She put her hands on his biceps, drawing strength from the hard warmth of his body. "We can get married as soon as you want," she said, and despite herself there was sadness in her voice.

He kissed her again, his mouth tender. "I'm sorry, darling. I know you wanted them to be happy."

"Yes, I did. But I found that I'm selfish enough to want my own happiness, too." With a little sigh she went into his arms; feeling them fold around her was like coming home. As he gathered her close she abruptly realized how thin the barrier of her night-gown was, allowing her to feel the heavy buckle of his gun belt and the extra cartridges shoved in the little loops, even the buttons on his pants. The last was so evident because of the heavy bulge behind them.

Once she would have been mortified had a man held her so close she could feel his body, but Luis had spent months accustoming her to his touch, teaching her the pleasure of physical love. A thrill went through her at the knowledge that he desired her, and without thought she moved her hips against him.

He slipped one hand down to her buttocks and urged her closer, bending his knees a little to bring them together. She sighed at the adjustment of their bodies.

Luis angled his head to fit his mouth on hers. Now. The time was now. She had made her choice, and he wasn't going to wait even one more night before making her his. Perhaps a gentleman would wait until they were married, but he wasn't a gentleman—he was a man who wanted his woman. The marriage rites were for society; the most basic vows would be sealed with their bodies.

She was no longer frightened by his kisses, or by his hands on her body. She shivered with delight whenever he touched her breasts. He led her through those things he had already taught her, feeling the delicious tension beginning to tighten her muscles. He unbuttoned her nightgown and slid his hand inside to stroke her satiny breasts, and she gave a soft moan as her nipples tightened.

He stepped back and unbuckled his gun belt, letting it drop to a chair. Then he pulled off his shirt.

Olivia moved to him, fascinated by the faint gleam of light on his smooth skin. It was too dark to see his expression, but she discovered that she didn't need light; she knew him, knew his wide shoulders and hard chest, his muscular abdomen. The bandage at his waist was a small splotch of white, and seeing it made her ache anew. She kissed him, brushing her lips across his chest to find his little nipples. "I love you," she whispered, her breath warm on his skin.

He tilted her head up and settled his mouth on hers, his tongue slowly entering and teasing. His hands swept across her shoulders, and the nightgown dropped to her waist, held up by the curve of her hips. Before she could do more than draw a quick breath he pushed it past her buttocks, and it dropped to the floor around her feet.

She stood frozen, her frightened eyes lifting to his face, and now she wished that she had light so she could see him. No, she didn't. She was naked, and if she could see him, he could also see her. She realized that he could see her very well, the paleness of her skin visible even in the darkness.

Her bareness was shocking. Her hands fluttered downward to shield her sex, and with inexorable gentleness he caught her wrists and moved her hands to her sides. "Have I ever hurt you?" he asked with his lips at her temple.

She began to tremble. "No," she whispered.

"I'm going to make love to you tonight. You're going to be completely mine. Do you know what's going to happen?"

She tried to think, tried to prod her stunned mind into coherency. "I . . . not really."

"Have you ever seen animals mating?"

"N-no. I mean yes. I saw a pair of dogs once." And she had been painfully fascinated before the impropriety of what she'd been doing had occurred to her, and she had rushed away in embarrassment.

Luis smiled against her hair. His innocent darling. "The concept is roughly the same," he said, soothing her with light caresses on her back and hips. "You've felt how I get hard when I'm with you. To make love I put my shaft inside you, here." And he moved his stroking hand to the front of her tightly clenched thighs, sliding one finger into the soft folds.

She jerked wildly, and he caught her to him with one strong arm. "Stop that," she moaned. "You mustn't." Her trembling had increased, and she felt weak, the muscles in her legs shaking and threatening to go limp. She couldn't believe that he was touching her between her legs, or that it was causing a violent firestorm to race along her nerves. She felt unbearably heated, her skin so sensitive that his touch almost made her cry out. Only the dim knowledge that she had to be quiet kept her from screaming aloud at this painful ecstasy. He had aroused her before, given her pleasure that had left her aching for more, but nothing had been like this. It was as if before he had given her only water to taste, and now he was giving her full-bodied wine. There was simply no comparison.

"Let's lie down, love," he coaxed, kissing her again. She stood rigid, and he persuasively rubbed his finger on the tiny nub between her legs, keeping his touch feather-light because she was so new to it all. She trembled again, and he felt the strength go out of her legs. He lifted her onto the bed and quickly removed his boots and pants. His entire body was aching with anticipation as he lay down with her.

She felt dazed by what was happening. He was seducing her, and she was helpless to stop it. She didn't want to stop it. But she felt as if she were on a runaway train that was going faster and faster, totally out of control, and she couldn't jump off.

She felt his hard length jutting against her hip, and

without thought she reached down to move it. As soon as her fingers closed around that alien flesh she jerked her hand away. Luis moaned, his hips arching a little. "Touch me," he murmured roughly, his breath coming fast. "Please. I've wanted to feel you holding me—"

She hesitated, for it seemed impossibly bold and wicked. But so had everything else he had taught her, and she loved it all. Shyly she folded her fingers around him again, and in the next moment she was fascinated by the feel of him, hardness covered by silky smooth skin. She felt the first faint edging of fear, for she didn't see how he could possibly enter her as he had said.

He moved over her, levering her thighs apart with his.

It took all of her self-control to lie still. Her hands twisted in the sheet.

He sensed her distress and soothed it with low whispers of reassurance and kisses that lingered. He fondled her breasts and kissed them, and soon the tension eased out of her muscles. Her legs relaxed so that they were no longer clamped on his. His talented fingers searched out the softness between her thighs, and the petals opened like a flower blooming. She made a soft sound, and her head rolled on the pillow.

He stroked her to passion, entering her with his fingers while using his thumb to keep her aroused. She arched and twisted, her body instinctively seeking his. He rubbed her to the very edge of completion, then removed his hand and guided his manhood to her opening.

Again she went still, though her chest was heaving. He leaned closer, letting her cradle his weight. The force of it pushed him a little way into her.

She closed her eyes, her entire body trying to draw back from him. He was inside her just enough for pain to threaten, and what she felt warned her that it would be true pain, not just discomfort. "It hurts," she whispered.

"I know, darling. But it's just this first time."

She lay beneath him, feeling the pressure as he eased deeper into her. She could feel her inner channel opening and painfully stretching to admit him. She felt a deeper stretching, and he was hurting her, the pain hot as her maidenhead tore to let him forge deep into her body.

He held himself still to let the pain abate. His shoulder was wet with her tears, and he set about soothing her even though his manhood was throbbing painfully. The soft clasp of her inner muscles was maddening, luring him toward a satisfaction he couldn't let himself have just yet.

The only true way to soothe her was to take her to the peak he denied himself, to show her the ultimate pleasure that was the reward for enduring this initial pain. His own climax would have to wait, for nothing was so important as giving her ease. He slipped his hand between their bodies and found her soft nub again, coaxing it from its protective folds with a whisper-light touch, luring Olivia back into passion. He pleasured her with hard-won patience, not trying to take her swiftly to climax but instead letting the pleasure build so that she felt first a gentle relaxing of her muscles, then the slow return of arousal. Only when her hips began to lift against his hand and initiate the movements of lovemaking did he increase the pressure and speed of his stroking fingers.

Olivia had been bitterly disappointed by the pain of his penetration even though Dee had said that the first time hurt. All of her previous lessons in sensuality had been full of heated pleasure, and despite her fear she had trusted him to make this final surrender as completely enjoyable as all the rest of it. Instead there had been pain, and the harsh shock of having her body invaded. But his experienced touch was bringing back pleasure so fast and so strong that it swept over her in waves. She surged beneath him, trying to take him deeper into her because somehow that had become part of the ecstasy; she locked her legs around his and writhed in increasing passion. Luis groaned aloud at the movement of her body on his length, trying to hold back, trying not to thrust hard and deep when every fiber in him needed to.

She cried out, and he put his hand over her mouth. She stiffened and shuddered, and he felt the soft internal shivers that heralded the onslaught of her peak. He couldn't stop himself then; he began to thrust, and in only a few seconds he followed her into mindless pleasure. The force of it emptied him and left him unable to move, sprawled heavily on top of her.

She moved her hand slowly down his back, luxuriating in the feel of his strong muscles. She felt dazed and dreamy. So there was pleasure after all, a pleasure so intense that she had thought she might die of it. She didn't regret that he hadn't waited until they were married, only that he hadn't completely seduced her before. This new intimacy was overwhelming in both the pleasure it afforded and the bond it had forged. She felt more utterly his than she had ever thought she would feel with a man, and more possessive of him than she had known was possible. She loved him, but this bond of their bodies was more primeval than that.

After a long while he stirred, lifting himself from her body. "I have to go," he said sleepily, "or I'll still be here in the morning, and that would have your father looking for a shotgun. I'll come for you at about ten. Will that give you time to pack?"

So it would be that soon. He had claimed her and saw no reason to wait even a couple of days for their marriage.

"Yes," she said, and she kissed him. "Where will we stay? Or will we be leaving town immediately?"

He didn't hear any hesitation in her voice, only curiosity. She truly didn't care where they stayed. Suddenly he felt like laughing out loud, exulting in the fate that had given her to him. "We'll stay in the hotel for a while until we decide what to do."

"So I won't need to pack all of my clothes right now?"

He grinned. "Well, I guess I can safely say that you won't need any nightgowns."

No, she wouldn't. She smiled as she watched him dress. She would have Luis to keep her warm. It was the most delicious future she had ever imagined.

She was calm when she went downstairs to breakfast the next morning. "Luis is coming for me at ten," she said. "We'll be married this afternoon."

Tears welled in Honora's eyes, and she hastily

blotted them away. "There's no need to be so hasty, dear. Won't you think this over for a little while longer?"

Olivia put her arms around her mother. "I have thought it over. I love him, and that isn't going to change. The only reason to wait would be if you and Papa wanted to give me a wedding."

Wilson sighed heavily and got up from the table. "You can't expect us to celebrate your marriage to a man like Fronteras."

"I wish you would, but no, I didn't expect it."

He bent his head, staring unhappily at the floor. Most of his objection was based on how unsuitable Fronteras was for Olivia, but part of it was an unwillingness to lose his daughter. He would have missed her at any time, but the parting would have been easier if he had been assured he was giving her safekeeping into reliable hands. Olivia deserved better than a life of insecurity.

She had always been the perfect daughter, adorable as a child, sweet and loving. She had never shown any wildness, had instead been precociously responsible and levelheaded. He knew doting parents never thought anyone good enough for their children, but it was painfully obvious that Olivia was marrying far beneath herself.

She was his only child, the light of his life. She would inherit his money. Was that why Fronteras was marrying her? Did he expect to be supported by his father-in-law? Olivia certainly deserved better than that. But she tended to see the best in people, and it wouldn't occur to her to be suspicious of Fronteras's motives. Wilson hadn't accumulated his wealth by being a fool. He knew a lot of men who had married because of money; he didn't want that to happen to Olivia.

He hadn't wanted to meet the man at all, but now he decided to delay his departure to the bank; he had a few things he wanted to say to Luis Fronteras.

Luis arrived promptly at ten, driving a buggy he had rented from the livery stable. Olivia, watching eagerly for him, felt her heart swell when she saw that he hadn't made any effort to impress; he wore his customary pants and shirt, a bandanna knotted at his neck, his gun belt buckled low on his lean waist and tied to his thigh. He looked exactly like what he was, and she loved him for not trying to put on a false front. Luis didn't need to impress anyone.

She opened the door and stood waiting for him, her face radiant with happiness. Luis smiled as he walked toward her, his dark eyes alight. The memory of their lovemaking shimmered between them, and Olivia's breath caught.

"I'm ready," she said, indicating the two cases behind her.

As Luis bent to pick them up Wilson opened the door of his study and cleared his throat. "I'd like to speak to you, if I may."

Honora came down the stairs, wringing her hands at the sight of the cases. Her eyes were red-rimmed.

Luis straightened, his dark face calm. "Of course."

Wilson stood aside and indicated his study. "In private."

"Papa," Olivia said, her tone alarmed.

"Hush. This is between us."

ANGEL CREEK

"No, it isn't!" she cried, stepping forward. "I'm involved, too."

Luis touched her arm, smiling down at her. "It'll be all right," he softly assured her. Then he walked into the study, and Wilson closed the door behind them.

He turned to face the banker. Perhaps Olivia had expected to leave without this confrontation, but Luis had known better. The man was concerned about his daughter; hell, Luis wouldn't have thought much of him if he hadn't been. If he could settle any worries, he was willing to try—it would make Olivia happier, and he would do anything to accomplish that.

Wilson drew himself up. "I'll give you five thousand dollars to leave here and never see my daughter again."

Luis's eyes narrowed, and a dangerous gleam entered them. "No" was all he said.

"If you think that marriage to my daughter will make you rich—"

"Stop right there. Don't even say it." His dark eyes were cold with anger. "I'm marrying Olivia because I love her. If you're worried about your money, then keep it. I don't want it or need it." Without another word he walked past the banker and left the room.

The sight of his face made Olivia's heart skip a beat, and she rushed to him, catching his arms in a grip so tight her nails dug into his flesh. "Luis?" she whispered, frightened.

His expression softened as he looked down at her. "Don't worry," he said. "We can leave now."

Behind them they could hear the study door open again. Honora took a quick step forward as if she

269

could keep them from walking out the door. Then she stopped, her anguished gaze locked on the man who was taking her beloved daughter away. Luis glanced up at her, his usual warmth toward women entering his eyes. He could understand Honora's distress and would willingly have done anything he could to alleviate it, except for leaving Olivia behind.

He crossed to the stairs and took Honora's hand. "I promise you I'll take good care of her," he said.

Even through her pain Honora responded to him, her fingers tightening around his; she clung to him as if for comfort. "But where will you live?" she wailed.

He shrugged. "Wherever Olivia wants," he said simply. "But wherever we are, I promise we'll bring the grandbabies to see you once a year, without fail."

Grandbabies! Honora's mouth opened and closed without making a sound. Her chest swelled with emotion. Grandbabies! Her own beloved Olivia's children.

And this man loved Olivia, truly loved her. Honora had been so worried, but now she could see it in those deep eyes. Well, of course, she thought suddenly. How could anyone not love Olivia? He might not be a stalwart pillar of the community, but he was a strong man, and sometimes that was better security than an uneventful life. More than anything she wanted Olivia to be happy, and, looking at this man, she was suddenly certain that he would make that happen.

"Do you think you could wait for me to arrange a wedding?" she asked.

"Honora!" Wilson said, shocked.

Luis gave her a devilish grin, one that made Honora's heart beat a little faster. "I'd rather not," he said. "But I'd be honored if you would stand up with us this afternoon."

"I . . . why, yes," she said, flustered. She gave Wilson a beseeching look. "Of course we'll be there. I wouldn't miss Olivia's wedding for anything."

"Honora!" Wilson said again.

She turned toward her husband. She seldom gainsaid him in anything, but what did men know about other men? It took a woman to know what another woman needed. "Don't 'Honora' me! Can't you see that he loves her?"

"Of course he does," Olivia said confidently. She smiled at her parents, her eyes shiny with tears. "What more could you want for me?"

Only the moon, Wilson thought, his chest painfully tight. But more than anything he didn't want to lose his beloved daughter, didn't want her to feel unwelcome in his home. Olivia had always been levelheaded, so why didn't he trust her judgment? It looked like the only thing he *could* do. His own eyes felt suspiciously moist, and he cleared his throat. "You're right. You have what's important. We'll be at your wedding, darling. Like your mother said, we wouldn't miss it for anything."

He and Luis shook hands, and though the look he gave Luis was hard, there was understanding between them. Honora began crying again, but this time her tears were much happier. Though she would miss Olivia dreadfully, she had always looked forward to this day.

And, of course, she always cried at weddings.

19

DEE GOT CAREFULLY OUT OF BED AND WALKED TO THE window. Sometimes she felt a dreadful sense of unreality and needed that view to reinforce in her mind where she was. There was a large block of time she couldn't remember; her last vivid memory was of crouching on the floor of the cabin and holding the rifle to her shoulder. After that there were only snippets of impressions until about a week ago, when she had awakened one morning and felt truly awake, though horribly weak, and the contrast between her last memory and her present situation was so sharp as to make her feel lost.

She hadn't asked questions, so she still didn't know exactly what had happened. She needed to know, but the need wasn't urgent. She would find out later, when she felt stronger. It was as if the immense weakness of her body had sapped her mind's energy, too; she didn't want to talk, didn't want company, she wanted only to sleep. She emerged briefly from the cocoon of sleep whenever the demands of her body grew too great, and as soon as the problem was solved—be it thirst or hunger or a need for the chamber pot—she drifted off to sleep again.

The periods of sleep were growing shorter, however, and for a few days she had been moving around the room with Betsy Acray's support. This was the first time she had gotten out of bed by herself, and though her legs were wobbly she was pleased that they supported her. It was a small milestone. If she had been presented with the task of walking down the stairs, she couldn't have done it, but as she felt not the slightest desire to go downstairs she didn't care.

She was in Lucas's house. She wasn't certain how she had come to be there. He visited her at least twice a day, in the morning and again at night. When he asked her a question she made an effort to answer, but the effort was apparent, and the answers were monosyllabic, so he didn't try to carry on a conversation. Sometimes when he looked at her she could see volcanic rage in his eyes and she wondered what was wrong, but the rage didn't seem to be directed at her, so she didn't feel it was worth the effort to find out.

It was the first time she had ever seen the Double C, and the contrast between the way Lucas lived and her own home was sharp. She had seen only this one room, but as it was a guest room the rest of the house was probably even grander. The bed was an immense four-poster, the linen sheets so smooth they felt like silk. The wood floor had been sanded to a satin finish and then polished, and a thick rug covered it to cushion her feet. There was an enormous wardrobe, a chaise longue upholstered in silk, a graceful cherrywood desk and chair, and a mirrored dressing table with a small bench. A big, comfortably upholstered chair had also been brought in for Betsy.

She had never felt inferior before, but Lucas's house made her feel that way. He would be at ease with women who wore silk dresses and perfume and jewels, while she milked cows and plowed and got dirt under her nails. He must have wanted Angel Creek very much to have been willing to marry her to get it. What would he have done after the wedding? Bought her a house in some city and sent her away so she wouldn't embarrass him?

She felt ashamed of herself for even thinking that. Lucas had been kind, taking her into his home while she recovered. He had never said or done anything that indicated he thought he was better than she; it was her own depression that brought the thoughts to mind. But seeing the Double C—as much of it as she could see from her window—and this room had made her realize how wide the gulf was between them.

"Oh!" Betsy said sharply from the doorway. "Miss Dee, you got up by yourself!"

Dee turned from the window. Betsy was carrying a tray with her noon meal, which meant that she had slept several hours after eating a few bites for breakfast.

"I'm going to get fat," she mused. "All I'm doing is sleeping and eating."

It was the first unnecessary thing she had said in the time Betsy had been taking care of her, and the girl threw Dee a startled glance as she hurried to deposit the tray on the desk and lend a supporting arm. "Miss Dee, you need to eat all you can. You're as thin as a stick."

Well, that was comforting, Dee thought wryly. Betsy was leading her toward the bed, and she rebelled. The bed was wonderful for sleep, but she had had enough of both sleep and that bed.

"I want to sit up and eat," she said. "The desk will do just fine."

Betsy looked worried, but Dee refused all attempts to change her mind. By the time they had crossed the room to the desk she felt as if she had run ten miles; her legs were trembling as she sank down onto the chair. Still, it was an accomplishment, and she would have to push herself if she ever expected to regain her strength.

Her meal was simple, a bowl of broth and a biscuit. She wondered why people thought that starving a sick person would help her get well. She was even more disgusted when she realized she couldn't eat all of it.

Still, it was time to make a change. "Who does the cooking here?"

Betsy still hadn't adjusted to a patient who was talking after two weeks of almost total silence. Her eyes were huge as she said, "His name's Orris, ma'am."

"Tell Orris that I appreciate his trouble, and that for dinner tonight I'd like to try just a little meat and potatoes in the broth. I won't be able to eat much, but it's time to start trying."

"Yes, ma'am," Betsy said.

"And are there any books in the house?"

"I don't know, ma'am. I ain't looked around." She had been too terrified of Mr. Cochran to risk his ire if he'd found her snooping around his house.

"Well, ask Orris or someone else. I'd like to have something to read, and I don't care what it is."

"Yes, ma'am."

"Are any of my clothes here?"

"No, ma'am."

"Then tell Lucas to get them. I'm tired of nightgowns."

Betsy's eyes rounded with horror at the thought of telling Mr. Cochran to do anything. Dee said, "Never mind. I'll probably see him as soon as you will, so I'll tell him myself."

Betsy slumped with relief. "Yes, ma'am." It had been a lot easier when Miss Dee hadn't done anything but sleep.

Dee's brief foray had exhausted her, but at least she still felt awake. She would have liked to continue sitting in the chair, but common sense told her it would be best to go back to bed before she toppled over. As she settled back down she looked toward the window. The sun was bright and hot, and she needed that brightness. After the dark weeks the sun told her that she was well and truly on the mend.

When Lucas came in to see her that night his eyes glittered with satisfaction. "I heard you've been sitting in the chair today."

She put aside the book she'd been reading. It was dull, but better than looking at the walls. She went straight to her request. "I need some of my own clothes. Would you get them from the cabin, or send someone else for them?"

He sat down in the chair and stretched his long legs out, crossing them at the ankle. "There's plenty of time for that."

She gave him a long warning look. "I don't intend to do anything more than sit in this room. I'm just sick of nightclothes. I can sit in regular clothes as well as I can sit in this." She tugged at the nightgown's long sleeve.

"Why go to all of the effort to change clothes when you're still spending so much time in bed?"

"Are you going to get the clothes or not?"

"No."

"Then get out and leave me alone," she snapped.

He threw back his head with a roar of laughter. Relief poured through him like sweet water, as delicious as when her fever had broken. These two weeks of withdrawn silence had been pure torment, because the frail woman lying so quietly in bed hadn't been the Dee he knew. This was his Dee, tart and headstrong, and he was going to love every minute of the next few weeks, with her totally in his control.

He got up and leaned over her, bracing his hands on either side of her hips. "You can't make me," he said. His eyes were alight with mirth.

Those green eyes narrowed dangerously. "Not right now, no."

"Not ever. When I've cared to fight with you I've won every time. No matter how much you dislike it, I'm stronger than you. And this is my land; what I say goes. You'll get your clothes only when I think you're strong enough to need them."

"I won't ever get that strong," she said sweetly, "if I don't eat."

He straightened with a scowl. She was herself again,

all right. She was just contrary enough to refuse to eat, and her health was too precarious for that.

"All right," he growled. "I'll get your damn clothes. But I want your word that you won't try to go downstairs by yourself."

She gave him an impatient look. "I've already said I didn't intend to leave this room. I'm not stupid. The only way I could get down the stairs would be if I fell down them."

"That's exactly what worries me."

"Then you're worrying for nothing."

He glared at her, aware that she hadn't exactly promised anything, but equally aware that if he pushed her she would only get more obstinate, and they would end up in a battle of wills. If she showed good sense in what she tried to do, he'd let her set her own pace, and the only way to find out was to let her do it.

"What kind of shape is the cabin in?" she asked.

He wished she hadn't asked until she was stronger, but there was no use in trying to evade the question. "All of the windows are broken, the back door is splintered, a lot of things inside were shattered or are full of holes."

Her lips tightened. "The bastards. Have you checked to make certain Bellamy didn't run his cattle back in there?"

"He hasn't," Lucas said with certainty. There wouldn't be any point in it now, with Angel Creek dry, but Dee didn't have to know that yet. He wasn't going to tell her until he had to; he intended to use the next weeks to spoil her rotten and bind her to him.

"Will you check on it for me?"

The anxiety in her voice made him feel guilty. He leaned down and kissed her forehead. "Of course."

He was so delighted that she was talking again that he was reluctant to leave her. He sat on the bed, talking and teasing, trying to make her eyes flash angrily again, until Betsy came in and gave him a shocked look. He sighed, chafing under the necessity of observing at least a semblance of propriety. He'd be glad when Dee was well enough to do without Betsy so he could send the girl home.

Dee set herself to recovering her strength, carefully pushing herself more and more every day. Lucas brought her some of her own clothes the next day, and though they looked out of place in the luxury of the bedroom she felt relieved to be wearing something other than a nightgown. It made her feel she was truly on the road to recovery. She hadn't lied to Lucas about her intentions; she kept to her room, slowly walking back and forth, forcing herself to stay up for longer periods each time. As she became more active her appetite returned, and her face no longer looked so pale and drawn.

Lucas began to devote more time to keeping her entertained, knowing that boredom would drive her to test her limits faster than anything else. He brought a big selection of books upstairs for her, and at night he taught her how to play poker. To his delight she already knew how to play chess, no doubt one of the benefits of having a schoolteacher for a mother. Playing with her kept him alert. Her philosophy in chess was the same as it was in life: She was aggressive and determined. The trouble was, he could never predict which battles she would choose to fight or when she would simply use defensive strategies. They were so evenly matched that more often than not the games ended in a draw.

She had been at the Double C for three weeks when she descended the stairs for the first time, to eat a real meal at a real table. Lucas kept his arm firmly around her and his attention focused on each step, ready to catch her if she should falter. She gave him a cool look that said she wouldn't let herself be so weak and walked steadily to the table with her head held as arrogantly as any ancient queen's.

The occasion signaled that Betsy's usefulness had come to an end, and he wasn't sorry to see it. He suspected that she hadn't been much use the past week anyway, that Dee had been riding roughshod over her. Little Betsy was helpless against Dee's iron determination, and ridiculously worshipful. Every time she opened her mouth it was "yes, ma'am" until the two words ran together into one. If she decided to emulate her new heroine when she returned home, poor old Sid Acray would have the devil's own time controlling his newly headstrong daughter.

So Betsy was sent home the next morning, with Lucas's sincere gratitude for her help and generous wages in her purse. She cried as she hugged Dee and left with tearful admonitions to "be careful!" wafting back to them.

Lucas chuckled as he watched the buckboard disappear down the lane with Betsy still waving. Then he turned to take Dee's arm and walk with her back into the house. "Well, sweetheart, you're on your own today, so try not to get into any trouble. Orris is in the kitchen if you need any help, and I'll be back this afternoon."

She sighed. "I have to admit I've been looking forward to the solitude. I'm not used to having someone hover over me twenty-four hours a day."

He looked down at her and smiled as he felt the familiar tug of desire in his groin. Tonight he was going to do something about it. She still looked so frail that a good puff of wind would knock her off her feet, but she was stronger than she looked. She was regaining her weight, and translucent color glowed in her cheeks and lips. He had searched through his mother's old clothes and found a few light day dresses that were so plain they hadn't had any particular fashion to date them; Betsy, who had proved able with a needle, had hemmed and tucked until the dresses fit Dee, who was wearing one of them today. The flimsy, pale yellow lawn cloth suited her, as did the way she had caught her heavy tresses high on the back of her head, baring the delicate nape of her neck. As soon as they were inside he bent and pressed his mouth to that innocently sensuous groove, and he felt the shiver that ran through her.

Her clothes weren't all he'd fetched from the cabin. The little sponges lay in a box in his bedroom.

Dee felt his arms close around her and caught her breath in painful relief. She hadn't realized how much she had missed being held, how alone she had felt. She had quickly become accustomed to his touch, to feeling his hard body warm against her, and the lack of physical contact had depressed her. He hadn't even held her or kissed her during all the time she had been at his ranch except for passionless pecks on the forehead, and she hadn't cared for those at all. Lucas's nature wasn't passionless, and neither was hers.

She turned into his embrace, letting her head rest in the hollow of his shoulder. "Tired?" he asked, rubbing his hand over her back.

"I'm always tired. I just try to ignore it."

He lifted her in his arms and carried her upstairs, where he deposited her on the chaise longue and arranged a pillow behind her head. "Don't ignore it. Rest when you need to. You'll get your strength back faster that way."

"I don't have a lot of time," she said. "It's been a month. The garden will be overgrown with weeds, and everything will be getting ripe in a week or so. I *have* to get strong enough to work."

He stroked her cheek, then let his hand drift downward until it covered her breast. "Get strong enough for this first," he said.

Her heavy black lashes drooped. "You can do all of the work."

"I intend to." He leaned forward and kissed her, his mouth slow and hot, his hand heavy on her breast as he leisurely kneaded her. "But I'd like for you to be awake."

She laughed, then sighed at the deliciousness of his touch. "I think I can manage that."

He left her with a wink, and she closed her eyes, letting herself drift. With the night to look forward to, she had no intention of exhausting herself during the day.

* * *

Lucas rode over the pass to Angel Creek that day. His own land had revived with the rush of water, renewing enough of the grazing so that the cattle would survive; they were leaner than he liked, but they were not starving to death or dropping dead from dehydration. The change in Dee's valley was painful. It was still green, but the vegetation was brittle. The sight of her cabin made his jaw clench. It had been such a tidy, sturdy little place, and now it was almost destroyed. The walls and roof still stood, but the wreckage of the windows and the contents testified to the amount of firepower that had been directed at her. It was a miracle that she had survived. If she had been any less of a woman, she wouldn't have. It was as simple as that. She had seen to her own survival by teaching herself how to shoot, and by being smart enough to stay behind cover.

He walked out back to the garden and stood looking at it for a long time. The plants that had been so lush and promised such a rich bounty of crops had shriveled in the dry heat. Dee had worked so hard, and it had come to nothing, by his own hand. The creek bed was completely dry, and the valley was strangely silent. It had been perfect, and he had deliberately destroyed it. He would do it again, for it was the only way he could force Dee into a safer life. That didn't mean he didn't regret the change. Angel Creek had been special. Now it was nothing.

He had had Dee's livestock taken to the Double C, except for the chickens, which could survive on their own. They had already disappeared, lured out of the valley in search of insects and water. The valley was abandoned, and the cabin showed signs that squirrels and other small critters had begun nesting inside. He looked in the barn and found spare lumber and nails, so he boarded up all the windows and reset the back door in its frame. Dee would be upset enough without finding the cabin taken over by animals.

The valley bothered him. He was glad to get back to the ranch, which was alive and busy.

20

L<small>UCAS CAME INTO HER BEDROOM THAT NIGHT AS SHE</small>
was brushing out her hair. He took the brush from her
hand and pulled it through the long strands, easing
out the tangles until it streamed down her back like
black silk.

She watched him in the mirror, her heartbeat
settling into a heavy thud. He was shirtless, and the
muscles in his torso flexed with every movement. He
was so intensely masculine that even performing that
very feminine chore for her didn't detract from his
virility, but then only a man as self-confident as Lucas
would have been so completely comfortable performing it anyway.

She wore the filmy pink gown he had brought her
when she had fallen out of the loft. The thin straps
barely hung on her shoulders, and the low-cut bodice
lay loosely on her breasts, inviting a man's hand to

slip inside. The fabric was just transparent enough to torment with what it didn't reveal, though she knew her nipples were plainly visible through the cloth.

Lucas's attention was focused on the mirror, and she watched the way his face changed, hardened, as he looked at her breasts. "It's been a long time," he murmured. Though the time could be measured in weeks, it had still been too long. He was beginning to think that even a day without her would be too long. He put the brush down and placed his hands on her shoulders, his rough fingers gliding over her smooth skin. He paused as he felt her thinness, the frailty of her collarbones.

Dee knew what he was thinking and let her head drop back against his abdomen. Their eyes met in the mirror. "This is the second time you've taken care of me," she said.

"And I hope the last."

She smiled, remembering how difficult it had been for her to accept his help that first time. But she had learned that she could trust his strength, and that had made this time of convalescence easier. If it had been anyone but Lucas caring for her, she would have forced herself to return to Angel Creek long before she was well enough. But he had said he would look after it for her, and she trusted him with her life as well as her valley.

She caught his hands and carried them to her breasts, closing her eyes in pleasure at the contact. "I won't break," she said huskily.

He picked her up and sat down in the big uphol-stered chair with her on his lap, her legs draped over the chair arm and her back supported by his left arm.

"I don't have much control," he admitted, his voice a little thick. "If I lie down with you, I won't have any."

"Do you need it?" she asked. She gave him a slow smile. "You could always make it up to me an hour from now."

He laughed roughly. "I'm trying not to tire you out too much. I'm not going to make love to you all night long."

"Pity," she said.

"Yes, isn't it?" Slowly he brushed his mouth against hers, lightly touching his tongue to her lips. She slid her hand around his neck and moved closer, firming the contact. He obliged, slanting his head and deepening the pressure, gliding his tongue inward to meet hers. It had been so long that the onslaught of sensation was a little overwhelming, a little frightening, as if it were all new again.

Knowing that she was his, that he had the complete freedom of her body, went to his head faster than whiskey. He had meant to take his time, but the thin silk barrier over her breasts was intolerable, and he pulled the straps down her arms with two quick movements. She gasped a little as the bodice drooped to her waist, then she freed her arms from the straps and leaned back against his arm, offering him unobstructed sight and touch. He took advantage of both, cupping a soft mound in his palm and lifting it slightly as his thumb rasped over the nipple, making it tighten and stand erect. He pinched it lightly, enjoying the firm resilience.

"Lucas."

"What?" The word was absently spoken.

"I don't need a lot of attention."

He looked up and noticed the color in her cheeks, the way her breathing had hastened. "It's been a long time for me, too," she said, strain evident in her voice.

He held her gaze and slid his hand up her thigh, pushing the gown high and baring her legs. When he reached the notch between her legs he expertly slipped his fingers in, sliding them along the soft folds. Dee's body jerked, and she let her legs fall open. "Don't close your eyes," he whispered when he saw her lashes start to droop. "Keep them open. Look at me."

She blinked, trying to focus, but her expression was dazed. He touched her soft opening and lightly circled it with his fingertips. She couldn't help it; her head fell back over his arm as her entire body tightened, the heated sensation coiling through her. He let her lie back with her head dangling backwards and removed the support of his left arm, leaving her lying across his lap like a sacrifice.

She felt helpless lying like that, totally at his mercy. She was bare except for the nightgown twisted around her waist, and totally boneless, unable to sit up even if she had wanted to. He pushed her legs further apart, and cool air washed over her sensitive flesh, telling her how exposed she was to his gaze. She heard a low, throbbing moan and knew it was hers.

"Are you ready for me?" he whispered, and he slid one big finger into her.

She arched and cried out, the hot tension radiating from her loins in waves. He moved his finger in and out, stimulating her almost beyond sanity, making her writhe on his lap in helpless, mounting ecstasy.

She was like fire, out of control and rapidly escalating toward climax. "Not yet," he said urgently, sitting her up and turning her so that she faced him, sitting astride his lap with her legs spread. He tore at the buttons of his pants. "Not yet. I want to be inside you, sweetheart, I want to feel you come."

"Hurry," she moaned, her hips undulating in search of the hot pleasure he had taught her.

He grunted as he freed his swollen organ and held it braced for her, his other hand on her buttocks bringing her forward, sliding her onto his shaft. She almost screamed at his hard, fierce heat penetrating deep into her. His big hands closed on her hips, and he moved her up, down, up again. The second downward stroke was all she required, and she was lost, submerged in the shimmering wave of sensation that caught her and tossed her in its upheaval, sending her inner sheath into spasms and making her soft muscles clamp down on him. He threw back his head with a harsh groan, fighting his response, but it was too late for him, too. He heaved upward, his fingers bit into the soft flesh of her hips as he ground her down onto his manhood, penetrating as deep into her as he could go, and his hot seed erupted with a force that convulsed him.

They calmed slowly, small aftershocks of sensation erupting along their nerve endings and prolonging the pleasure. Fatigue settled on Dee like a heavy blanket, and she slumped forward, her face buried against his throat, unable to move.

Lucas held her cradled in his arms. He felt pretty damn weak himself. He rubbed her back, luxuriating in the aftermath of release. "Dee? Honey, are you all right?"

She made a noise, but nothing that resembled words.

He gripped her arms, holding her back a little from his chest. She was utterly boneless. "Dee? Damn it, answer me."

"Leave me alone," she mumbled.

He eased her back down onto his chest, stroking her hair away from her face. "Do you want to go to bed now?"

"Mmm."

He smiled and closed his eyes. God, it felt good to hold her, to feel her safe and warm in his arms. It felt good to thrust into her and let go of his control, to feel the deep linking.

He shifted her in his arms so she was lying sideways again and awkwardly pulled up his pants with one hand while he supported her with the other. She looked blissfully asleep and didn't stir even when he got to his feet. He placed her on the bed, removed the nightgown, shed his own clothing, put out the lamp, and got into bed beside her. He settled her against him, feeling the contentment now that she was where she belonged. If he had his way, she'd never spend another night away from him.

He normally woke before dawn, and the next day was no exception. He was achingly hard. Dee stirred against him, and he mounted her, sliding into her with a total lack of haste.

This time it was slow, almost leisurely. She responded drowsily, and he tried not to make any great demands on her. The demands of her own body, however, eventually dispelled her lassitude, and she began moving under him with increasing urgency. The morning sun, already hot, was rising over the mountains by the time they relaxed, mutually replete.

Realization of what he had done hit him like a poleax. He propped himself up on his elbow, his hand going to her belly. "Damn it, we didn't use the sponges."

Her eyes opened, and they looked at each other in silence. He didn't say, "If you get pregnant, we'll get married," because she didn't respond well to ultimatums, and that's essentially what the statement would be. What he said was, "If we had a kid it would have to be a pure hell-raiser," and a slow grin spread across his face as he contemplated the idea.

"Don't look like that," she grumped.

"Like what?"

"Like the idea tickles you."

"It does. Just think what a fighter a son of ours would be."

"It would serve you right if you only had girls," she announced, "and every one of them was just like you. Just think of all the young men prowling around."

The idea was mind-boggling. He fervently hoped he never had any daughters, because he didn't think his heart could bear up under the strain, especially if they were anything like their mother. Dee didn't know it yet, Lucas thought to himself, but she was going to be the one having his kids.

Two days later they had visitors at the Double C. Dee was sitting on the porch, and Lucas, who had made a point to stay close by since she had truly begun recovering, was in the barn. He walked up to the house when he saw a pair of riders approach.

Dee got to her feet and walked to the steps. One of the riders was Olivia. Betsy had been full of the gossip about Olivia marrying a Mexican gunman who just happened to be the very same man who had risked his life to help Dee during the fight with the Bar B men, of which he had been one. All of that had confused Dee, because she hadn't known anyone was helping. It certainly explained why she had been able to hold them off for so long, however. And she had never even met the man whom Olivia loved.

But she was about to meet him, for the man riding with Olivia was tall and lean and darkly handsome, and the way he wore his gun said that he was very proficient with it. She looked at him curiously and felt a little shy.

"Oh, Dee, you're looking so well," Olivia said warmly as she slid from her horse. With a small sense of shock Dee realized that Olivia had been riding astride, something she would never have suspected her of doing. It was something that she herself did all the time, but Olivia was different.

"I feel fine," Dee said, smiling as she went down the steps. "I don't have my full strength back, but every day I'm a little stronger."

They hugged each other, aware as they did so that their lives had changed over the course of this summer and would never again be the same. Olivia's eyes misted over, and Dee bit her lip to keep her control.

Luis dismounted and stood beside Olivia, his dark eyes surveying Dee with obvious approval. She felt herself blushing a little and was surprised at herself. There was something in that very male look, which was in no way insulting, that made her soften. "This is my husband," Olivia said with pride. "Luis Fronteras. Luis, this is Dee Swann, my best friend."

Dee held out her hand, but instead of shaking it Luis folded her fingers tenderly in his and carried them to his lips. "Miss Swann, you were amazing with that shotgun. It was something to see."

Her hand still tingled where he had kissed it. She looked down at it in amazement, then back up to Luis. "I owe you my life," she said simply. "Thank you."

"Thank Mr. Cochran," Luis said, nodding toward Lucas, who was striding toward them. "If he hadn't arrived when he had, I think we would both be dead."

Lucas shook Luis's hand and kissed Olivia's cheek. "Congratulations," he said to Luis. "You have a wonderful woman for a wife."

"I think so," Luis said peacefully.

"Come inside and have something cool to drink," Dee invited. "It's too hot to stand around out here."

Lucas put his hand on Dee's elbow as she went up the steps. She was feeling the effects of the heat far more than anyone else, which indicated how far she was from complete recovery.

There was iced tea to drink, for Orris had been making it for Dee. Lucas and Luis each took a glass, and their eyes met ruefully, but they didn't say anything. Dee and Olivia, of course, saw nothing unusual in drinking tea.

"I wanted to see for myself that you were recovering," Olivia said to Dee, "and to tell you and Lucas good-bye. Luis and I are leaving tomorrow."

"Where are you going?" Dee asked. "Will I ever see you again?"

"Of course you will! We won't be gone forever. We're going to go to St. Louis and take a train ride." A look of ecstasy came into Olivia's blue eyes. "We're going to go as far as the tracks will take us. It's something I've always wanted to do."

Dee thought about it. She had always thought of traveling as what you had to do to get to a definite destination; she had never considered traveling just for the sake of traveling. If that was Olivia's dream, she could scarcely have picked a better husband for herself. She wished them all the happiness in the world.

Lucas and Luis were talking quietly, and without being able to hear what was said Dee knew they were discussing what had happened at Angel Creek. Their faces were too serious for it to be otherwise.

"Bellamy hasn't been seen in town," Luis said. "Opinion is pretty strong against him." He eyed Lucas. "I heard you beat the hell out of him."

"I tried hard enough," Lucas replied grimly.

"Tillie has been staying out at the Bar B with him, taking care of him."

"She loves him," Lucas said. "I don't understand it myself, but she does."

"Yet she still rode out here to get you to stop him."

"And she was crying the whole time. She begged me not to kill him. I guess I would have if it hadn't been for her. If Dee had died, I'd have killed him anyway."

"Is Dee truly all right?"

Lucas glanced over at her. "Stronger every day. She'll want to go back to Angel Creek pretty soon."

Luis grimaced. He knew what Lucas had done, because he'd heard rumors and had ridden out to Angel Creek himself to see if they were true. He hadn't told Olivia, knowing that she would be very upset on Dee's behalf. His dark eyes were grave. "I don't envy you, my friend, when she finds out."

Lucas grinned. "It'll be interesting for a while, but she'll eventually see reason."

"If she loves it so much," Luis said, "she may be too hurt to see anything but the pain. You took a big risk."

"And I'd do it again," Lucas said quietly. "I'd sow every acre of it with salt if that was the only way I could keep her safe."

21

Dee woke up and stretched lazily, deliciously
aware of Lucas next to her in the bed. They had slept
together every night for over two weeks, and she had
cherished every moment of it because she knew it
couldn't last. She lay in the early-morning darkness
and faced the knowledge that the time had come for
her to go home. She was fully recovered; there was no
need to stay and every reason for her to leave. She had
so much work to do that she didn't know if she would
be able to handle it, but she had to get started or lose
her entire garden. Vegetables wouldn't wait indefinite-
ly without spoiling.

Lucas stirred and reached for her, tucking her in
close against him. "I'm going home today," she said
quietly.

He stiffened beside her, then got up and lit the
lamp. His beard-roughened face looked harsh in the
mellow light. "Why?"

"Because it's my home. I can't stay here forever. People are already talking, not without good reason."

"You could marry me."

She looked both rueful and sad. "You don't have to offer. Kyle Bellamy's sense of timing couldn't have been worse. I had just decided to let you graze your cattle in the valley, to get you through the drought. From what I've seen, though, you're still in good condition. You don't need Angel Creek."

"You don't either," he said roughly, stricken by her offer. Damn her generosity; she made him feel doubly guilty. "If you hadn't lived out there, none of that would have happened."

"It doesn't matter now. I just wanted you to know that you don't have to marry me to have access to the valley."

"Marry me anyway." His eyes were fierce. "You know it isn't just Angel Creek I want."

"I know." She thought of his ambitious plans, his fine house, and knew that she was out of place. "You want the Double C to be an empire. I can't be part of that, Lucas. I couldn't bear it in Denver, not even temporarily. I would make you miserable. People would ridicule you because of me. I'm not very good in social situations," she said with a wry smile that did nothing to ease his expression. She tried another way to make him understand. "When—when my parents died I was terrified. All of a sudden I had no one, and I thought I might die, too, because I had no reason not to. But I had the land. Somehow, living there, making things grow—it helped. It isn't just that I love it, but that I need it. Angel Creek valley doesn't belong to me nearly as much as I belong to it."

"Damn the valley!" His outburst was violent. He thrust his fingers through his dark hair, wishing it could have been put off for another week. "There's nothing out there now. I diverted the creek."

Dee blinked at him, not certain she understood. "What?"

"I diverted the creek. Angel Creek is dry now. Your valley isn't worth a hill of beans without water."

Dee got out of bed, her face blank with shock, her mind reeling from the enormity of what he'd done. She reached for her clothes.

"I'd do it again," he said harshly. "I would have eventually done it anyway, to keep the ranch going. Come hell or high water, I'll do what I have to do to protect the Double C. But that damn valley was going to get you killed, and you're too stubborn to admit it. Without it you'll be safe, you can sleep without having to keep one eye open. I did what was necessary."

She didn't look at him as she finished dressing. She spoke slowly, still feeling numb from the shock. "Then you should understand that I'll do whatever's necessary to keep my garden."

He lost control of his temper in the face of her obstinacy. "Forget the damn garden!" he yelled. "You don't need it. I'll give you the money you would have earned from it."

She straightened and faced him. Her eyes were terrible in their glittering clarity. "Keep your money, Cochran. I told you the day I met you that I wouldn't make a good whore, and nothing's changed."

It was worse than a nightmare, because she could wake up from a nightmare. She had imagined the

garden overrun with weeds, the vegetables overripe.
She could have salvaged something from that, put by
enough to get her through the winter even if there
wasn't enough to sell at the general store.

What she saw was the complete opposite of the
overripe bounty she had expected. The vegetables had
literally withered on the vine, seared by the heat,
deprived of the water that had nourished the earth.
The ears of corn hadn't filled out. When she examined
the stunted ears she felt only a few dried kernels
beneath the husks.

Angel Creek was dry, and the valley was turning
brown. She walked out into the meadow, the one that
had been full of wildflowers that glorious dawn when
Lucas had made love to her lying on the soft meadow
grasses. There were no flowers now, no sweet, rich
scents to delight her.

Without the rushing whisper of water the valley was
eerily quiet. She walked up the creek bed. She could
see it was dry, but somehow she had to verify it. How
could she mourn unless she truly understood the
depth of what had happened there?

And Lucas had done this to her, deliberately destroyed her home.

She wanted to feel the energizing rush of anger,
clean and hard, but this went beyond anger. She felt
numb, as if a part of her had ceased to live.

She went back to the cabin and stared at the
boarded-over windows. That would also be Lucas's
doing, she guessed. She supposed she should be glad
he had made the effort.

The cabin was in ruins, but remembering the bar-
rage of bullets that had assaulted it, she hadn't ex-

pected anything else. She had been prepared for that. It was the death of the valley that shook her to the base of her soul.

Work had always soothed her, so it was a good thing she was facing such a mammoth chore. She hardly knew where to begin in the cabin. So much had been damaged, and little of it could be salvaged. She swept out all of the broken glass, then drew up a bucket of water and spent an hour on her knees trying to scrub the bloodstains from the floor.

It took an hour before it registered. Water. She sat back on her heels and looked at the water bucket. The well was still good.

Hope ran wild, making her giddy. Dropping the scrub brush, she dashed out to the garden and walked down the rows, examining each plant.

The corn was totally lost; it was too dependent on water during the growing stages. But what about the beans and tomatoes, the onions and squash? Some of the plants had been sturdier than the others and still had life in them.

She ran back to the well and dropped the windlass, listening for the life-giving splash as it hit water.

All of her determination centered on the well. It took more strength than she had ever realized to draw up a bucket of water, and she was trembling after she had done it three times. Three buckets of water, at half a bucketful to each plant that looked as if it had a chance at survival, equaled only six plants. The intensely dry heat seemed to suck it out of the ground almost as fast as she poured it on, but she was careful to pour at the base of the plants so the root systems could get as much as possible.

The sun was too hot. She paused and looked up at it,

wiping her face on her sleeve. It was wasting water to pour it out in this kind of heat. Nighttime would be better; the plants would get more of it that way, and she would be able to work more comfortably in the cooler hours.

With that decision made she returned to the cabin and the work there. The results were discouraging. There was so little left that didn't have a bullet hole in it, even the pots and pans. Her iron skillet had survived, of course, but other than that she found only two pots that were usable. Even her biscuit pan was a casualty, and the coffeepot had so many holes in it that it resembled a sieve.

But no matter how useless it seemed she didn't let herself stop. If she stopped, she would think about Lucas, and she would break. She would sit down and howl like a lost child. If she could just stay busy and numb, she would be all right.

She had become soft during the past weeks. When the night finally cooled it was all she could do to force herself to move instead of collapsing in bed, as her body kept insisting she do. Everything was too dry for her to risk carrying a lamp out to the garden, so she worked by starlight.

She found that after a while she became so numb that she no longer felt her exhaustion. She hauled up bucket after bucket of water and trudged to the garden to empty it on what seemed like endless rows of plants.

It was some time after midnight when she realized she had been standing at the well in a stupor, holding an empty bucket in her hand. She didn't know how long she had been standing there.

Her legs felt as if they had lead weights attached,

and her hands had no feeling. She was so tired she couldn't lift her feet. She went back to the cabin, fell facedown on the bed, and didn't stir until noon.

That first day set the pattern for the days that followed. She tried to sleep as much as possible during the day, and at night she hauled water to the garden. She didn't think about it, didn't try to assess her progress, she just did it. She knew that if she ever stopped she would have no hope left.

Eight days after she had left, Lucas rode over to Angel Creek. It was late in the afternoon, but cooler than it had been in weeks. He figured eight days had been long enough for her to stew; now they could have a thunderous fight and clear the air.

Every day he had resisted the urge to check on her, to ride out there and see if he could talk sense into her. Damn, he missed her. He hadn't had nearly enough time with her. It would take a lifetime to satisfy him.

The first thing he saw when he rode up was Dee carrying a bucket of water out to the garden and carefully pouring it around the plants.

Anger seared him. That damn garden! He should have pulled the plants up by the roots and burned them. Why couldn't she see how useless it was?

He strode to meet her as she walked back to the well. She would have gone past him without even glancing at him, and his temper erupted. He jerked the bucket out of her hand and hurled it across the yard. "What in hell are you trying to do?" he yelled. "Kill yourself?"

She pulled her shoulders up very straight. "Thanks

to you," she said softly, "I'm having to water my garden by hand."

"Goddammit, Dee, it's too late!" He grabbed her arm and dragged her over to the garden. "Look at it!" he raged. "Open your eyes and look at it! You're pouring water on dying plants! Even if you could get some of them to bloom again, winter will be here before they can bear."

"If I don't have a garden, then I don't eat," she said. She tugged free of his grip and walked over to pick up the bucket.

He followed her and kicked it away from her outstretched hand. "Don't pick it up," he said with clenched teeth. She had been almost back to normal when she had left him, now she was noticeably thinner, and dark circles lined her eyes. Her face was pallid and drawn. "You've lost," he said. He put his hands on her shoulders and shook her. "Damn it, you've lost! It's over with. There's nothing left out here worth having. Get your clothes, and I'll take you home."

She jerked away from him. "This is my home."

"This is *nothing!*" he roared.

"Then *I'm* nothing!" she suddenly shrieked at him.

He tried to regain his control, but his voice was iron hard when he spoke. "You have two choices. You can take the money I offered you for the land and live in town, or you can marry me."

She was taking deep breaths, searching for her own control. Carefully she said, "Why would you want to buy worthless land? I don't want your conscience money, and I won't take charity."

"Then we're getting married."

"Those are your choices, not mine." Her hands were knotted into fists. "If I won't take your money to ease your conscience, you can bet I won't marry you for the same reason. My choice is to stay on my land, in my own home."

"Damn it, you'll starve out here."

"My choice, Cochran."

They faced each other like gunfighters. In the silence that stretched between them they heard a deep rumble, and a cool wind played with her skirt.

Lucas lifted his head, a frozen expression on his face. He sniffed, catching the unmistakable scent of dust and rain.

Dee looked up at the bank of dark clouds advancing toward them. The sky had been clear for so long that she stared at them in stupefaction. Rain clouds. Those were actually rain clouds.

They saw it coming, a misty gray wall sweeping down the slope. Within a minute it had reached them, slapping at them with scattered raindrops so big that they stung when they hit and made little dust rings fly up from the earth.

Lucas took her arm and propelled her up on the porch; they reached it just as the rain became a deluge. Thunder boomed so loud that the ground shook.

They stood in silence on the porch and watched the rain blow in sheets. It became apparent that it wasn't going to be a brief summer thunderstorm as the rain settled down to a hard, steady downpour.

He had seen it before and knew it for what it was. It was a drought-buster, the signal of a change in the weather, and just in time, too. None of the surrounding ranches had gone under, but another week would have seen cattle dying. Everyone had survived the drought.

Everyone but Dee.

The hard rain would replenish the ground water and refill the wells. It would save ranches and herds, bring grass springing back to life. Runoff from the mountain would fill Angel Creek again, but it would only be temporary. The valley would revive, but it would be too late for her, too late for the garden. When it was all said and done, everyone had made it through the drought except her.

She turned and walked into the cabin, quietly closing the door behind her.

She hadn't cried before, but now she did. She had kept herself under strict control, forcing herself to work automatically instead of thinking, but she could no longer keep the thoughts at bay.

Lucas could not have chosen anything designed to hurt her more. She had fought so hard for her independence, had carefully carved out a life for herself that she had loved, and he had destroyed it. If it had been Kyle Bellamy, she could have understood it; she could have been angry and hostile, she would have done what she could to prevent it, but she wouldn't have been so totally stunned by betrayal. It wouldn't have devastated her emotions if she hadn't loved Lucas, but she did. Even now she loved him. And he had demonstrated more clearly than she could ever have imagined that she meant nothing to him at all.

Lucas stood outside the door and listened to her crying, the sound mixing with that of the rain until sometimes they were indistinguishable, or perhaps they were the same.

He had never imagined Dee crying. He had never imagined that the sound of it would tear at his soul and leave it ravaged.

He had never imagined that he could hurt her, and now he knew just how stupidly arrogant he had been.

22

Lucas remembered what Luis had said: If Dee loved Angel Creek so much, she would be too hurt to see beyond the pain. He had known she loved it, but he had disregarded her feelings, assuming that he knew what was best for her. The truth was, he had done what was best for himself, not only in securing water for the ranch but in trying to manipulate Dee so that she had no choice but to marry him. Not once had he considered that losing Angel Creek would break her heart, though he should have; he loved the Double C in the same way. He loved it so much that he would never, ever forgive anyone responsible for destroying it.

But he had done exactly that to the woman he loved.

He had been so arrogant that he had blithely assumed living on the Double C would more than compensate her for losing Angel Creek. He had assumed that she would merely be angry, and that he would eventually be able to wear her down.

He should have remembered her deep, fierce passions, and the way she had looked that morning when he'd found her in the meadow, her face so radiant it had hurt him to look at her. He had discounted the strength of her love and made the worst mistake of his life. How could he convince her that he loved her after he had deliberately smashed the very foundation of her life?

Everyone was jubilant about the rain, almost giddy as they watched water holes refill and streams begin to run. Even the Bar B had managed to get by. Lucas felt savage as he watched it rain again the next day, and the next. It had all been for nothing, everything that Dee had endured. Bellamy had attacked her for nothing. He, Lucas, had destroyed Angel Creek valley for nothing. Fate and nature had mocked them by sending the rain just in time for the ranchers, but far too late for one woman.

He had her bull and two cows returned to her, and he bought some chickens to replace the ones that had left when he'd diverted the creek. He didn't take them himself because he didn't think she would be glad to see him under any circumstances just then, and maybe never.

Dee forced herself to go through the motions of living. She was too stubborn to let herself give up, but she did everything automatically, without hope or purpose. As Lucas had so caustically pointed out to her, she had been wasting her time pouring water on dying plants. None of them had recovered enough to bear.

No matter how she looked at it, she was in a hopeless situation. She still had some of last year's bounty that she had canned, but not enough to last through the winter, unless she could live on milk and eggs. She didn't have enough money to repair the cabin and buy food, too, but she wouldn't be able to stay in the cabin through the winter without repairing it. If she repaired the cabin, she would starve. Every alternative she explored brought her to a blank wall.

Unless she could find a job, she didn't know how she could live through the winter. And even if she did, what about next year? Could she manage a large garden without Angel Creek to nourish it, relying only on what rain came? Perhaps, though it would inevitably mean watering by hand again. A lot of families got by like that. But families were just that, families. By definition there were at least two people to share the work. Though she was strong, she knew her limitations. If she tried to grow a garden as large as she normally did, she would wear herself down trying to tend it, and exhaustion led to clumsiness, which led to accidents.

She could grow just enough for herself and manage to eat. But there wouldn't be any money for repairs, or for clothes. Not that she had that many clothes now, she thought, picturing her utilitarian garments, but she had always been able to replace them as they had worn out.

If she found work, she could survive, but it wouldn't be much more than that. She wouldn't be able to garden, wouldn't have the time.

She had loved it so. The rich scent of the earth in the mornings, the cool, silky feel of the dew, the tangible rewards of harvest, the almost blissful satisfaction of seeing the life and bounty that, with her care, the earth had given so generously. There had been a sublime rhythm to the seasons. She had followed nature's timing, renewing in the spring, flourishing in the summer, harvesting, then lying dormant through the long winters. No matter what she did now, it seemed she had lost that, the very thing she had most loved.

But people all over the world faced shattering disappointments, even tragedies, and went on with their lives. Time was inexorable. She had to either cope or give up. She knew how to do the first, but not the second.

The first person she went to see about a job was Mr. Winches at the general store. He peered sharply at her. "What's that?"

"A job," she replied calmly. "It doesn't matter what. I can do your books, put up stock, sweep the floor."

"I can do all that myself," he grumped.

"Yes, I know."

He was still staring at her. He chewed on his lip. "Sorry about what happened to your place. Guess that's why you're here."

"Yes."

He sighed. "Wish I could help you, but the plain fact is it would be stupid for me to pay anyone to do what I can do myself. The store just ain't big enough to call for it."

"I understand," she said. "Thank you."

She didn't even feel disappointment, because it was exactly what she had expected. If she did get a job, no one would be more surprised than she would.

She tried the dry goods store, but Mrs. Worley was just managing to support herself. An employee was out of the question. It was the same situation at the hat shop.

She walked up and down the streets, going into every business. The bank didn't need any more clerks. The two restaurants were family-owned, and hiring anyone to help meant a family member would be left with nothing to do. Likewise at the two hotels. It was a fact of life. In a family-run business the jobs went to family. She had known the situation before she began asking, but she asked anyway on the off chance that someone might be laid up and unable to work.

The one seamstress in town didn't need any help. Most women did their own sewing; there just weren't enough people in Prosper who paid to have their sewing done.

Dee even asked about cleaning houses, and Mr. Winches let her put a notice up in his store. No one contacted her. The people who could afford to have someone do their cleaning already had someone to do it.

What she had told Lucas when she had first met him was the literal truth: The only job for her in Prosper was in one of the rooms over the saloon.

The one asset she had had—the land—was worthless now. She might be able to give it away, but no one was interested in buying it. She knew that Lucas would give her his guilt money in exchange for the deed, but it would be nothing more than disguised charity, because he certainly didn't need it. He had plenty of water—the sweetest, clearest water imaginable, inexhaustible. He had the Angel Creek water.

It wasn't called Angel Creek over on that side of the mountains. She didn't know if it even had a name. It wouldn't have the same character over there, for the Double C was wide grazing land, and the effects of the water would be muted. In her narrow little valley it had been miraculous, creating a small paradise. That was why it had been called Angel Creek. She had never thought of it as just a cut in the ground with water running through it; Angel Creek had been alive, with its own personality, its mystery, a full partner in the bounty her garden had produced. She grieved for it as if a person had died.

If there was anything she had it was pride, yet as the days passed she was forced to the realization that she might yet have to swallow that pride and accept Lucas's money. There was nothing for her there, but she would be able to start again somewhere else.

Lucas! She still couldn't let herself think about him. The pain was still too fresh, too enormous. She lived every day with the knowledge of it, but she didn't take it out and examine it, or try to understand it. It was simply there. As long as she could ignore it she could function, but if she ever let it out it would destroy her.

Her body, whose rhythms were as inexorable as the seasons, told her that she didn't carry his child.

She should have been relieved.

Yet, against all logic, she had hoped. A baby now would be a disaster for her, but still she had hoped. Those two unprotected times with him had been her last chances to conceive. She no longer cared about her reputation, if any of it was left; she would have loved his baby with all of the fierceness of her nature, just as she loved him. She wouldn't hurt so much if she didn't love.

It took Dee a moment to recognize the woman who rode up to her cabin. She wore a stylish riding habit and an impossibly chic little hat with a plume curling around the brim and sat gracefully sidesaddle. But the dark red hair was the same, and the liquid brown eyes. It was Tillie, the saloon girl who had ridden to the Double C for help. Dee supposed she owed her life as much to Tillie as she did to Luis Fronteras or Lucas. They had all played their parts.

The two women faced each other. "Good morning," Dee said quietly. "Would you like to come inside?"

Tillie dismounted and walked up on the porch. It was the first time in ten years that she had been invited into a respectable home. The cabin was humble and severely damaged, but not many people would have asked her inside or even greeted her civilly.

"Thank you for what you did."

Tillie gave a little smile. "It was only partially for you. I couldn't let Kyle destroy himself that way."

"I heard you're living on the Bar B now."

"Yes. We're getting married. But we may not stay in this area. I don't imagine folks will ever forget what happened, or forgive him. It's lucky both of us are good at starting over. And thank *you*. You could have stirred people up against him even more, but you didn't."

"There didn't seem to be much point in it. Lucas

almost killed him." Colorado was a state now, she realized, but statehood hadn't changed the way folks handled things. If there was a dispute, people settled it without bringing the law into it. Kyle had received more punishment than the blows from Lucas's fists; he was virtually an outcast, his reputation destroyed.

Looking around the cabin, Tillie said, "You'll be starting over, too. I came to offer you some reparation for the damage. I know I can't make up to you for what happened to your place, but it will help you get by."

Starting over. Dee's heart thumped. How could she start over? "Kyle didn't cause this," she said. "Oh, he's the cause of the damage to the cabin, but Lucas Cochran is the one who ruined this valley."

"He wouldn't have done it if it hadn't been for Kyle," Tillie said gently. "It was a hard decision, and a hard thing to do, but then Lucas is a hard man. He knew that as long as you had Angel Creek there would be someone trying to take it away from you, and you'd always be in danger. So he took away the only reason anyone would have for wanting the valley. He did it to protect you."

A look of utter desolation came into Dee's eyes. "I would rather have taken the risk."

"*Lucas* couldn't have risked it. He loves you too much."

Dee said slowly, "When I walk outside, what I see doesn't look like an act of love."

"I know. Like I said, it was a hard thing to do. It was hard for me to ask Lucas to help you that day, knowing that Kyle might be killed because of me. Not many people would have seen that as an act of love, but it was. I would have done anything to have stopped him, even if he had hated me for it."

"I don't hate Lucas," Dee said, and it was the truth.

"But can you forgive him?"

"No. Not now. Maybe not ever. I just feel empty, like a huge part of me is gone. But it isn't a matter of forgiveness, it's a matter of living. Right now I'm not very interested."

Tillie had seen that look before in other women's eyes, even in her own eyes on occasion. It was the look of someone who had nothing to lose. That kind of bleakness went deep, and if the person ever recovered, she was different, changed in ways that were hard to understand.

"I brought the money with me," Tillie said briskly, changing the subject.

"I don't want Kyle's money."

"It isn't his, it's mine."

Dee looked at her in surprise. "All the more reason not to take it. You shouldn't have to pay; you aren't responsible for any of this. If anything, I owe you for saving my life."

"But Kyle's debts are mine," Tillie insisted. She smiled wryly. "It's part of loving someone."

"Thank you, but no." She might eventually have conquered her pride and accepted Kyle's money, she thought, because this was partially his fault, but it was out of the question to take money from Tillie.

Tillie hesitated. "I hear you've been looking for work in town."

"Yes, but there isn't any."

"Then take the money. I can afford it, and you need it."

Dee thought about the money and starting over, but it wasn't money she needed; it was water. She went still, staring at Tillie as if she had never seen her before. What was wrong with her brain? Anything that had been done could be undone. A creek that had been diverted once could be diverted again.

She must have been in a stupor from shock, from the pain of Lucas's betrayal. It was the only excuse she had for sitting there instead of *doing* something about the situation. She had never been one to sit and rail at fate; she rolled up her sleeves and took matters into her own hands.

She felt alive for the first time since Lucas had told her what he'd done, the old glitter returning to her eyes.

Watching her closely, Tillie said, "What? What is it? Do you have an idea?"

"I do. And there's something you can do to help me."

"Anything. I'm at your disposal."

A slow smile broke over Dee's face. "Can you get me some dynamite?"

Always interested in an adventure, Tillie went with her when Dee followed the creek bed up into the mountains to the source. It wasn't an easy trip by any means; Dee was certain there had to be an easier way, but she didn't know what it was.

They both wore pants, which was a good thing because several times they had to proceed on foot, leading their horses. They climbed and skirted and detoured, sometimes losing sight of the creek bed and having to work their way back to it. But when they reached the fork it was unmistakable. The earthen dam curved across the east fork, sending all of that beautiful water down onto Double C land.

Dee stared at the structure that had killed her farm. If Lucas had needed the water to survive, she would have built the dam herself, a handful of mud at the time. She had been willing to sell the valley to him. But *damn* if she would let him destroy something so beautiful, something that she loved so much, just because he thought he knew what was right for her better than she did!

"Have you ever used dynamite?" Tillie asked.

"No."

"Oh, my God."

"Don't worry. I asked in town. The blacksmith used to do some mining and showed me how it's done."

"Do you just light the fuse and throw it on the dam?"

"No. I'm going to plant it on the east side of the dam, at the bottom of it. That way, when it blows, it'll lower the creek bed, too." She understood very well the dynamics of what Lucas had done, and she was going to do the same thing.

It took her a while, using a knife, to gouge out two holes in the hardened clay. She wedged the sticks of dynamite in and stretched out the long fuses. She had taken the precaution of burning lengths of fuse so she could time how long it took to burn a foot, and she estimated how long the fuse would have to be to give her time to get safely away from the blast.

"You'd better start on down the mountain," she said to Tillie. "I'll give you five minutes before I light the fuses."

"I'd like to watch," Tillie said. "I came this far. I want to see you do it. I'll leave when you do."

They looked at each other and grinned.

Dee lit the fuses.

They ran for their horses, swung into the saddle, and rode for all they were worth. Dee silently counted the seconds.

Lucas was walking along the creek bank, looking at the water rushing along, oblivious to the battles that had been fought over it. It was deeper than he'd ever seen it before, in some places deep enough to swim.

He wondered if it was worth it.

Dee had been going from door to door in town, asking for work rather than coming to him. The irony of it was that he was the one person who couldn't deny her anything, and she would rather die than ask him.

He had hoped, despite everything, that she would come to him, that she would cool down enough to realize that he'd done it to protect her. But it wasn't a matter of temper, it was a matter of a hurt so deep that she was still reeling from it.

And it was pride. There had never been a prouder creature born than Dee Swann. That didn't make it easy to love her, but if she had been less proud, less fierce, she wouldn't have been the same person, and he wouldn't have loved her to distraction. If she hadn't been so strong, she wouldn't have been able to match him in strength of will, and he couldn't have loved her otherwise. She was exactly what he needed, a true mate.

But he had struck hard at that pride, and at the independence that was such a large part of it. Dee *would not* forgive him for Angel Creek; she couldn't do that and remain the same person. He had expected —demanded—that she be less than the person she was. She had to have the freedom of independence; it fed something within her, was part and parcel of the spirit that made her so strong. How had she put it? Angel Creek didn't belong to her as much as she belonged to it.

If he forced her to come to him, to surrender her pride, it would kill something within her.

The only chance he had was to give it back to her, that independence and pride. She would never come to him except as an independent woman with her dignity intact. She would always insist on maintaining that independence, on keeping some part of herself separate. How could he blame her for that when he was the same? He would never subordinate himself to anyone else, and neither would she. She might be his partner, but never his dependent. He had never wanted it otherwise, but it had taken losing her to make him realize it.

He looked at the water again. Precious stuff, but not as precious to him as Dee.

She had turned down his marriage proposal even after he'd told her it wasn't because of Angel Creek. At the time he'd been so angry that he hadn't thought about it, but suddenly it hit him. Even if he somehow made it up to her for Angel Creek, she still wouldn't marry him. He had told her all about his plans, how he intended to make the Double C an empire by using his money to influence political decisions. He had talked about the social functions in Denver, the balls and receptions he and his wife would have to attend because deals had a way of being made in social settings. He had been thinking of Dee at his side, had actually been arrogant enough to think he could make her over into a proper little socialite.

But Dee couldn't live that way, and she knew it. It wasn't just that she wouldn't enjoy the life; she had to be outside, free, unfettered by the suffocating rows of buildings and the unending rules of society. Had he truly been so blind that he had imagined she would fit in just because that was what he wanted? She had never asked him to change. How could he have been so stupid as to expect it of her?

He thought about all of his plans, his ambitions, and he weighed them on a mental scale. He had wanted influence only because of the Double C.

But hell, he was already rich. And Dee would bring much more to the ranch than his ambitions ever could. She would bring herself, her spirit, the children they would have.

He had to choose, and with blinding clarity he knew that there was no choice at all. He would take Dee over any amount of power or influence he could ever hope to build. He would sign the Double C over to her completely if that was what it would take to get her back. He wanted her as his partner for life.

His partner.

He blinked, astonished at the idea that had come to him. It just might work. It was the only thing he'd thought of so far that would even begin to make it up to her.

He heard the boom, low and rumbling, that came from the mountains. He looked up, expecting to see clouds, but the sky was clear. He didn't know where the thunder had come from.

Thunder, hell! Abruptly he realized exactly what it was. His mouth fell open, and he stared at the mountains. Then, helplessly, he began to laugh.

He should have expected that she would do something about the situation. That big boom was a signal that she was back in fighting form.

It was the next day when Dee heard a horse being ridden right up to the cabin. She looked out and saw Lucas swinging down from the saddle. She had expected him the day before and wondered what had taken him so long.

She picked up the shotgun and walked out on the porch. "What do you want?" she asked without preamble.

He stopped with his boot on the first step, warily eyeing the shotgun. "Now, Dee. If you were going to use that, you should have done it the first time I saw you. It's been too late ever since then."

She smiled. "It's never too late to correct a mistake."

"Exactly." He jerked his head toward the sound of running water, where Angel Creek once again flowed clear and deep. "Who set the charges for you?"

She jerked her chin up. "I didn't need anyone to do it for me. I did it myself."

Lucas stared at her, aghast. His heart almost stopped as he thought of the danger she had been in. Damn it, didn't she know how unstable dynamite was? He hadn't even considered that she had done it herself, though now that he thought about it he realized that he should have expected it. When had Dee ever asked anyone to do anything for her?

"Are you crazy?" he yelled, his face flushing with anger. "You could have been killed!"

She gave him a scornful look. "I suppose you think I didn't know what I was doing."

"Did you?" he shot back.

She lifted her eyebrows at him. "Evidently," she drawled. "I'm still here."

He felt like banging his head against the wall in frustration, and then suddenly he laughed, because he hoped she would be driving him crazy like that for the rest of his life. Maybe he was already crazy, because he could swear he'd seen a glint of amusement in those witch-green eyes. She loved making him lose control.

"Tillie helped me," she volunteered.

"Tillie!" He took off his hat and wiped the sweat off his forehead with an agitated motion. "Jesus." But it made sense. Tillie would do it because she would feel obligated to atone for Kyle's sins. In this instance, Lucas knew that his own transgression had been much greater than Kyle's, even though he had done it out of love.

Dee gave him a challenging look. "If you build another dam, I'll just blow that one up, too."

"I don't intend to build another dam," he said irritably. "Hell, I should have blown that one up myself. I just didn't think of it in time."

Startled, Dee stared at him. "Why would you do that?"

"Because I was wrong." He gave her a level look, their gazes locking. "Because I didn't have any right to build it in the first place. Because I'd do anything to get you back."

She had never seen his eyes so blue, so determined. Her heart began thumping in her chest, but she didn't dare let him see it.

He moved up one step, and she brought the shotgun up. "Stay right there," she warned.

He didn't even look at the shotgun. "Will you marry me?" he asked.

Involuntarily she glanced toward the creek.

"No, not because of that damn water," he snapped. "Keep this valley. I don't need it. What I need is you. I'll have papers drawn up so that the valley remains yours, and I'll sign the Double C over to you. Just marry me."

Dee was astounded by the offer. Her arms went limp, letting the shotgun waver and the barrel point downward. Before she could take another breath Lucas was on the porch, cautiously removing it from her hands and setting it aside.

"What did you say?" she asked dazedly.

"I said Angel Creek will stay your personal property, yours to do with as you see fit without any say-so from me. I don't know why I didn't think of it before. And I'll give you my ranch. I'll give you whatever you want if you'll just say yes."

She had never imagined he would say anything so astounding. He simply couldn't mean what he was saying. "But . . . *why?*"

He drew a deep breath; it was damn hard to put himself on the line, staking everything he had and his future happiness against her answer. "Because I need you, sweetheart. I need a wife who'll knock me in the head when I try to ride roughshod over her, and you're the only one who has ever dared. I've lost count now of how many times I've asked you to marry me, but let's get one thing straight right now: I've never asked you because of this valley or the water. I asked you because I love you. Is that clear?"

She couldn't think of anything to say. She gaped at him, her mind as blank as a chalkboard that had been wiped clean.

"I said, is that clear?" he barked.

"You can't want me," she blurted.

"Why the hell can't I?"

"Because . . . because I'm not what you want," she sputtered. "You're going to spend a lot of time in Denver, and I couldn't live like that. People would make fun of me. I wouldn't fit—"

"No, you wouldn't," he agreed maddeningly. "To hell with Denver. I'd rather have you."

"I can't ask you to give up—"

"Goddammit, you aren't asking me to give up anything!" he roared, at the end of his patience. "I know what I want. Now answer my damn question!"

She blinked and tried to gather her scattered thoughts. "I don't want the Double C," she said. "I wouldn't marry you because you offered me land."

Lucas threw his hat on the porch and considered stomping it. Instead he seized her arms and shook her. "Then forget the damn land," he said, his teeth clenched tight. "Just say you'll marry me."

It began unfurling slowly, a bloom of joy swelling inside her chest, and she tried to contain it. If she didn't, she'd be in danger of bursting. He meant it. Incredible as it was, he meant it. He would never offer to part with an inch of his beloved Double C unless he thought it was the only way he could convince her to marry him, yet he had offered to give her the entire ranch. He loved her, and the hot look in those blue eyes told her that he didn't feel even a tinge of regret for giving up his ambitions. He had made up his mind, and when Lucas Cochran made up his mind about something no one could change it.

"All right," she said.

He shook her again. "All right, *what?*"

She began to laugh. "Yes," she said.

"Yes, *what?*" God, she would make him a raving maniac before the year was out.

She gave him a smile of blinding sweetness. "Yes, I love you, too. Yes, I'll marry you. But not because of the Double C or any other reason, except that I love you. Was there anything else?"

Lucas hauled her against his chest, his arms so tight that her ribs were constricted. He closed his eyes as tears burned. He had gambled his entire life on this and had been in terror that she would refuse him. "God, you're stubborn."

"I know," she said placidly, the words muffled because her face was against his chest. "As stubborn as you."

"I meant it about Angel Creek. It stays yours. You need it, sweetheart. I didn't understand before." He kissed her hair. "As new owner of the Double C, you're one of the richest women in the state."

She lifted her head and gave him a blinding smile. "No," she said.

"Of course you are. I know how much the ranch is worth, damn it."

"I don't want the Double C."

"A deal's a deal."

"Not until I say 'I do' it isn't. I won't take the Double C. You need it just the way I need Angel Creek." Her hands crept up his back. "This doesn't have to be a surrender, you know. Why can't it be a partnership?"

"Hell, I don't care," he said impatiently. "Just as long as you marry me."

She felt surprisingly peaceful. "It doesn't matter whose name is on the papers as long as I can still come here," she said, and with a start she realized that it was true. Angel Creek was hers even if the title had Lucas's name on it. She trusted him, and because she did she wouldn't have to fight to maintain her independence. The respect he gave her as a person was a measure of her true independence, and that was all she'd ever wanted. Marrying him couldn't change that at all.

"That's what I realized about the Double C," he admitted. "The name didn't matter. Having you mattered, and the land would still be there. But we'll do it however you want," he said, tilting her face up for a hard kiss. "It can be your legacy to our kids, if you want."

Her entire body rippled with pleasure at the thought of the hours of lovemaking that would be necessary to get those kids. Lucas absorbed the movement, his own body responding.

"We'll fight a lot," he said, thinking of it with anticipation. He could barely wait.

"That's almost certain."

"And make love when the fighting's over."

She drew back to give him a long, green look. "That remains to be seen."

"No," he said, lifting her in his arms. "It doesn't." He strode down the steps and over to the creek bank, where the crystal water of Angel Creek swirled and glittered just as it had before, but with a certain giddiness to it, as if it were glad to be back. With a deep shout of laughter he tossed her into the water, then jumped in himself. It was cold, but they didn't care. Shrieking with laughter like a child, Dee jumped on his back and forced him underwater again, and they grappled together until the laughter died and something else came into his deep blue eyes.

He pulled her up on the bank and covered her there, shoving her skirt up and stripping her wet drawers away, then unbuttoning his pants and tugging them down only as far as was necessary, because he couldn't wait a minute longer. He linked them with a hard, single thrust, groaning as the tight heat of her body enveloped him. This was nothing less than paradise.

Dee's legs embraced him, then loosened. She pushed at his shoulder, and he rolled, taking her with him. She sat up and pushed her wet hair out of her eyes, and he caught his breath at the look of ecstasy on her face. It was the same exalted expression he'd seen there one dawn, and he had put it there. With the bright sky behind her and her eyes as green as emeralds, she was the most beautiful thing he'd ever seen, and she was his.

"We're getting married tomorrow," he said.

She leaned forward to kiss him, her mouth tender. "Whatever you say, darling," she purred.

He wasn't fooled for a minute.

EPILOGUE

KYLE AND TILLIE BELLAMY EVENTUALLY SOLD THE BAR B and moved back east. Dee received one letter from Tillie saying that they were happy and were considering a move to New Orleans. She never heard from Tillie again.

Luis and Olivia Fronteras traveled for two years, then to her parents' delight returned to Prosper and bought land just west of the Bar B. Though Wilson Millican was never certain just how his son-in-law supported Olivia, they always seemed to have money and he didn't think he should inquire too closely. Olivia was happier than he'd ever seen her, and that was all he asked. He never would have imagined his sedate daughter as having a streak of adventure in her, but he had to admit it suited her. Then, in swift procession, Olivia presented her husband with three daughters. She couldn't have made him happier, because Luis was always delighted to be surrounded by females.

Lucas and Dee Cochran had five children. Three boys came first, hell-raisers just like he had predicted. The next two were girls, and by the time the oldest one was a year old Lucas was worrying. His baby girls were so much like their mother that he knew he wouldn't draw an easy breath for the rest of his life.

He and Dee fought and yelled and made up. The house rang with noise and passion. He wouldn't have had it any other way.

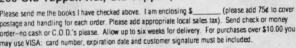